I0746334

THE SECRET

A HIGHLAND NOVEL

WHERE TIDES RUN DEEP

Alan Dunlop

Dedication

To all those individuals and organisations who protect and promote the continuance of all our field sports—hunting, shooting and fishing—and our 'Courtesy of Choice' and inalienable right to enjoy them.

THE SECRET & WHERE TIDES RUN DEEP

Published by
Maurice Wylie Media
Your Inspirational & Christian Book Publisher

For more information visit
www.MauriceWylieMedia.com

The Secret

CONTENTS

Chapter 1

The estate had fallen on hard times. Things were not as they once were since before the Great War, and now a Second World War lay heavily on the nation. Lady Eleanor herself had sadly changed too, and the house, stables and lodge each reflected, in their own way, the downward spiral of inner decay and ruin it was fast coming to be.

Before the Great War and after, it had been good. Continental parties of sportsmen and anglers had sampled the secluded yet welcoming atmosphere of Strathmore Lodge, and the meat from their trophies and culls[i] had graced many a table in poor Highland homes.

Strathmore Lodge was different. It had always been different, ever since Lady Eleanor had taken a bad fall on the moors, and an ill-clad child appeared out of nowhere it seemed, with a brace of moorfowl and a bedraggled rabbit by the heels. The youngest girl of the well-to-do Hamilton family of the Curragh in County Kildare, Ireland, she was not long married at the time, and a newcomer to the Lodge which her husband, Colonel Archibald McNabb, had inherited. A lover of the wild and oftentimes windswept moors of her new bridal homeland, she had come initially with her father on a hunting trip, and had fallen in love with this Highland scene, and with the still recuperating son of its owner!

Thereafter, she was accustomed to riding out for hours on end, sometimes daily, and it was on one such occasion that the accident happened. Suddenly and without warning she found herself on the ground with a searing pain in her back, and she knew she was badly hurt. Unable to move, and with the warm blood beginning to trickle from the corner of her mouth, she turned her head, only to see the boy running towards her. Raising her hand as if to implore, she weakly breathed, "Cuidich mi, please"[ii].

The boy was quick to respond. Running to her, he threw down his birds, rabbit and snares, and in earnest and knowing tones replied, "Cuidichidh mi thu."[iii] The horse's leg was broken, that was evident, and the boy saw at once just how serious the situation was. Very quickly unsaddling the horse, he placed the saddle where the woman's head could use the skirt and knee roll for a pillow. Untying the saddle blanket, he covered the now trembling woman, and left the water bottle, rifle and ammunition beside her. He was well aware that a shot could guide a search party. Then he was gone, just as quickly and mysteriously as he had appeared.

That was a full forty years ago now, but Lady Eleanor never forgot that; but for the boy, she could not have lived. A broken rib had punctured a lung, and the doctor said that but for the child's timely intervention, he could not have saved her. When she was well enough to receive visitors, she sent for the boy and had him brought to her. His name was Rab Mackenzie, and he was ten years old. His mother was a widow with a small bairn to care for, and young Rab was the breadwinner. That's why he was out on the moors that day. He said he wasn't stealing, just trying to get something for the supper, and have a little broth off it for the child. His mother took in washing from the local timber mill, and they had some potatoes, but no milk for the bairn that day.

There were many such days for Rab, meeting with Lady Eleanor, and it was from these weekly talks that she built up a picture in her heart and mind of the poverty of the local peasants around Strathmore. There were many widows. Husbands killed in their employment through unscrupulous men taking advantage of them. Others through common accident, and still others through careless disregard for their health and a too great a liking for the bottle. Most leaving behind small children, hungry, ill-clad and pitiful. Rab was very articulate and mature for one so young, and it was clear to see how he had become the mainstay for his mother and family.

"I could tell your ladyship of very many within a ten-mile distance who are worse off than we are. We go to Kirk on Sunday and hear much of God's Election of Love, but Mam says we don't get to see very much of it. We go hungry very often, your Ladyship, and it appears to Mam that God's Election of Love only refers to those who have the most. Can you explain that to me please? Does God only elect those with land or does he elect people to give land to? It seems everything is against us, Mam says."

Rab was full of questions, and each week with Lady Eleanor he brought a new supply.

"How can one person own all as far as our eyes can see, and own all the beasties that graze on it too? Did you know they once hanged a man up north for eating a piece of venison? Eating a piece of meat made him as guilty as the man who killed it. They couldn't find that man, so they hanged the man who ate the meat."

During these talks the earnestness and innocence of the child's demeanour forcibly struck Lady Eleanor, and she mostly just listened, for she found Rab's homespun logic and argument sometimes defeated her. She never defended either the land or game laws, lest she appear to be as unfeeling and uncaring as those who formulated them, but she felt obliged to counsel the child on the somewhat skewed view he had of Christian doctrine. It was important to her to make him understand that the sins and excesses of mankind were not to be used as the measuring rod of the Saviour's attributes of love and mercy.

"Rab, I am understanding very well what you are saying, and you might be surprised to know that on the basis of justice alone I entirely agree with you and your Mam, but I want you to know this. Never take your Christianity from other Christians, or from those who say they are Christians. Even the church that we both belong to is far from perfect.

Why is this, you may ask? Simply because men have organised religious systems through which to serve the Master. Sometimes they work quite well, but very often they fall into disrepute, and those in charge have not the moral courage to rectify matters, and unfortunately it is the people in the pews who suffer most. The minister has his stipend, his church furlong or his close, and sometimes the cash from these lands is not shared as it was meant to be, and clergy greed has deprived many a hungry child of its rightful portion.

But never allow those things to interpret Scripture, Rab. Scripture stands alone and pure from all the corruptions of mankind, and the Lord who gave it will one day bring every hidden thing to light, and hold men accountable for how they have abused His revealed truth."

It was through such conversations with this very interesting and articulate young lad that Lady Eleanor purposed in her heart that if others could be comfortable with such a cold, unfeeling attitude to the poor, whether in church or state, she could no longer subscribe to it, or indeed remain silent concerning it, nor indeed could Strathmore Lodge.

It was around that time that she formed a child support programme whereby a significant portion of Strathmore's wild provision was shared with the poorest in the parish. All this was done with utmost secrecy, for Highlanders would be quick to take offence at open public charity. Trusted ladies and trusted butchers therefore made sure that what was given to this programme, whether venison, salmon, pheasant or grouse, made its way to the right tables. The church was excluded from all this, for by and large, the people's confidence was not warm towards the clergy, and in too many instances, the people were not wrong in their reading of this unfortunate situation. As a pattern for her benevolence Lady Eleanor took her mother's plan, that which she used in the time of the Great Irish Hunger, when the poor died by the tens of thousands due to the potato blight. She remembered, from the stories her mother told of the tragedy, how she and some other concerned women had begun a scheme to help where they could, and the child had listened intently as the history was told and retold over the years.

It was through these weekly meetings with the young Rab Mackenzie that Lady Eleanor first realised that her time had now come to emulate her mother's example, for the circumstances in which she found herself demanded a response, and what was more pitiful and needy than hungry children, when the means to help them was on hand and plentiful.

It was these same weekly meetings that led the young Rab to become involved in the activities of Strathmore, and he became a very useful pair of hands at whatever he was asked to do. Whether in the harness room, picking-up or driving on the pheasant beats, or the handling of deer carcasses, whatever it was, the boy was not only willing but very able. This ability was never more clearly seen than in the gun room after a day's shoot or stalk. He became adept at the handling of firearms, and could be trusted to make safe, clean and store safely any firearm it held.

All this was not lost on Colonel McNabb, and when the time came to employ a new Land Steward, young as he was at 18 years old, Rab was given the job. At that time there was another lad who had been around Strathmore before Rab, and who could likewise turn his hand to whatever was needed, a boy by the name of Stewart McDonald, Stu he preferred to be called, but it was Rab who was chosen for the new post.

Chapter 2

It was a long time ago now, but Rab remembered very clearly the events of the accident. He had been out on the moors with his snares, braided horsehair for the pheasant and grouse, and stout twine for rabbit or hare. The twine, soaked in hot animal fat and allowed to cool, took on a rigidity when pulled through the fingers, and this rigidity allowed it to maintain its shape when pegged out on an open rabbit run or game trail. They worked well, and Rab was rarely short of meat when he daily checked his traps.

He had become the breadwinner of the family at an early age, ever since an accident had robbed him of his father. His father had worked in forestry, and their little wooden shack was part of the job incentive. Jock Mackenzie was killed as he walked past a pile of logs that were improperly built, and when they slipped, they killed him outright.

Due to an unscrupulous and ambitious lawyer, the company refused to pay Mrs Mackenzie compensation. The lawyer found a very early addendum to the initial workplace regulations which stated that any worker killed or injured outside of their actual shift would be treated as trespassers, and therefore not entitled to compensation in the event of any injury. Since Jock was walking home a few minutes after his shift ended, this law was cruelly upheld, and the widow, five-year-old Rab and a new bairn were evicted without a penny piece to their name.

The young Rab did not understand much of what was taking place at the time; all he knew was that his father had been killed through the company's carelessness, and they were protected from any blame by a point of law. It was no surprise therefore, that the young Rab grew up with a deep-seated animosity and suspicion of the law and its lawyers, and he made no bones about it either.

In their extremity at this time, it was Jock's aged father who provided shelter for them, so they were not left without a roof over their heads. It was not much, a small bothy, but it meant safety from the winter winds and Highland snows, and they were grateful for it. It was built of rough-hewn stone and thatched, and it became a home to the little family. When the old man passed away the bothy came to them. In the passage of time this became the family home, and Rab always considered it such.

As the crow flies the bothy was only a couple of miles from Strathmore, and unless one wanted to walk the moor, a cattle trail road of sorts was the only other way in, and it was about five miles longer. Rab knew the paths of course, for he rode them daily with his snares. His mount was an old animal that had passed its useful working life and had been turned out on the hill in retirement.

This particular pony had taken to wintering in their turf shed, and one day Rab put a rope halter on it and sallied forth. From then on it became his mode of transport and, being unshod, it was largely this factor that had allowed him to hear clearly Lady Eleanor's mount that day as she urged it along a straight stretch of bridle path at a canter.

The bridle path was flinty ground, and as she passed Rab, who had hidden himself in a gorse thicket, the tragedy happened. The winter rains had eroded a deep narrow gully across the path, and entering it the foreleg of the animal snapped like a twig. The unfortunate beast went neck and croup[iv] over and its helpless rider hit the rocky ground hard.

After the shocked child had seen to the injured lady, he immediately mounted his own animal and made directly for the Lodge, where the first man he encountered was Hamish McInnes, the gamekeeper.

"Sir, there's been an accident," Rab cried out. "Lady Eleanor's horse has fallen and she has been badly hurt."

"Where lad?" McInnes was quick to reply.

"At the Crags sir, just past the Crags on the way to the High Moor- You can't miss it."

Thus it was that Lady Eleanor's rescue was underway even as the doctor made his way to the Lodge, for staff moved as one to facilitate the Colonel as he called for this and that, and it was a very relieved party that made its way back to Strathmore with a very sick lady on an old army stretcher, whose canvas still bore the evidence of similar duty in days gone by.

Such was Rab's introduction to the McNabb's of the manor, and in the process of time he became part of it.

The Colonel worshipped his young bride and was only too pleased to have Rab brought to her as she grew better. He was greatly impressed when he heard from Hamish McInnes how the galloping messenger gave a very detailed account of Lady Eleanor's whereabouts and injuries, and he was just as interested as his lady to hear more from the young boy himself.

Unspoken of course, the young Rab became the son the Colonel would never have.

In the decades that followed, there was no aspect of Strathmore that Rab was not made familiar with, and slowly and almost imperceptibly, he became the linchpin, the centre and moving force of the whole business. As for Rab, he knew little of the hidden respect and growing confidence in him. As far as he was concerned, he worked for two people whom he had come to love and cherish, and he enjoyed the work as only someone born to that lifestyle can.

He was just a few years there when the Colonel put him under the tutelage of Hamish McInnes, who was instructed to take him to the hill and teach him the art of a successful stalk and all that it entails, both before and after.

Hamish had now grown a little past his vigour for such work and knew he must soon relinquish it to a younger man. It was with genuine earnestness and cheerfulness, therefore that he took on his new role as Rab's mentor, and it became one of the most enduring friendships outside of the McNabb's that Rab ever made. It was indeed an idyllic time for the young boy. His mother and sister were now well provided for and he had no worries from that quarter that might have spoiled his happiness.

If there comes a time in every life that makes a man or woman wish it might continue, then these years were so with Rab Mackenzie. But fate found him, as it very often does, tragically and suddenly, and his providential idyll became crushed and broken in an instant.

Chapter 3

The Great War had passed into a memory, leaving in its wake indescribable pain, loss and lasting grief. Slowly but surely however, the country found its feet again, and, while a new generation would soon forget, the hearts of those who lost flesh and blood would always weep. Strathmore had felt the impact of the Great War too. International guests had been reluctant to come, as suspicion and anger still smouldered in many hearts, and the Kaiser's aggression would not soon be forgotten.

Now, another war, and with the same enemy too, had engulfed the nation in another bloodbath. Old wounds were opened up again as nations took sides and made alliances and pacts. But paradoxically, as the young men fought it out on the fields of blood, life at home continued much the same, and Strathmore was no different in this respect.

Colonel McNabb was now nearing eighty years of age, but still maintained a youthful spring in his step. The leg wound however from the Second Boer War had begun to trouble him more and more, and it bothered him. He tried bravely not to let it interfere with his daily work, and he engaged as much as possible in Lodge life. He still carried with him an air of military bearing and the discipline that came with it, but his greatest attribute was his generosity and kindness. If he had a fault, as most men have, it was through his kindness and forbearance.

It was Rab who was with him the day he was tragically killed. The Colonel had insisted on taking an old army friend to the hill. Rab had demurred, but the Colonel was not going to pass up this opportunity with his visitor. "Nonsense Rab, nonsense. I'll walk the legs off you boy, just wait and see."

Rab could understand the situation of course, and so against his better judgement he let it pass.

All went well until it came to the shot. Rab beckoned the visitor to his side and pointed out the beast they had been stalking now for about two hours. It was a good animal. Rab had chosen it especially for the Colonel's friend, a royal[v], a year past his best in Rab's opinion, but still a worthy animal for any man's trophy room.

As he passed the rifle over to the man now lying at his side, Rab once more gave him the benefit of his assessment. "That is a two-hundred-yard shot sir. The rifle is zeroed at 100 yards, as you will remember from the range. A high shoulder shot will give you approximately a 4-inch allowance for bullet drop, which will be right on target. Keep well forward and you will drop him where he stands."

The old soldier took up a comfortable prone position in readiness for the moment. Making sure his left forearm was evenly rested on the turf below, and that the rifle was steady on the aim, he slowly removed a sprig of heather that was obscuring his sight line, and he was ready.

This was Rab's worst moment on any stalk. Hours of work and fieldcraft now condensed to a few seconds that would be crucial, absolutely crucial, between success and failure. Rab glassed[vi] the stag again, and held fast his vision on the animal in its totality, and he was very glad he did so. When the shot[vii] was taken, he both heard and saw the strike, much too far back, and certainly not in a spot that would give any hope of a quick and relatively painless death. After a jump of surprise, the animal took off at speed, much to the dismay of the ghillie who had worked so hard to secure it.

After explaining to the Colonel and his guest that the beast was a very fast runner, Rab took the rifle and went after it, telling them that they would be better to have lunch now and wait until he returned. It took a while to come up on the wounded animal, and he had to stop several times to glass the hill until he at last spotted it. It was now among a small herd of hinds, head down and blowing, but Rab knew that if scared again, it could take off and run for miles and be lost to him before it finally dropped. Caution was needed, more so now on account of the other animals with it. If only one of them got wind or sight of him he could bid the stag goodbye.

A deep and rocky gully ran from the valley floor past where the little group of deer were grazing. There was a fresh flow in it from recent rains, but, while it would be wet and cold, it would serve his purpose well. The noise of the rushing stream would greatly assist him and allow him to move a little quicker to a firing position.

At almost two hundred yards, Rab at last had an opportunity to pluck victory from the jaws of defeat, and he determined to take it. He would only get one shot, and it was longer than he could have wished. There were other animals in close proximity, not usually a satisfactory situation, but the wind was in his favour and it was good light, and he must take the shot, for the circumstances demanded it.

It was now down to him. Success or failure had come into his hands, and the burden was a felt one. He took another long look at the stag. It had not moved. He looked very closely at the tall grasses and bog cotton that grew near the animal, and they were not moving either. Now was his time. He had only three things in his head at that moment: his rifle, his ammunition and confidence in his own experience. He had proven all three things before; now he would do so again.

The rifle bucked and the stag staggered, stumbled forward a few feet, then fell, front legs folding under its weight. It never moved, and Rab felt the sense of relief that was always released in those final few seconds.

Following the wounded beast had brought Rab closer to a path that led to the Lodge, and rather than retrace his steps he made straight for it. The light was fading now with overcast clouds, and he was anxious to get back to the Colonel and his guest.

As he entered the courtyard he met Stu MacDonald, and in a few brief words told him to get Ben the pony and bring him to Braeside Hill. He requested lamps and asked him to come as quickly as possible. "I'll go on ahead and let them know what's happening, and I'll gralloch[vii] the stag while I'm waiting. Hurry Stu, for the Colonel has been out too long already." By the time Stu MacDonald arrived it was full dark, and the Colonel and his visitor had now made their way to the kill. Brigadier Brodie's request!

What happened next could never have been dreamed of. As Stu and Rab finally pulled the last knot on the now roped and loaded stag, the pony suddenly shied and reared, falling backwards with the heavy load on its back. The Colonel, behind the animal, could only raise his hands as if to ward off the falling pony, but he was not fleet enough of foot to jump aside. The pony fell right back and the antlered head of the trophy beast fell on top of the old gentleman. A tine from the antlers' cup[viii] pierced his temple through, killing him instantly.

For once in his life Rab Mackenzie was almost bereft of reason. He could not immediately fathom what had taken place. The light from the lamp in the Brigadier's hand showed a picture of unspeakable horror, and Rab was distraught at the shock it brought so suddenly and tragically. He knelt beside the man who had been a father to him since he first came to the Lodge, and when the pony was cut free from the load and the stag removed, he cupped the dead face in his hands and wailed loudly and long. It was only when the Brigadier put his hand on his shoulder that he came again to himself, but still stood sobbing and gazing on the scene in unbelief.

Chapter 4

It was a sad and sorry party that entered the courtyard that evening. Stu MacDonald was sent to run ahead with the news and to call the maids to Lady Eleanor's aid. Rab himself led the pony with the dead Colonel across the saddle, and made sure that the body was laid out in the drawing room before Lady Eleanor, now beside herself with grief, was allowed to see him.

For the next few days, the accident and the shock it brought were palpable among the staff. Bookings were cancelled or suspended, and an air of unprecedented sadness and loss pervaded the estate. The day of the funeral brought scenes of unimaginable woe, as Lady Eleanor was literally borne up behind the horses that pulled the funeral carriage, borne by the loving hands of the widows and women that made up her group of Strathmore Children's Aid. It was all too much for Rab, and he hung back as far as he could and spoke to no one.

The day after the funeral the enquiry began. Lady Eleanor herself sat in her chair, flanked by close professional friends and well-wishers. It was not a large meeting, but those who were invited were important to the credibility of the proceedings.

Strathmore staff were there, as were the local solicitor and Chief Inspector of Police, Duncan McEwen. The family doctor, Angus McCabe, was chosen to record what was said and Edgerton, the solicitor, was given the task to follow up on any questions fully and thoroughly so that the truth might be established.

The Chief Inspector was invited, for although it was not actually a police matter, Lady Eleanor wanted the affair closed properly so as not to allow rumour or gossip to flourish by reason of neglect of information. Rab was there of course, as was Stu MacDonald. The Brigadier was very noticeable by his absence, leaving a note to explain a very sudden recall to Edinburgh!

Lady Eleanor made it very clear from the beginning that the purpose of the meeting was not to build a criminal case against anyone, but simply to honour the memory of her dead husband by setting the record straight as to what exactly took place that dreadful day, and the circumstances that led to her husband's death. Anyone would be free to speak if they could help the proceedings, and were encouraged to do so, but first of all the Lodge manager and ghillie, Rab Mackenzie, would tell the story of the hill stalk he had organised that day.

Rab then stood, and in his own simple yet concise manner began with the guest gun, the Brigadier. He was, as all already knew, an old friend of the Colonel's; nevertheless Rab felt it proper to speak with him as he would any other guest, and go through the various protocols of a hill stalk and recovery, and some of the problems and dangers that can accompany such.

On the day before the stalk, Rab took him to the Lodge shooting range and allowed him to become familiar with the rifle he would use. It was an old .303 calibre Lee-Metford, in excellent condition. Rab explained that the rifle was zeroed at 100 yards, and for a shot of, say, 200 yards, a high shoulder shot would give the Brigadier a 4-inch bullet drop margin that was perfectly adequate for a kill shot at that range. The rifle was fitted with a box magazine that held five rounds and Rab had the guest try the gun on the range test plate, which was done in an acceptable manner. Rab could not explain why the guest placed such a poor shot on the stag. It was a cold barrel shot and ought to have been the best shot of the day. The ghillie further stated that familiarity with a weapon is only part of the skills needed to complete a successful kill, and since it was the Brigadier's first attempt at live quarry, Rab could only conclude that perhaps his nerve gave at the last moment, or that he 'pulled the shot'[ix] inadvertently as he squeezed the trigger. He had seen it before: grown men overwhelmed at the prospect of a first kill. He had also seen men overwhelmed on the range as they prepared to demonstrate that they could indeed hit a target at 100 yards plus. Some even had to take a long walk to compose themselves!

Rab went on to tell of returning to the Lodge at 7:45 pm and meeting Stu MacDonald, giving a brief account of the instructions he left with him. "Bring the gelding Ben, and a riding pony for the Colonel, and hurry, for the Colonel had been out too long already."

It took Rab an hour to get back to Braeside Hill and the kill, around 8 pm, and Stu did not arrive until 9:30. He did not bring Ben as instructed, but brought a younger, inexperienced animal that had never yet been on a solo extraction. Rab felt the pony skittish from the outset and laid the blame on the fact of its inexperience. After the accident, Rab had enquired as to why Ben was not brought as requested and was told he had already been groomed and stabled for the night and so the younger animal was brought instead.

As Rab continued it began to be apparent in the meeting that had Stu MacDonald done as he was told there may have been a happier outcome.

It was at this point that Edgerton the solicitor intervened with a question, asking Rab to clarify his remark concerning a 'cold barrel' shot. Rab stated that it was a law of ballistics: that from a properly zeroed rifle in competent hands, the first shot will always be the best, for as the barrel warms the zero sometimes shifts.

"Of course, I should add that I used the phrase out of habit, for in all fairness it would not have applied to the Brigadier's shot, nor indeed in a stalking situation. It comes into its own particularly in a target rifle, when multiple rounds are fired and the barrel gets hot. But in a stalking situation with a light hunting rifle, one-shot kills are the norm, and even if it took more, the kill area is big enough to absorb any zero shift."

"Now you have me flummoxed, Rab. Two rifles are mentioned, a hunting rifle and a target rifle. I thought a rifle was a rifle. Is that not so?"

"Sorry sir for the confusion, but there is a difference between the target rifle and a hunting rifle. The barrel of a target rifle will be much heavier, noticeably so. This gives it stability on the bench or in a prone position, and the heavy barrel helps to absorb the heat generated from firing while reducing the shimmer that comes off a hot barrel. At long range in a shooting competition, where the closeness of each strike is measured in paper thicknesses, rather than inches, the cooler the barrel can be kept the more accurate the shot will be. There may be other not so obvious differences, but the weight of the barrel will be the most obvious.

A hunting rifle must be light enough to carry all day if need be, yet robust enough to function as to its purpose. Can that help you sir?"

"Hmm, very interesting Rab, very interesting indeed. Thank you for your help. Before you sit again, can I ask another question?"

"Of course, sir."

"Would you care to give your opinion on the Brigadier's test shots on the range? You described them as acceptable."

"Yes sir, acceptable is the only word I could use."

"Why so, Rab?"

"Well sir, our rifles are all zeroed at 100 yards, but we always give a degree of allowance for the shooter. That is to say that if he can place his five shots within a six-inch circle, that is acceptable for a kill shot. In the kill area of course."

"How far was the Brigadier's shot from the imaginary 6-inch circle Rab?"

"Nearly two feet sir."

"Two feet Rab?"

"Yes sir. The beast was a very large one, 20 stone plus, and the stomach is beyond the rib cage, well toward the rear."

"It was a poor shot, Rab."

"Very poor sir."

"Was he drunk Rab?"

"No sir."

"What would you have done had he been drunk?"

"I had already settled that question early on in the stalk. I heard him open his pocket flask and turned and confiscated it there and then."

"One last question Rab, and you have been very patient. What was the terrain like at Braeside Hill where the shot was taken?"

"It was very good underfoot with short grasses, which was why the deer gathered there. It is a favourite place."

"What was the terrain like where the animal eventually fell?"

"Dangerous going sir, rock-strewn gullies and boulder-covered slopes. Treacherous underfoot."

"Who told you the Brigadier wanted to go to where the beast fell?"

"The Colonel, sir. I think the Colonel humoured him as his guest, for the Colonel was not steady enough on his feet for such terrain."

"Was he unsteady Rab?"

"Well sir, it was a very bad war wound. The shell that hit the Colonel took away the calf of his leg in its entirety, and the surgeons removed what was left. The leg from the knee down was merely the leg bone covered in healed tissue, skin that is. There was no muscle, no tendons, nothing. His leg was merely a stiff peg, so you may imagine how difficult it was to move swiftly or manoeuvre, especially on rough ground."

"Thank you again Rab. You have been very patient and very thorough in your explanations. Throughout this whole tragic incident one name keeps coming to the fore in a negative way, and that man is not here to help us in our enquiry, or to offer a word of condolence whereby a grieving widow might take a crumb of consolation. I take great exception to people who take all that is offered by way of friendship and then take off at the first sign of trouble. With Lady Eleanor's permission I should like to write to the said gentleman and make him aware of how we view his absence today."

Lady Eleanor then spoke. "Stu, why did you not go immediately to my husband's aid when Rab asked you to?"

"I couldn't see the reason for such a hurry ma'am. And I thought Rab was a wee bit rude in asking it in such a way. I have brought a few stags in myself on many an occasion, and know a wee bit about it too."

"I see." Is that why you remained for supper before setting out, and is that why you didn't take Ben when asked to do so?"

"Aye, you could put it that way I suppose, but I think it fair to say that I was here before Rab some years, and a man likes to be given his place and not spoken to like a bairn concerning work he has known all his life."

The atmosphere in the room suddenly changed, shocked into silence at the very evident resentment, now revealed, that had manifested itself.

Lady Eleanor sat stoically, she had heard enough. Her husband was not yet cold in his grave and this staff member's callous indifference to it was spoken of in such a manner as to be inexcusable. When she did speak, she addressed Edgerton the solicitor.

"Mr Edgerton, your thoughts on writing to Mr Brodie are quite natural and commendable, and I thank you for your concern. However, I would be dishonouring my dead husband if I did not relate the full story concerning Mr Brodie. I know the Brigadier had his weaknesses, weaknesses that became more apparent since his promotions through the ranks came to him his based on family connections, rather than his military accomplishments. But my husband was very fond of him, for he had seen another side to his character.

Mr Brodie served under my husband in the Boer Wars. He was not a Brigadier then of course. One day as the company were in the field, the scouts spotted what they thought was a Boer encampment out on an open plain. There was a large fire going, tents pitched and horses tethered, and, when the scouts reported all this back, preparation was made to attack.

It was all an elaborate ambush, however. The Boers, knowing the routine of patrols in the area, had set up the camp in the open plain to draw the attention of the British forces. What my husband's company didn't notice was that the only access to the plain was through a narrow and rock-strewn gully.

It was in this gully that the Boer riflemen had hidden, with an artillery piece, having left their horses in the camp half a mile away. As the mounted troops came within range, the first fusillade from the hidden riflemen cut them down like grass before a scythe. Men and horses in a writhing bloody mass now blocked the way forward. Having nowhere to run and no cover for themselves or their horses, the company did the only thing they could do. They turned and fled back down the ravine. It was later described in the company report as a tactical withdrawal!

The Colonel did his best to rally the troops, encouraging them to leave the horses and take cover, but the situation was too late to remedy, for once the company could see safety before them, there was no stopping them.

Mr Brodie was among the fleeing troops, and as he glanced backwards, he saw the Colonel's horse collapse from under him and the Colonel himself trapped under it. A shell from their captured artillery piece had almost severed the Colonel's leg and killed his horse, leaving him stranded and forsaken in the heat of the engagement. The Colonel told me it was the worst moment of his life. He had given up all hope in those few seconds, and he expected no mercy from the men whose wives and children they had been rounding up and putting in concentration camps[x].

It was just then that it happened. The Boer rifle fire, that had now ceased at the departure of the fleeing troops, suddenly erupted again, and as the Colonel raised his head to see what was happening, he saw a lone rider leading a second horse coming at full gallop up the ravine.

It was Mr Brodie. He had turned when he saw my husband fall and, catching the reins of a loose horse, returned for him. The Colonel said the rifle fire was like a curtain of death. It was madness, suicide, to hope to escape such withering and accurate fire, but escape he did, and Brodie came on headlong until he reached my husband. It was just then that the rifles once again fell silent, as the Boers began to realise what was happening. Not a shot was fired as Mr Brodie got my husband mounted and carried him from the field, the Boers giving this heroic act the recognition it deserved.

So you see gentlemen, the Colonel was greatly indebted to Mr Brodie, and would have done anything for him to make his visit to Strathmore as pleasant as possible. He saw him as a victim. A victim of nepotism and cronyism. A sad and tragic culture that is all too prevalent in the armed forces, and which in times of war leads to untold losses and bloodshed. Let's not blame Mr Brodie for the Colonel's death, tragic though it was. He died at a sport he loved, and with two friends he knew and trusted."

There was a stillness in the room that could be felt as Lady Eleanor finished her report. All this was new to the staff and guests that day, and they were stunned to silence at the lengthy and reasoned speech that the otherwise quiet and serene Lady of the Manor had made. It gave them all a very different viewpoint than what Stu MacDonald had planted in their minds, and not a little comfort to know that their beloved employer had died as he would have wished, on the hill, and with friends.

Dr McCabe now quietly intervened, inviting the Chief Inspector to bring a conclusion to the proceedings, and the inspector did not mince his words.

"Lady Eleanor, thank you for the words you have just imparted to us, and thank you for the wisdom and courage to do so. We were all privileged to know the Colonel, and his loss will be felt by all in this room for some time to come. This is indeed a tragic time for us all, and we have heard some tragic things, but let me remind all here today that this is not a court of law, nor is it a Coroner's court.

This meeting is merely a gathering of professional people, friends and staff of Strathmore Lodge, met together to confirm the details that led to the untimely death of Colonel McNabb. Lady Eleanor has done well indeed to call such a meeting and to have it recorded, and to let us hear with our own ears the statements from those who witnessed the accident that claimed the life of a good man. The events of that day are now settled, and the findings of this meeting make it clear to me at least that Colonel McNabb lost his life in an accident that, but for a few seemingly innocuous circumstances, might have been prevented. I say, might have been prevented.

No one in this room intentionally or knowingly brought about the Colonel's death, although the behaviour and attitude of some leave a lot to be desired. The two employees who witnessed the accident have given their testimonies, and since neither have contradicted the other in those testimonies, we must conclude therefore that the testimony of the ghillie and manager, Mr Rab Mackenzie, is to be taken as the definitive version of what exactly happened, even as to times and conditions on the day.

I commend him for a duty well done, and at the same time exonerate him from any blame whatsoever in this unfortunate affair. We are at one with Lady Eleanor in her grief and loss, and assure her of our every support and help as she hopes to continue in the work of the Lodge, difficult though it might be for her.

Thank you, one and all, for your patience today."

Chapter 5

It was two days later that Stu MacDonald was asked to come to the Manor. As he entered, he noticed Rab already there, with the stable boys, housemaids and butler, all seated in the drawing room. Lady Eleanor sat at her desk and beckoned Stu to her desk. He was not asked to sit. She handed him a letter with words quietly spoken. "Stewart, this is a full and final payment for your years of service at Strathmore, and the reason for your dismissal today. If you sign and date this you may take the money and go."

Stewart MacDonald, when raise was not a man to be trifled with. A surly individual at the best of times, he was well known in the local taverns and had been barred from many of them. Strong and wiry, he was hard as nails and stubborn as a mule, and would not take dismissal lightly.

Reaching over the desk he first read the brief message: *"Unsuitable for the post as groundsman."* Nothing was said about the accident and, taken unawares by this surprise, he signed and dated the copy letter and stuffed both it and the money into his pocket. He then glowered around the seated figures, many of whom chose not to meet his gaze, heads hanging[xix] rather than face his baleful stare.

"So that's your game, is it? Looking for a scapegoat for the old man's death? Well, I'm not taking the blame. If you want someone to blame, try his drunken army friend. A windbag and blowhard if I ever met one. Aye, the Colonel was certainly fooled by that one all right, but he didn't fool me, not for one second. Now he's taken off and old Stu takes the blame. Well, I'm not having it, d'ye hear. The Colonel paid for his own mistake, that's what I say. He was old enough to know an old fraud, army friend or no."

At this, Rab stood and moved to Lady Eleanor's desk, where Stu MacDonald stood raging like a cornered animal. "You have said your piece, Stu and you have said enough. Now get out."

"You have not heard the last of this, Mackenzie. I'll see you in my own time and in my own way. Then it will be settled, and only then."

Rab walked around the desk to where MacDonald stood and looked him in the eye. "Get out, Stu, now."

MacDonald, faced with an imminent drama wherein he did not have his favoured surprise advantage, chose not to get involved, and turned and walked out, leaving a badly shaken Lady Eleanor trembling in her seat. That same night Stu MacDonald was found dead in the Lodge vehicle; a single shot to the head had severed his connections to Strathmore forever.

After the meeting was over that day Lady Eleanor was a broken woman.

Stu MacDonald's outburst and the slur he had cast on her dead husband had taken their toll on her. But she had work to do in the immediate aftermath, and she prepared herself to do it.

Sending a maid to the stables with a message to have her horse brought over, she dressed for the ride. It was not far, two miles at most, and the weather was good. Her destination was the home of Stu MacDonald, for Stu's wife was a loyal and staunch supporter of the Strathmore Children's Aid programme, and highly thought of on that account alone. Moreover, Rachel MacDonald was a close confidante of Lady Eleanor, and it was her who was entrusted to come and do the washing and cleaning of her personal quarters.

For this, she was paid, but the bond between them was a genuine one and had grown and matured over the years to a sisterly affection and love, and the two women often sought solace in each other. As her mount made its way down the last stretch of bridle path, Lady Eleanor heard a raised voice, and she could see a figure outside Rachel's door.

It was Stu, and he was now very obviously in a drunken rage. As Lady Eleanor reined in the gelding, she could hear a few words of his obscene outburst. "I'll show them all," he screamed through the closed door. "Just wait and see, I'll show them all." As her horse grew restless, Lady Eleanor patted its neck and spoke soothingly to it to quieten it down. She did not want Stu to see her, and she waited until he took the mountain trail that led to Strathmore Lodge, or to the tavern, depending on which fork he would take where the paths met.

After tying her horse in the lean-to, she knocked lightly on Rachel's door. The two women never spoke, but embraced, sobbing on each other's shoulders, until Rachel finally pulled her visitor inside and closed the door. Sitting now at the rough deal table in the tiny and sparsely furnished room, Rachel spoke first.

"Don't say anything, my lady. There is no need. I have heard it all already and I am not surprised. My husband is unhinged and has been so for a very long time. He has begun to steal, spends most of his time in the tavern and has been spoken to by the police a few times concerning threats he has made. It is a great pity it has taken the death of your husband to unlock Stu's real character.

Only last year, he saw old man McHenry fall on the hill in the snow, and walked past him when he could have saved him. The old man was not found until the spring thaw. What kind of man would do that, my lady? Be very careful please, for my husband has become a very dangerous man and I am afraid for you. Sometimes I am even afraid for myself. Please be careful. Promise me you will."

Lady Eleanor reached across the table and let her hand rest on Rachel's careworn fingers, stroking them affectionately." I promise, Rachel, I promise."

As she gave her horse its head for the return journey, Rachel's words caused the grieving widow to fear. Had she not heard those words, spoken so earnestly, things might have had a different outcome! As she came to a halt at the rear entrance to the Manor, she dismounted and tied her riding crop to the cantle. This was a sign to the stable hands that all was well and to stable the animal. Then, with an affectionate pat on his neck, she let the animal go to find his way to the courtyard. It was a practised and natural end to a day's ride, and as Lady Eleanor turned from her mount, she saw him!

It was still early in the evening and the moon was just breaking above the walled garden, and it was the silvery glint of moonbeam upon the vehicle window that first drew her attention.

Chapter 6

For those few initial seconds, raw fear struck deep within her stomach, and Rachel's words came again to her with an even greater intensity: "Please be careful. Promise me you will."

Stu Macdonald had parked the Land Rover behind a large and leafy garden shrub, which was why Lady Eleanor did not immediately notice it, but she saw it now, and Stu was standing with his back against the driver's door, watching her. There was nothing she could do, and he was too close for her to try to outrun him. It was when she saw the rifle that all hope left her. Even if she could manage to outrun Stu, she could not outrun the rifle.

"Not so high and mighty now, eh?" The drunken man leered. "Friends all gone." Just you and old Stu, the unsuitable groundsman, and that after 40 years' hard work. Just sign it and go, eh? Well, we shall see about that, won't we? Only old unsuitable Stu can save you now, if he had a mind to, that is."

As he rambled on Lady Eleanor began to compose herself, for she knew she must compose herself. The Colonels of-repeated advice came back now with a clearer intensity than ever before. From beyond the grave, his concern reached out in a comforting and clear vision that took her beyond Stewart MacDonald and his drunken intentions, and brought her to execute a plan.

"In a dire situation, don't panic. Never panic. Panic blinds, and panic kills. Think and rationalise the situation. A plan, any reasonable plan, is always better than blind panic."

If she could keep him talking her plan might just work. If she could get him into the vehicle, she could slam the door and run. He was drunk, and she was sure he could not have time to exit the vehicle and catch her, or indeed have time to aim and shoot. It was now or never, while he was still ranting and boasting.

Calling him by his name, she began to walk forward to where he stood, and she put a hand on his arm. "Stu, spare a thought for a widow tonight and talk to me. Not once in all your years here have, I ever said an angry word to you. Not even once, Stu. Surely that must mean something. Surely we can talk this over in a civilised way and come to an arrangement on it.

Get in the truck for me. You can even take the pony home tonight, and I will send something for Rachel with you. Get in Stu, and put the rifle in the rack. Put your bottle over on the passenger side and climb inside and we will talk."

As he stood there in the moonlight, the former groundsman looked at her with glazed and unfocused eyes, puzzled and wondering, no doubt trying to figure out just how the conversation had been turned around to this. When Lady Eleanor saw this opportunity, she took it. Opening the door, she took his forearm and pressed it forward to assist him to enter, saying at the same time, "Come Stu, in you get."

Climbing clumsily inside, he reached over and placed the bottle on the other seat, rifle still in his right hand with barrel pointing upward, and still looking at Lady Eleanor. It was enough! The rifle stock was clear of the door, and she pushed it with all her might.

She remembered nothing more, not even the shot, but the crash of the closing door coincided with the crack of the rifle as it sent its high-velocity load upwards through Stewart MacDonald's brain, killing him instantly.

When Lady Eleanor next opened her eyes, she was lying on the floor in her living quarters and Rab Mackenzie was pressing a cold towel against her brow, trying to bring her round. It took a moment or two, and as she came to she spoke. "Oh Rab," she whispered tearfully. "Where is Stu, Stewart MacDonald, where is he Rab, where is he? He has a rifle; he has a rifle."

"Listen, m' lady, and listen very carefully. Stewart MacDonald is dead, dead by his own hand, and we have only a couple of minutes before others become involved. What happened to Stewart MacDonald happened behind the closed door of a Land Rover. All I can tell you is you didn't do it and, quite apparently, you didn't see it either. On hearing the shot I ran round to see what was happening and found you lying unconscious at the door of the vehicle.

Stay inside. Do not talk to anyone until I get back. Do you understand?"

"But Rab."

"But Rab nothing M'lady. Do you understand? You know nothing of Stewart MacDonald's death but what I have told you, absolutely nothing."

She nodded her head weakly and Rab, before he left, bade her again to stay in her room and send a maid to ask the doctor for a sedative. Then he was gone. When he reached the stable yard it was empty, but he noted the gelding still standing at his stall, so he quickly unsaddled him and led him in, closing the door behind him. "Out of sight, out of mind," he muttered as he made his way to the reception telephone.

Carrying the phone to a quiet corner he phoned the local police.

"Inspector McEwen, please."

"Just gone sir." Anything I can help you with? Who is calling, please?"

"Rab Mackenzie, Strathmore Lodge. Can the inspector be reached?"

"Just hold sir, and I will check he has indeed gone."

"Hello Rab. What's happening with you up there? You just got me going out the door."

"It's bad, Inspector. Stu MacDonald has just been found dead of a gunshot wound in the Lodge Land Rover."

"That's bad Rab."

"Yes sir, it is."

"Anyone else involved?"

"Not that I see sir, and I saw him just seconds after I heard the shot. The vehicle door was closed and it appears to be a tragic accident."

"We cannot handle this alone Rab; I am obliged to call central on this."

"I know sir, but I want to have this cleared up properly for all to see."

"It will be done Rab, and we will do what we can of course, but it is too late tonight to begin investigation. I will send a couple of constables up to preserve the scene and expect us all there tomorrow morning at 8 am."

"Thank you, sir, I will be waiting."

"How is Lady Eleanor coping, Rab, or is it too soon to ask?"

"She is very badly shaken sir, and in Dr McCabe's care. I would prefer in the circumstances that she be not involved in this. I cannot see her being of any material help. As a matter of fact sir, I would ask you to leave her out of this entirely. I do not wish to be blunt, but that's how I see it sir."

"It will be done Rab; it will be done. See you tomorrow."

The inspector looked long at the phone after he had replaced the receiver. Although he felt what Rab had asked of him was a little odd given the circumstances, he nevertheless trusted Rab Mackenzie. As a matter of fact he owed Rab Mackenzie. Just before the war the inspector had a problem. He was a lowly sergeant then, and it was Rab Mackenzie who solved that problem for him.

Chapter 7

It had been a common issue that brought the whole thing about for the sergeant. The McNaghtons, a neighbouring estate, had been losing deer to poachers, and someone from the estate had the ear of police HQ.

Once the complaint went up to HQ, it was the hapless Sergeant McEwen who became the scapegoat. The communication was civil, but the threat was crystal clear. If this poaching cannot be stopped, then the recent application for promotion will not be considered. How could one expect to rise in Her Majesty's law enforcement ranks if something as simple as poaching is allowed to go on under your noses down there? On paper, it looked very convincing, but only those who know the way of the forest and the habits of deer can fully comprehend just how difficult it is to apprehend a cunning poaching gang.

Transport and manpower are needed. Surveillance is required. A knowledge of the highways and byways used to and from the killing ground is essential, as is community help and support. The problem here being, that since the McNaghtons were not particularly liked, who in the community would be willing to speak out at a McNaghton deer going missing? Police HQ had laid a heavy burden on the young sergeant, and he felt powerless to change the situation. It was while in this dilemma that Colonel McNabb's ghillie came to mind.

The sergeant was well enough acquainted with the Colonel, but his ghillie always seemed to be absent whenever the sergeant had occasion to call, and he had begun to think this was deliberate, if for no other reason than that it could hardly be a coincidence! Things being what they were with the sergeant however, he found himself making an appointment to speak with Rab Mackenzie at Strathmore Lodge.

McEwen had decided from the beginning that he would be very frank with Mackenzie, for he had heard he did not suffer fools gladly, and although McEwen did not think himself a fool, yet he considered that if Mackenzie once thought he was being deceived or blindsided, the visit would be short and fruitless.

When McEwen and the ghillie met that day there were few pleasantries, and it was Rab who set the tone of what would take place by commencing with a curt question. "Well sergeant, what can I do for you today?"

Sergeant McEwen immediately picked up on the ghillie's mood and temperament and replied, "I have a problem Mr Mackenzie, a problem I cannot deal with. I don't have the manpower or the confidence of the community in this instance, and I am stymied as to knowing what to do." As the sergeant outlined his predicament, he noted a sudden distaste in Rab's demeanour at the mention of the McNaghton estate.

"The McNaghtons haven't changed, have they," he said to the sergeant. "Looks like as if they still haven't got enough. Now it's a deer or two they cannot abide losing." McEwen was taken aback at this somewhat hostile remark and asked Rab what he meant. Was it something he ought to know about for his investigation or was it merely a personal opinion being expressed?"

Rab was only too willing to supply the young sergeant with the opinion he held. "Whatever way you want to take it, sergeant, but since you are now a victim of McNaghton greed and overbearing authority you might be interested in having the history before you proceed any further."

"Tell me, Mr Mackenzie, and let me decide on the issue for myself."

"Well, long before you were born sir, my father was killed in an accident at the forestry works. The chairman of the company was a McNaghton, and also a major shareholder. That would be the grandfather of the man in charge now.

Due to a cruel and unjust point of law, my mother and her two bairns were turned out of the little forestry shack they had for accommodation while my father worked there. We received not a penny piece of compensation, and but for my grandfather, we might have died on the moors.

Now the same selfish attitude is against you and all that you have worked hard for, all for a few poached deer. How many deer have they lost, sergeant?"

"One a month for the past three months. The poachers are careless with the gralloch and the gamekeeper's dogs are finding it and giving them away every time."

"Hmm, not professionals then; at least that's something in our favour. Three deer, eh, out of the thousands that roam these hills. It could only be a big loss to a greedy man. The McNaghtons are still using the same tactics, willing to sacrifice you and your family for their own personal greed. Your future career will be destroyed if you don't catch McNaghton's poachers; you can rest assured of that. Have you anything to go on, anything at all by way of evidence that might pinpoint the culprits?"

"Nothing, Mackenzie, nothing at all. Plenty of footprints and entrails, but what evidence is that? They must use a vehicle, for those animals are big ones, and I couldn't see them just carrying the carcass off."

"That's right, sergeant; they will have a vehicle. The operation is simplicity itself. The shooter is dropped off at a spot known to hold deer in the late evening. Once set and rifle ready, a lamp man will do a sweep with the light and once the pale orbs of the deer's eyes show, an animal is picked out and shot. It is all over in seconds. The shot beast will be a near one, an easy shot, for they cannot afford to be chasing a wounded deer in those circumstances.

Unless a keeper, or yourselves, were right on hand in those few moments, apprehension of the gang will be almost impossible. When the shooter and his mate have dragged the carcass to the roadside, the vehicle is called up from its hidden location for the pickup, and off they go! A wild night is favoured most often, the wind muffling the sound of the shot and also any little noise the poachers might make. Even the most zealous gamekeeper will hardly venture out on such an evening. Yes sir, Mr McEwen, you have a problem on your hands. I can say that without fear of any contradiction, and I cannot see how I can help you further." The sergeant looked crestfallen at the news and had no reason to doubt Rab Mackenzie's word on any of it.

"So, nothing from these scenes of the crimes at all then that might at least scare them off if it was made known in the village?"

"I was only at the last scene, for McNaghton wanted me to see it for myself, as if that would make any difference, and all I found was this old cartridge which I picked up and slipped into my pocket, not wanting to add to my grief by telling him what I found, for he was in a foul mood."

The sergeant held up the live round for Rab to see. It was old and heavily stained with age, and seemed misshapen and dented compared to modern cartridges. "I never saw one of these before," continued the sergeant. "Dropped no doubt in the hurry of the moment, but what can it tell us of our poaching gang, It's only an old cartridge?"

Rab stood as if transfixed at the sight of the old cartridge in McEwen's hand. He never spoke for a long time, but eventually reached out and took the round from McEwen's palm.

"Sergeant, if these poachers could be identified, what would happen to them?"

"Well, as you know this has been ongoing for a while now and has reached HQ, and McNaghtons themselves have become involved. If caught they will no doubt feel the weight of the law, for old man McNaghton is out for blood on this."

"But suppose this could be stopped without the law becoming involved? Suppose you could solve this and put an end to it without going through the courts; would you do so?" The sergeant was somewhat put out at this rather blunt question, but he had no one else to turn to with his problem. He had come here today for advice, and he felt he must answer the question truthfully if he was not to lose the confidence of the ghillie of Strathmore.

"That's an awkward question, Mackenzie, as I am sure you must be aware. But, if I knew the poaching could be stopped for sure, then yes, I would be willing to do so without the criminal aspect coming to light."

"Can I have your word on that, McEwen?"

"You have my given word. Upon my honour"

"Well then, I can identify your poacher, at the very least the shooter, and I have seen that rifle a few times. "Sergeant McEwen stood slack-jawed at this revelation. He was not expecting this, and this crucial information coming so soon after the impossibility of the problem was a little too much to take in. "What... what do you mean, Rab? Can I call you Rab?"

"Certainly, sergeant. I have just given you my trust, so I ought to have no difficulty giving you my name. I could count on the fingers of one hand how many men use my first name, and I don't give it lightly, I assure you. What I have to tell you involves good people, and I will not have them destroyed or tarnished by the likes of a McNaghton, especially for the taking of a wild animal for the bairn's table."

"I will not let you down Rab, whatever the story you have, so feel comfortable in confiding in me. I have bairns too remember, and I have already suffered from the McNaghtons interference."

"Again, this all happened before you were born, before I was born too as a matter of fact."

Chapter 8

There was once a man in Connan Bridge by the name of Jack McGregor. Jack had a wild way with him and a little place like Connan Bridge was just not big enough for a man with such a nature. Things began to unravel for him when a keeper from McNaghton's estate, where he worked at that time, accused him of not looking after the birds that were being reared for the coming season. Apparently a fox or marten[xviii] had gained access to a pen and killed the lot. One thing led to another and Jack hit him. While at his tea that same evening Jack answered the door to two policemen, who had come to arrest him for the assault on the keeper earlier that day.

Jack listened to them as they outlined the charges and knew from their tone that they were not interested in the facts of the case, but that their sole sympathy lay with the McNaghtons. Jack knew then that he was up against it, and that prison awaited him very soon, and so he decided to do the only thing available to him. Asking the officers to wait until he retrieved his coat and boots, he made straight for the rear door and entered the forest behind the little cottage. Jack was never seen again. Stories abounded about this, but there was nothing of any relevance brought forward to account for Jack's sudden disappearance.

Then one day when I was about eight years old an old man came to our door. His face was so disfigured that we were afraid of him. Asking him to wait, Mam called to Grandfather that someone was here to see him. Imagine our surprise to hear the almighty howls of recognition that seemed to explode at our cottage door. Badly disfigured though he was, Grandfather recognised his old friend immediately; Jack McGregor had come home. We all sat until morning as Jack told the story of those missing years, and what a night it was. Even Mam sat through it, eyes drooping with sleep many a time, but yet not wanting to miss a word.

After he had entered the forest that night Jack knew there was no going back. He was savvy enough to know that the poorest of the parish would not have much by way of sympathy from the magistrate; the McNaghtons would see to that, and he could not abide the thought of prison. So he took the best option open to him; he ran off and joined the army to fight the Zulus in South Africa. When the war was over, he got employment as a merchant seaman and saw the world while he worked! Eventually he did come back to Connan Bridge near the end of his life, and such were his colourful tales of Zululand in the local taverns that he acquired the name that can still be read on the stone marker in the local graveyard: 'Zulu' Jack McGregor.

The Colonel had a great liking for him, for he provided an eyewitness account of the tragic loss of life at the Battle of Isandlwana[xii], where 1,300 British servicemen were overwhelmed by Zulu forces and perished, largely because of the incompetence and inept leadership of its commanders. Jack told of the ranks being so thinned out that they could not possibly hold the line and that the Zulus several times ran through and attacked from behind!

When I first came to Strathmore as a young boy Jack was a frequent visitor. He was very old then but the Colonel always welcomed him, for his very straightforward manner struck a chord with the Colonel. His tales of the battle were a sad reflection on the commanding officer, who had given orders that a new ammunition box could only be opened when the old one was empty, and it was too late then in the heat of battle. It was bayonets and hand-to-hand fighting against men who knew no fear and who were only too willing to trample on their own dead to get to the front where the action was hottest. Jack was still bitter about this even as an old man, and often said that had they had the leadership their comrades had at Rorke's Drift[xii], things would have been much different.

One day Jack appeared carrying a rifle wrapped in a piece of sacking. It was his rifle, he said, the one he used against the Zulus, and which saved his life when a Zulu spear almost took his face off, but for being deflected by the rifle butt.

He wanted the Colonel to put a pin in the split stock, and he brought a few rounds with him to 'try out' on the range. The Colonel was delighted to see the rifle and he and Jack spent a long time discussing those times. The Colonel offered to buy it from him but Jack said he had promised it to his nephew and wouldn't like to sell it on that account. I am of the opinion that the rifle now belongs to the son of that nephew, Jack's grand-nephew, and he still lives in Connan Bridge. The rifle is a Martini-Henry[xiii], firing a very heavy slug, and more than capable of thinning out the McNaghton deer.

There's not another rifle like that north of the border, I wager, and Jack's grand-nephew is your poacher, sir."

Sergeant McEwen had listened enthralled as Rab gave this background story, which so clearly and positively identified the poacher. "Looks like I have a long way to go Rab, if I am to serve this community as I would like. I am indebted to you, truly indebted, and if I can ever do you a good turn you only have to ask. Any ideas as to how I should approach this grand-nephew?"

"Remember these are good people sergeant; they are not of the criminal class. It is not a crime in my book to provide for a hungry family from the wild beasts that roam these moors. Go to him in plain clothes, and have a word with him. Show him the cartridge and tell him you know the story of his grand-uncle, Zulu Jack, and that you don't want history repeating itself in his family over a McNaghton deer.

Don't mention my name; let him wonder where you got the information. I think you will see the problem solved, and sure if you make a friend out of your good turn to him, all the better for you." Tell McNaghton that he will not have any more trouble from the poachers, but not a word of what I have told you, not a single word. You will get the recognition of stopping the gang, McNaghton will be mollified, and Jacks nephew will have learned a lesson too. A good result sergeant for all concerned.

Leaving the station for home, as the inspector now considered Rab's request relating to Lady Eleanor, strange though it appeared, he purposed in his heart to honour it.

"Yes Rab, it will be done, he thought. "I owe you that much."

Chapter 9

Central Division arrived promptly at 8 am the next morning. Rab and the inspector had already visited the scene at first light and it had not got any more pleasant from the evening before.

The inside cab had been liberally coated with blood and brain splatter, and from what they could see through the gore the rifle still lay angled upward and backward from where the butt stock rested in the footwell. It appeared that the deceased's head had been over the muzzle when the gun discharged, and a very evident scorch mark ran for a few inches up his bare neck before the bullet had taken the complete cranium off just above his right ear. "Heavy weapons do heavy damage Rab," the inspector said. "Indeed they do sir, and if more people were aware of just what damage they can do there would be fewer accidents."

"Central will look at every aspect of this Rab, even though it is quite apparent to me that this discharge took place behind a closed door and therefore rules out foul play." "Let them ask sir, and we will do our best to answer, but I want this cleared up in a positive manner, and no loose threads left hanging."

Rab had already visited with Lady Eleanor that morning and told her he would be busy all that day, but that he would come and explain all to her tomorrow. She did not say much, but it was plain to him she was still suffering shock, and he determined that she would not be dragged into this by any officious outside influence if he could help it.

As the small group stood around the scene, two men suddenly appeared in plain clothes and introduced themselves from Dingwall Central: Detective Shields and Detective Ross.

"Would you have a rough time of death?" Ross asked no one in particular. "I have the exact time of death, sir," Rab replied. "And you would be, sir?" Ross asked.

"The ghillie, Rab Mackenzie, and I am the one who found him."

"Not often we have such a clear and positive witness, is it, Shields?" Ross said with a smile. "Exact time, no less!"

"Well, before we move........."

"Excuse me, Mr Ross and Mr Shields. Just before we do go any further with this investigation—this is the second very tragic death we have had here in one week, and we are understandably in a bad way through it all.

Now I can help you by being co-operative, which I want to be, or I can give you the keys of the vehicle and go about my work, but keep a civil tongue your heads, and don't mock me or make light of my assistance, for I will not be mocked by any man." Ross and Shields looked at one another; it was clear they were not used to such plain speaking, but they both realised that the ghillie before them was no country bumpkin, and could perhaps make things more difficult if he chose to do so, so they accepted the rebuke and Ross spoke.

"Mr Mackenzie, I am sorry for the offence given, and I assure you it will not happen again, and yes, we would value your assistance in this matter, very much so."

The police inspector allowed his former intake of breath to exhale slowly. He had wondered just where this standoff would end, and he saw in Rab Mackenzie something he never saw before in any investigation. He saw a man with truth on his side and nothing to hide, and, standing in the confidence of that knowledge, was willing to rebuke even law enforcement.

"Well Rab, can I call you Rab?" "Of course, sir." "Before we move from here to taking statements and have the body removed, I would like some photos of the inside of the cabin. Notably where the rifle is positioned and where Mr MacDonald's hand is in relation to the trigger mechanism.

May I open the door?" "I would be obliged," Ross said. "See if you can open it without disturbing anything inside."

Rab pressed the door handle down very slowly, and suddenly the catch gave a loud click and the door sprang outward from the door jamb. Rab put his fingertip into the now open door and gently eased it open for all to see. It was not a pretty sight.

The rifle butt was resting forward in the footwell, and the weapon, upside down, still angled back to the deceased's shoulder. His right hand was down by his side and clasped around the trigger mechanism, his thumb actually inside the trigger guard. It was a common hold, if not a safe one among hunters, especially when handling a rifle within a vehicle, while in the process of arranging it alongside the seat for rapid availability. The bolt was forward and closed, and Rab told those present the empty case would be inside and could be retrieved for examination. After photos were taken, and the cabin measurements carefully noted, Ross said, "Can you bring the rifle and we will get it cleaned for further handling?" "Certainly, but my fingerprints will then be on the gun, sir!"

Ross laughed: "Don't worry, Rab. The photos are enough for our purposes; you are in no danger." With that Rab took hold of the weapon and wrested it from Stu's cold and lifeless hand, and, using a rag brought for the purpose, wiped the blood from off the woodwork and trigger. "Can we have the empty case?" Shields asked, and Rab, pulling back the bolt, ejected the bright brass case. Picking it up Rab reached it to Shields: "There you are, sir."

The men from Dingwall were very glad they had retained the assistance of this ghillie. As the morning wore on his willingness to oblige was noticeable and very welcome. These men had learned lessons already from the ghillie of Strathmore, and no doubt before the day ended, they would learn even more!

Chapter 10

The large table in the Lodge annex was heavily laden with a variety of breakfast favourites, all piping hot. Bacon, eggs, venison cutlets, black pudding, fried tomato and mushrooms, and an assortment of breads and cheeses. Tea and coffee to wash it down, or a glass of milk, or even a cold, home-pressed Strathmore cider.

It was unpleasant work they were engaged in, but Rab couldn't see the point of making it more unpleasant by being inhospitable or niggardly. Hospitality and courtesy were always part of Strathmore, and Rab made sure that those around the table got what they wanted. Even the maid who attended the table was a winsome lass and had a way of making people feel at home. It was after a hearty breakfast and the table cleared that the men got down to business.

Ross from Dingwall took the lead initially, asking who was who around the table and getting acquainted with the general atmosphere of the room.

Rab introduced the two stable lads and an old man described as a woodcutter. He kept the fires going, Rab explained, and, with the help of a pony, past its best for hill extraction, he chained in windfalls and timber which was then run through the sawmill for the Lodge and the Colonel's needs. A young lass was there also who had come just a week before to gain experience for a university course, and the butler and a couple of maids rounded off the gathering. It was by no means all the staff, but they were chosen from among the staff to better carry the results of the meeting.

Rab further explained that a few of those present were alibi witnesses if such were needed, for he was actually talking to them when the fatal shot was heard. "Gossip is the death of any business, Mr Ross, and I do not want that for Strathmore." To that end he was willing to undergo any reasonable investigation that the Lodge may get back to normality.

Ross spoke again. "Thank you, Mr Mackenzie. You and your staff have been more than helpful already, and we would hope to conclude this affair today and save ourselves a return journey if possible. Now, if I could move forward in a series of steps, I think we can get a full picture of what exactly led to this tragedy. For the sake of our note-taking could I ask you to repeat what you told us when we were at the scene this morning, about you hearing the actual shot?"

"Well, sir, I was in the stable yard with five of these people here present at exactly five by the clock on the 1st November. I was reassigning some work for the next morning and had just finished when I heard a muffled gunshot. I immediately left the group to continue their duties and made my way to the rear of the dwelling house. I was not at all alarmed, but I was curious as to who would be on the estate with a rifle at that hour and without permission. The rest you know, having seen it for yourself this morning."

"Yes, indeed I have seen it, unfortunately, and I shall never forget it. Let's talk now about the rifle we recovered, and I see you have it here for us. When we examined the estate log books, there was no mention of this rifle. Can you explain that to us, please?"

"The rifle is not in the estate register because it is not an estate rifle. It belonged to the Colonel, and he used it in a personal capacity."

"Can you enlarge on that?" "The Colonel brought that rifle home from South Africa when he was invalided out."

"Oh, I see, a war trophy." "No sir, a trophy yes, but not a war trophy, for the Colonel did not look on the Boer War as a war." "But we won, Rab." "But what did we win against, sir? Half-naked Dervishes in the Sudan, brandishing spears and cowhide shields against long-range artillery, rifles and cavalry, and innocent women and children in the Boer Wars." "Surely the Colonel would not share your views, Rab?"

"I am giving you the Colonel's views, Mr Ross. The Colonel thought that Lord Kitchener was a man of blood. A great strategist when it came to herding Boer women and children into concentration camps, where tens of thousands died from disease and hunger. The Colonel told me that he would rather suffer another disability than to take orders from Kitchener again."

"You had a high regard for the Colonel, didn't you, Rab?" "Very high, sir."

"What school did you attend?" "I never attended any school, sir."

"How did you come by your knowledge then?"

"I came to Strathmore in about 1910, when I was ten years old, and the Colonel and Lady Eleanor put me under the care of the former butler. The Colonel's words to the butler were: 'Teach this boy how to read, and read well. 'After that it was easy. I just read, and still do."

"Well, Rab, for what it is worth, you have not disappointed your benefactors."

"It is worth a lot, sir, and I thank you." "Can we get back to the Ma.... Mann....Mannl...." "Mannlicher, Mr Ross." "What is so special about this gun?"

"It was only special to the Colonel because it was a memento, and for a few certain features it has. It is a carbine, a very short rifle, less than 40 inches, and very light, just under seven pounds. In a vehicle all this becomes very important, and the Colonel's shooting activity revolved around his vehicle. You can see how the wood of the butt stock runs all the way to the muzzle. This leaves it very pleasing to handle and a lot warmer in winter than exposed steel. It has another feature, sir, concerning reloading. It has a straight-pull bolt. That means a single pull-back and push forward reloads it.

None of the up, pull back, forward and down again as in most rifles. This feature allows for speed in reloading and also for the shooter to keep his eye on the target in case a second shot is required. It is a very useful feature indeed."

"Does the gun have any disadvantages in your opinion?"

"It is a military rifle, not a sporting rifle, so my opinion could only be from a sporting point of view, and it is hardly a fair comparison."

"Well, Rab, considering it was being used in a sporting sense, and a man has died tragically by it, perhaps your opinion may be useful here."

"Just so, sir. I see the point. The rifle was not made to be loaded in single rounds, as we sometimes are accustomed to doing in field sports and with ordinary bolt-action rifles. The ammunition is fed in from a preloaded clip that fits into the magazine box, and when the last round is chambered, the clip is released. This means that the shooter cannot just put a couple of rounds in his pocket and use one when an opportunity presents itself. He must have the clip already loaded in the magazine, or else carry a clip and load it when necessary. As this can be a nuisance when time is of the essence, a loaded magazine at all times is the drawback in safety terms only."

"What about the safety catch?" "A safety catch on a loaded rifle certainly has its uses in certain circumstances, but it can never be compared to an unloaded chamber and a safe gun.

Do you think the Colonel behaved wisely in having this weapon in his vehicle when we consider the danger it presented?"

"The Colonel was a military man with a military mind. Military men take calculated risks within the sphere of their work. It is allowed. The vehicle belonged to the Colonel, for his use in the field, so it was his choice to make. But over and above all this, the Colonel had a procedure that allowed him to have a military rifle, with a second safety capacity."

"That sounds interesting, Rab. We would like to hear about that."

"There is nothing profound or scientific about it Mr Ross, just plain common sense and wisdom. When the Colonel used the Mannlicher, he never recycled another round unless another shot was required. He always left the fired and empty case in the breech, and only recycled it the next time he needed to. He was very strict in adhering to this procedure."

"Hmm, I see.) So, that being the case, how did Mr MacDonald manage to discharge the weapon?" "There was only one way he could have done that, Mr Ross. He deliberately brought the rifle into readiness to fire."

"Why was the vehicle in the walled garden Rab, beside Lady Eleanor's door?" "If I could read a dead man's mind I could answer that, but I cannot say for sure what was in his mind, sir, but I do know he was drunk. And he had threatened that his dismissal would be avenged." "Just one more question on a firearms issue. When we looked at the Lodge registration list, we found 12 Lee-Metford rifles. But these are all antique rifles, using black powder. Surely the Colonel would have upgraded to something more modern, or are we missing something here?"

Rab smiled. "Not at all, sir, and well noted. We here at Strathmore never use any other rifle than the Lee-Metford, except of course if a guest wishes to bring and use his own gun. When the Colonel returned from the war he took a few years to recover from his wound, and when he eventually opened for business, he did so on a very economical and common-sense budget. He was not dependent on the sporting amenities of the estate for financial independence, nor was he impressed with the American advances in sporting weapons, excellent though they are. He also considered that had his plans for the estate been dependent on overseas supply for parts or ammunition, he may have been at a disadvantage, and since bolt heads, barrels and ammunition were readily available for the Metfords, he stayed with them.

The Colonel was nostalgic about things, many things, and he was at home with the Lee-Metford. He ran the estate very much as he would a working hobby or pastime, and that brought him enjoyment. To send one of his ghillies with a guest, and a black-powder rifle, and to see them bring back a fine stag, brought him great satisfaction. He was a practical man too, and he recognised from experience the value of a reliable military weapon.

Subsequently he purchased 12 brand-new rifles from the manufacturer and customised them for hill use. As far as the black-powder issue was concerned, he found that the extra velocity given by the Lee-Enfield when the new advanced propellant came into use, necessary though it would be in military terms, was far and away above our needs here, and the Lee-Metford never let us down. A quick look at our stalking record says it all, sir.

However, the success of the rifles here at the Lodge came not without thought and preparation. It was no hit-or-miss strategy. The Colonel knew what he was doing. He first stripped each weapon down, and bedded the barrel all along the wood of the fore-end before reassembly. He also brought each trigger pull to a set and exact break-away, and, zeroed carefully by the same man, in the end he had 12 identical rifles.

This meant, of course, that if a rifle got damaged, very wet or mud-caked, it could be left on the repair bench for attention and another identical one used for the next day. When the Lee-Enfield came into service the Colonel was well enough pleased with the performance of the Metford to remain with it, even though it was less powerful than the new Enfield. He did not believe in overkill, and as I have said already, the Metford more than met our needs."

"Well, I think our investigations have proven very thorough, and both Mr Shields and I are satisfied as to all relevant aspects of this tragic incident. If we might have a word with Lady Eleanor before we go, I think our investigation would be complete."

After a respectable moment or two of silence Police Inspector McEwen spoke.

"To all here today, and to these men from Dingwall who have been so thorough and understanding, I express my appreciation. It has been a long and very difficult few days for us all. Let's now put this behind us and go forward. Lady Eleanor needs you all more now than ever before. I am glad it is over, and I can promise you that we will not be far away in the event of any future problems.

I had a word with Dr McCabe this morning regarding Lady Eleanor, and he tells me she is emotionally frail, and it has been advisable to keep her under partial sedation to allow her to come to terms with this second sudden death within a week, as it were. In such circumstances, he tells me it cannot be advisable to interview her, and since she did not even hear the shot, so close to her dwelling, he considers it totally unnecessary to do so. I hope our visitors, Mr Shields and Mr Ross, will see the situation as it is, and accept what we have given them as all they need and more to finalise their report."

Ross spoke now, and concurred with all that the inspector had said, thanking the Strathmore staff for their hospitality and help in what must be a severe trial for them all. With that the meeting broke up slowly, Rab and the policemen being the last to leave. As he walked them to their car he surprised them with a very generous offer.

"Why don't you two men come up after Christmas when we are culling hinds, and I will take you out on the hill? After all this you might be interested in the day-to business of hunting lodge, or a day at the salmon if you prefer." "That would be very interesting Rab," Ross said, "and I think I'll take you up on that." "You do that. I'll be here. What about you, Mr Shields?" "Thank you, Rab, sincerely, but I am more interested in painting a scene than stalking or fishing for it. I might, however, bring my easel and paints and attempt a sketch or two. How would that sound to you?"

"Come and welcome, Mr Shields, and don't bother about bringing lunch. Be my guest at the Lodge on that day."

Chapter 11

As soon as their car had turned onto the road that led to Dingwall, Rab turned and strode purposefully towards the walled garden. Something that was asked during the meeting struck him forcibly. The others had not picked up on it, but when asked the question it immediately registered with him, and he decided to follow it up in the hope of a positive outcome. If indeed his guess was right, it would be a major contribution to his promised meeting with Lady Eleanor.

Walking to where the vehicle had been parked, he saw the trodden grass that had been right by the door, and where he and each policeman had stood, to get a view of the inside before the door was opened. The ground was worse now—trodden flat by the local undertaker, who had removed the body, the truck itself having been taken to be hosed down and cleaned. But Rab knew that if he was correct in his thinking and was patient, he would succeed. He was sure Stu McDonald would have first driven the vehicle here, then alighted, and out of habit would almost certainly have reloaded the weapon immediately where he stood.

Rab went down on all fours for his search, for he knew the difficulty of finding a brass case in grass, even in good conditions. Using his fingertips to part the tussocks and weeds, he did indeed eventually come upon it. Partly buried by the weight of men standing on it, it was there just the same, and he prised it out gratefully, gazing at it in the palm of his hand. The empty case of the last round the Colonel fired and was replaced by the one that took Stu McDonald's life. A live round meant for the Colonel's wife!

He would go now and meet Lady Eleanor as promised, and seek to allay her fears.

It was a great relief to all when they said goodbye to the detectives, but for Rab MacKenzie the relief went much deeper. Stu McDonald had caused great disruption and public scandal to a household that had been so good to him throughout his working life, and Rab considered it a just and proper outcome that the man's final moments remain settled on himself and his own misdeeds.

He had no regrets about having deflected a very embarrassing and potentially damaging investigation with Lady Eleanor. As far as he was concerned she was already a victim, an innocent victim, and he could not see any justice in putting her through a legal protocol for protocol's sake. There was no criminality involved, unless the concealment itself was so accounted, but that meant nothing to the morality of the situation as he saw it, and he dismissed it on that basis. In Rab's mind justice was much better served by common sense. He had lived to see common sense turned on its head in matters legal, and many of those who mistakenly followed such ill-advised procedures were all too often unjustly treated by the same law they had tried innocently and honourably to uphold. He was not going to allow that to happen to Lady Eleanor.

Rab had not come to this decision lightly. He had lain awake throughout the small hours pondering the events of the past few days. He was not an outwardly religious man, certainly not prominent in church activity. But he was a conscientious man and lived by the principles of the Gospels as taught by Christ himself. As a child, he had accepted the Son of God as his Saviour, and it was important to him therefore to meet his fellow man based on honesty, integrity, and transparency. To give a fair hearing to all regardless of their station in life, and to accept hypocrisy and prevarication from none.

He was not a man to ingratiate himself into the company of the well-to-do, but was known more for his dealings with the downtrodden than for his attention to the privileged. It was this very characteristic that brought about a reputation he had in Strathmore and beyond. It all came about at one Autumn fair in Connan Bridge. Livestock of all varieties—pigs, sheep, donkeys, turkeys, geese, and goats—lined a street that was fast becoming a quagmire that wet October morning. Horses, too, were on view for those who wished to buy either a working draught or a riding hack, and Rab had come early to see if he could perhaps get a foal whose temperament would be suitable for hill extraction.

It was as he was engaged in looking over a potential purchase that he saw it happen.

An old woman was coming down the street with three chickens under her right arm, tied by the legs and held carefully, supported by her left hand. It was obvious to all who saw her that her means of livelihood were slim indeed. Behind her came a heavy wagon from a neighbouring estate, a two-horse team pulling an assortment of produce. Potatoes, a crate of lambs for slaughter, wicker baskets of chickens, and bags of grain and vegetables filled out the remaining space. As the wagon trundled along it took up the width of the thoroughfare, and both people and livestock hastily gave it space to pass.

The old woman however did not hear the wagon coming. Coming up behind her, the nearside horse knocked her aside and off her feet. The chickens however were not so fortunate. They fell, still bound, under the feet of the heavy draughts, and what was left of them went under the wheels of the wagon. The broad iron tyres utterly destroying any meat value they may have had. The old woman was unhurt, but the look of shock and horror as she saw her chickens gone was a sight to melt the hardest heart.

Rab saw it all, as did many more that day, but the wagon never slowed or acknowledged the incident, the driver seemingly oblivious to what had taken place. No one went to her aid as she gathered herself together, and tried to brush off the mud that now covered her skirts and shawl, causing them to hang in wet folds around her.

Behind the wagon, one of the chickens feebly kicked a dying farewell to the scene, while the old woman looked around her in utter shock and bewilderment. While the crowd looked on with idle curiosity, Rab stepped forward. As the horses drew alongside he caught one by the bridle, bringing the wagon to a standstill. With oaths and curses the driver now shouted angrily at Rab to let go of the horse and get out of the way or he would feel his fist on his jaw.

Rab never spoke, but taking the short length of rope he had brought for the foal, he tied one end to the bridle and the other to a stationary cart. He then walked forward to the driver and said, "We have seen what you can do to an old woman, step down and let's see what you can do with a man".

By this time the throng had seen enough to know something was amiss, and a hush now swept over the market babble—the silence itself could almost be heard. The driver looked hard at Rab, slack-jawed and doing his best to comprehend what was taking place. "You almost killed an old woman there, and you have destroyed her means of living. You owe her, mister, and you are going to pay before you move another inch down this road."

Rab kept the man in his gaze, and the man under his gaze knew he was in trouble. He never spoke, and he never moved except to transfer a chaw of tobacco from one cheek to the next, and direct a squirt of tobacco juice between the horses before him. He was buying time so that he could figure out what he could do, but for once his wits failed him.

Finally Rab spoke. "I am going to take a basket of your hens now for that old woman, mister. You can try and stop me if you will, or you can pay your employer for them. I advise you to pay your employer!" Rab MacKenzie was not a violent man, but he gained a reputation that day that remained with him for the rest of his life.

Yes, Rab had come to a decision, and he would not flinch from carrying it out. It was in this same frame of mind that he knocked on the door of Lady Eleanor's quarters and waited for admission, as he always did. He did not have long to wait, for Lady Eleanor herself was waiting and anxious. "Thank God you are here Rab, she said tearfully. This has been a terrible day for me. How did the day go, is it over?"

"Yes M'Lady, it is over, and I thank God too, for it has been a heavy burden on me. But grace was given in my hour of need to answer truthfully all I was obliged to, and I did so with a clear conscience."

"Can we speak of God's grace in this, Rab? Are we not being a little presumptuous in doing so? After all, we have hidden a very important piece of evidence."

"No M'Lady, we have hidden nothing evidential, absolutely nothing that was relevant to the truth of the matter. What we have hidden belongs to us, and to no other. We have a secret, yes, but it is not a guilty secret, and the Word of Life itself abounds with instances of those who carried lawful secrets."

"What do you mean, Rab? What about the authorities? Do we not have a moral obligation to them?" " M'lady, I know the depth of your faith, and I know the sincerity of your heart, and I would never ask you to compromise either of those two things, never. There is a crucial difference between legal codes and ethical principles, and we must sometimes differentiate between the requirements of law and those of morality.

It was I who brought you from the death scene, and you were unconscious when I did so, so you have nothing to hide or feel guilty about. As for myself, I have not the lightest regret at having done so. I am a believer too, and if you will just give me time to put the case to you, perhaps you might be led to see it differently.

Chapter 12

Very gently Rab MacKenzie began to counsel his grief-stricken employer. She was in no state for more trauma, and Rab was very aware of just how much all this had taken its toll on her health.

"M'Lady, we cannot pick and choose what we want to believe from the Good Book, and we cannot be more Christian than Christ himself. Some things are easy for us to accept and follow, and other things we refuse under the belief that it is not Christian for us to accept them. We did not wish for this to happen. We did nothing to bring this on ourselves. We are innocent of any complicity in it.

Stu McDonald is dead, killed with the weapon he had already loaded and made ready for your death. Now, if we believe that *'Whatsoever a man soweth, that shall he also reap'* we must believe that the Lord in His overriding grace and mercy delivered you from Stu McDonald, and brought Stu himself to His judgement bar. It is not a pleasant truth when we see it come to pass before our eyes, and the bloodshed involving us so to speak, but it is God's truth nevertheless. Will we then take God's gracious deliverance and throw it back in His face because it offends our sensibilities to accept it? God forbid, M'Lady.

Stu McDonald could have easily throttled you with his bare hands, but he chose to play cat and mouse before he shot you."

"But Rab, maybe he didn't know the gun was loaded; perhaps he was only trying to scare me." "Well, I can tell you a different story, M'Lady." Reaching into his waistcoat pocket, Rab pulled forth the empty and muddied brass case. "Do you know what this is?" he said as he handed it to her. "It is an empty cartridge case from my dear husband's rifle. Where did you get it?"

M'Lady, no one knows better than you where this could have come from. This was the last round fired by the Colonel, and left in the breech as was his custom, until Stu McDonald deliberately reloaded the Mannlicher just outside your door. I picked this up on the way here. I found it in the grass.

You have been delivered M'Lady; it is very evident to me, and Stu McDonald has gone to meet his Maker and give account there.

Do you realise what would have happened if we had allowed the authorities the knowledge of those few minutes of talking with Stu? You could now be facing a murder charge. All that was needed was an unscrupulous prosecuting counsel out to make a name for himself, as the McNaghton lawyer did concerning my father, and it would be very easy to show how a drunk man could be lured to his death and the whole thing made to look like an accident. Stu McDonald has caused us much grief here at Strathmore, and I was not going to allow him to cause more mayhem by his death.

Have you thought of Rachel, his wife, in all this M'Lady? There is another side to this. Had we allowed Stu's murderous intent to be known, we would have robbed her of every memory she may have taken comfort from, and left her and the bairns to live out a life of shame by being the relatives of a would-be murderer. If we cannot add something good to a widow's grief, we ought not to remove what little good they may have."

Lady Eleanor sat through all this, eyes fixed intently on Rab, listening to every word and noting every nuance of his argument. She felt ashamed of her weakness, and her fear and her lack of understanding of the real issues at stake in this. Rab was right. What would the world be like if men and women of character and principle allowed evil to flourish, and refused to shoulder arms in the battle for the Crown rights of King Jesus? Would she show the same sympathy for Ananias and Sapphira[xiv] that she had shown for Stu McDonald? Or Judas Iscariot, who had a heart of ungrateful wickedness?

As she pondered these things, a whole array of Bible characters suddenly began to come to mind, those who had paid a heavy price for their sins, and she realised for the first time just how much she needed to lay hold of these revelations also, and accept them as inspired waymarks and warnings. Many things are included in the Scriptures, and set before the Christian in life's pilgrimage, to keep them in the narrow way, and to remind them of satan's malice, and the Lord's retribution for disobedience.

"We haven't included the clergy in this, Rab. He has not been asked for his advice; ought we to do so, just to be sure?"

"No, M'Lady, and we shall not be approaching him for advice on this or on any other matter concerning Strathmore. I noted he was not asked to join the staff enquiry into the Colonel's death. You must have had a reason for that omission!"

"You do not have a very good opinion of the clergy, do you, Rab?"

"No, M'Lady, as a matter of fact I have a very poor opinion of them generally."

"Why is that Rab? You must have strong feelings to think as you do."

"I have very many reasons, M'Lady, and I have had fifty years to have them confirmed over and over again in my mind and heart."

"Even here in our own parish, Rab?" "Particularly here in our own parish."

"Do you care to tell me about it?" "I don't like dwelling on them, as I don't want my heart to become bitter or hard as a consequence. But in the circumstances M'Lady, I will recall an incident that may serve to show my suspicion of the clergy, and I will leave you, M'Lady, to judge for yourself whether or not I have just cause.

I was just four or five years old when my father was killed. He had just finished his shift and was walking past a pile of logs near our cabin when a ground stay gave way and they rolled over him. He was killed instantly, and Mother couldn't even open the coffin. When we were evicted from our cabin, some good folks made a protest to McNaghton. The local doctor at that time and the undertaker Sowerberry were the ones to the fore in helping us. In fact, it was Sowerberry who went to see the clergy on Mother's behalf.

My father never missed church when he was alive, and my earliest memories are of that. When the clergy was approached to enter a plea for some kind of compensation for our family, he refused on the grounds that Mr McNaghton was also a member of his congregation, and it would not be fair if he were to show favouritism between members of his own flock! The morality of the situation was ignored; favouritism had nothing to do with it.

That was in April I think, but just six months later another event took place that brought my father's death to the fore again. It would have been just before you came to Strathmore M'Lady.

One beautiful autumn afternoon the McNaghton nanny took their two children for a walk in what was then called the High Meadow. It was a common thing for her to do, a regularly repeated custom. There were always a few hinds that frequented that meadow, I suppose because it was quiet and secluded, and the children had often been taken to view them as a treat, and perhaps have a picnic while they were there.

On this particular afternoon however, a rutting stag had joined the group, and, seeing the children, began stomping[xv] towards them menacingly. As it drew closer it became apparent that the stomping was no showy ritual, such as can be seen sometimes, but the animal was indeed aggressive. The nanny gathered the children behind her and screamed loudly, for there was nowhere to run and no cover for her to take refuge. A young man tending pheasant pens not far away, hearing the screams, saw it all happen in a few terrible seconds. At the stag's first charge it seriously injured the nanny and the young boy, aged seven. At this the little girl ran, and the animal, now emboldened, charged again and lifted her like a rag doll on its antlers. The child's clothing however, became entangled on the antler tines, and instead of falling to the ground she fell back within the antlers themselves.

It was a terrible sight, M'Lady. The child, still alive and screaming, and the stag now trying to shake itself free of the awful burden. Finally it ran off in a panic and disappeared, taking the child with it.

Every man who could hold and fire a rifle made their way to the McNaghton's that night. There was nothing they could do in the darkness, but they came just the same, determined to do what they could to help in this time of extreme tragedy. The community felt for them, and I remember Mother crying in her prayers for the situation. It took two full days to find that stag. He had run himself to exhaustion and died with his grisly load still entangled on his head.

The McNaghton's blamed the nanny. They said she ought to have known of the danger. That it was a case of gross negligence, taking small children to where a rutting stag had hinds to protect, and that she might have known so. They dismissed her in disgrace. The fact that she had sustained a broken arm and had put herself in harm's way to protect the children did not seem to register with them.

The funeral was the biggest ever seen around these parts. They buried her in what is now the old graveyard, right at the top in a secluded corner. Mrs McNaghton wrote a few lines to put on the granite pillar they erected a little later, and nicer words would be hard to find, M'Lady."

"Do you know what it says, Rab?" she asked. "Have you read it?" "Many times, M'Lady." "Tell me, Rab, for your story is so remarkable and touching, that I would love to hear what the mother wrote for the headstone."

"Well, M'Lady, from memory it went something like this:

> *'Beneath this grassy hillock, my darling Annie sleeps.*
> *Nothing now can hurt or harm her; Jesus safe her spirit keeps.*
> *Shall I wish her back to mourning?*
> *Shall I wish her back to weep?*
> *No, I'll joy because my Saviour, placed my lamb among his sheep.'"*

There was silence in the room as Rab finished speaking, and it was so for long moments. A tear rolled down Lady Eleanor's cheek and fell on the desk, fragmenting into tiny droplets on the red leather inlay. Rab himself hurriedly wiped a hand across his face, for the sight of Lady Eleanor's evident emotion had affected him. "That was lovely, Rab," she said at last. "Thank you for sharing that with me, and thank you for coming in tonight to give me the report."

"But the story is not finished yet, M'Lady. Not quite.

The girl belonged to the same parish as the McNaghton's, and when she became well enough to attend again, she was immediately called aside that Sunday morning and told by the clergy that in view of the great tragedy, it would be advisable for her to attend another church, for her visible presence was a source of greater grief to the already grieving parents.

So yes, M'Lady, if I may respectfully go back to answering your previous question, I do have a dislike and suspicion of the clergy. Just because a man wears the garb of religion, it does not make him a man sent from God. After all, we have only their word for it! In my judgement, those who put on the livery of religion must prove themselves to be true, and that can only be done through their behaviour, example, and character. Robes, titles, and colourful vestments alone are no substitute for Christ-likeness, and no proof whatsoever that Christ sent the wearer of such! Many aspire to be religiously employed, but employment in things religious is not proof of discipleship.

The Word of God nowhere states we must give allegiance to those who merely wear the garments of piety, but makes it very clear that we will recognise the true from the false by the fruit they bring forth. That being so, M'Lady, we are at liberty to decide for ourselves who deserves our respect and recognition as servants of Christ.

Do you ever wonder M'Lady, why the taverns are full and the churches almost empty? There is a reason for that, and it is not always the fault of people who frequent the taverns. Men, even rough, ungodly men, are quick to recognise a hypocrite, and I have known a few of them in Strathmore over the years. Is it too much to expect that a man who claims the authority of God ought to have the characteristics of Christ about his person? Yet what do we see? Self-serving, and moral cowardice when it comes to defending the wronged. Indifference to the needs of those who have the most need—the widow and fatherless children, the poor of the parish, the unimportant of this world.

No, M'Lady, I could never accept that those clergy who neglect these things were ever sent from God. They have made an industry out of religion, an employment, an easy living, and this nation has suffered as a consequence. The decline in church attendance has its roots in the clergy themselves, and it is there they must begin to find a solution.

Excuse me, M'Lady, I did not mean to say as much as I have done, but my heart is heavy when I see how unjustly people are treated by clerics that I cannot contain my distaste for them. Please forgive my outburst."

Lady Eleanor rose and approached the ghillie standing before her.

"On the contrary Rab, there is no need for forgiveness. I thank you rather. I have listened to you with great attention, and admiration too. You have spoken well, but the sad thing is it is all true, and I have learned more from you tonight than I have in a lifetime from the clergy. It grieves me too, and it grieved the Colonel. That is why he was so supportive of the Strathmore Widow and Child Programme. He knew more than he ever said, and he never once invited the clergy to Strathmore.

You have brought great comfort to me today. To hear from other lips what I had known for myself, but was afraid to admit for so long. I see things now more clearly than I ever saw them before, or ever will see them again. Thank you again; I am indebted to you for your candid, honest, mature judgement. Before you go, can I ask you something?" "Certainly, M'Lady." "Will you bring me my husband's rifle?" "It is in my cottage; I'll bring it tomorrow. Let me clean it first."

Chapter 13

ab MacKenzie lived alone in a cottage at the main gate to Strathmore Lodge. It was a small cottage, consisting only of two bedrooms, a living area, and a scullery for cooking and washing up. Another small room leading off the scullery served as a pantry. There were no glassed windows in the pantry, but on three sides the window space was covered with very fine mesh wire, and this allowed perishable foodstuffs and meat to be kept fresher for longer. In the wintertime it froze!

A small porch shielded the front door from the worst of the winter gales, and the roof, steeply sloped, was finished with a tasteful mixture of grey and blue slates from the Luss quarries. Built of local stone, well pointed, each of its three front windows was made up of six small panes, and although modest, it was nevertheless impressive.

It was called 'The Gate Lodge'; most, if not all, estates had them, and, as the name implied, lodged the man at the gate. This necessary security function doubled as a status symbol to the community, and it was this factor that ensured the building was kept in good repair and appearance.

Strathmore had long since ceased to use the cottage as a security measure, and so Rab became the new tenant when he was given the job as Land Steward by the Colonel. It was within this snug and private dwelling that Rab MacKenzie spent his evenings. The large iron range, an old original Esse Doric model, well supplied with seasoned timber cut small, provided him with warmth and comfort. He rarely cooked, for the Lodge kitchen provided his needs, but on those occasions when his sister visited, he himself prepared a savoury dish for both of them.

His evenings were spent reading, either from his Bible or one of the many volumes he had acquired over the years. An oil lamp, with a tall glass chimney, gave forth its light from a little table at his elbow. He could have used the electricity, put in years ago by the Colonel for his ghillie, but the lamp had belonged to his mother, and he preferred it.

However, as it so often proves to be, Rab MacKenzie's solitary and comfortable lifestyle was not all unalloyed happiness, for he carried a secret grief within his heart. The trauma that he suffered in his early childhood affected him deeply, and the older he became the worse it seemed to be.

Rab never socialised beyond his duties as estate manager, and while he never had a lady companion throughout his life, he carried a hope within his breast that it might be so one day. Someone who would understand him, someone who would be a soul companion. Someone he could trust implicitly. He had a yearning in his heart for mutual companionship, shared ideals, and aspirations.

With this future hope within, and his daily energetic commitment to employment, Rab overcame those dark and brooding visitors from the past. No one would have guessed that the ghillie of Strathmore had this hidden affliction, but beyond the business-like exterior lived another being altogether, the *"old man"* as the Scriptures described it, and it was only by the grace of God that the *"new man"* prevailed.

Rab understood that solitude was not always the best answer to his hidden problem, but he did prefer to be alone, and sought to keep his mind constantly busy, always planning tomorrow's work today, and thus leaving no room for those negative things to take hold of his mind and heart. It was this very circumstance that led him to take a renewed interest in the game fishing aspect of Strathmore, and in doing so opened up a challenge that even he found daunting in its eventual outcome.

Although a neighbour, and a close neighbour to the McNaghton estate, Strathmore had a feature that was the envy of the successive McNaghten dynasties. Flowing slowly northeast towards the Firth, the Ringhorne River, by a quirk of nature's fancy, suddenly veered away from the McNaghton acres, and for six miles meandered through Strathmore's lands. The Ringhorne had another cruel twist for the McNaghton's. It was not a shared river. Strathmore owned the land on both sides, and, try as they might, the McNaghtons failed to either purchase or rent either the land or the fishing rights on it. The Colonel was not a self-serving landowner, and he resisted the temptation to sell off any of the land or fishing rights. He always said that the very best of fishing would always be affordable on the Ringhorne, and year by year the clientele grew until Strathmore salmon beats were the last word in the fishing fraternity. The Colonel's own thirty-year-old record still stood, and was there on display in a prominent place in the Lodge dining area. Underneath, in a neatly framed plaque, were the words:

> *"58 lb hen fish. Fresh run with sea lice[xvi] still attached. Taken on beat 6, north bank, Strathmore. Lure was a hand-tied 'Willie Gunn', fished slowly down the ripple.*
>
> *The rod was a Hardy ten-foot split cane, and the reel was from the same manufacturer. The leader was fifteen fifteen-pound breaking strain and it took 1 hour and 15 minutes to net."* Archibald McNabb, July 22, 1930.

The Colonel liked to share, and he knew those who sought the 'king of fish' would want to know the details.

Many were the eyes that looked longingly on that fish over the years, a constant reminder to all hopefuls of what they might expect. Rab could not guarantee them success, but he could make the way to success possible by his close and diligent attention to each and every salmon beat Strathmore had.

Given that the tree line sometimes reached the riverbank on Strathmore's six-mile stretch, only nine beats were possible, but using both banks, this doubled, and these beats were identified as North and South for clarity of purpose. Each beat was a proven and productive companion to the others, and Rab had decided to utilise them to their full, attractive potential. Shelters, stiles, beat numbering, and distance indicators to the Lodge were all helpful, cheaply provided additions that proved welcome to all those who visited Strathmore's Ringhorne, and this kept him busy. It was while he was engaged in this renewed interest that the first inklings of trouble manifested themselves in the county.

A neighbouring estate had suffered the loss of a gamekeeper when he came upon a poaching operation. The gang, raiding a pheasant roost, beat him so badly that he died at the scene. It was sad news. Such news is always sad, but when little children are left fatherless on the run-up to the Christmas season, it seems to resonate more deeply with the public. Yet, paradoxically, it was the same public that encouraged such greed and criminality through their readiness to buy black-market produce! Wherever there is an opening for such trade, there are always those who are willing to meet its needs. Here in the Highlands, the coveted desire for ill-gotten gains, be it fish, fowl, or flesh, was an ever-present threat to those whose honest endeavours put them in harm's way while protecting their lawful interests, and there were men desperate enough to kill to avoid capture and jail.

At times like this, estates pulled together in order to apprehend the culprits, and extra men were temporarily employed to patrol the woodlands and riverbanks in the dark of night, hoping to catch, or, at the very least, scare off the thieves. The real difficulty for all the estates was the random habits of the poachers. The estate management did not know when or where they would visit next, and so any success they may have had with the patrols was limited indeed.

The knowledge of a gang now operating in the area was bad news for Rab MacKenzie. He knew how vulnerable Strathmore was, for while all estates in the area provided venison and pheasant, only Strathmore provided salmon! Rab knew that in the approach to the Christmas season, Strathmore would be a target.

Since the Colonel's death, Rab had taken on the Colonel's weekly habit of riding the river and checking that all was in order. It was not an onerous duty, and Rab always looked forward to it as a welcome break from the intense activity of the hill stalk and all the preparation that goes with it. Every Monday morning, therefore, after the work for that day was designated to staff, Rab saddled a quiet pony and, with a flask of tea and a sandwich in his shoulder bag, he set off. He did not carry a gun on these rides, preferring to give all his attention to the work at hand, and not be distracted from it by the temptation a gun may have had if he encountered crow, fox, or magpie on his travels. Vermin control was important, but today it would be the river that would get his full attention.

Chapter 14

The ride that early October morning was uneventful. All was peaceful and serene as he gave the pony his head and let it follow the path. On these rides, he never failed to note that, while only four feet higher, one could see much more from horseback than from walking, and the experience was a pleasant one. He enjoyed the wider view the elevation gave him, enabling him to better see the otter track running along the riverbank, or the dew-marked fox trail in the grass. Here and there, a fish head or bony remains were visible—picked clean, for what the otter left the crows and magpies finished off.

It was as the pony veered to skirt the tree line close to the water's edge that Rab saw it. A flattened area, caused by many feet, and entering the trees and undergrowth. This was not usual, for the area was unsuitable for fishing, and yesterday being Sunday, meant that no fisherman had been here from Strathmore. Dismounting for a closer look, Rab noted a cigarette end and some spent matches. The cigarette end was of the hand-rolled variety, such as is common with those in society who are among the working class—miners, dockers, and forestry labourers. Rab was aware, too that criminals, and especially those who had done jail time, were given to this particular method of tobacco use, and the thought perturbed him, certainly in the light of the recent murder of the gamekeeper. Carefully putting the cigarette stub in his pocket with the spent matches, he mounted again to continue his ride, and had not gone very far when he saw the boy.

Of slight build and not more than ten or twelve years old, Rab noted he had a boy's usual fishing tackle—a long pole and a line of equal length. Here, where the river was not far from its headwaters, such a fishing rig could easily span the river, and in the right hands, and with the right lure, could be every bit as effective as the more expensive outfits of the well-to-do.

As Rab came into the boy's vision, he noted that the child never wavered from his purpose, but fished on without as much as a look at the new arrival on horseback. Suddenly the truth dawned on Rab. The boy was not expecting a ghillie to be on horseback, and had thought of him as some stranger out for a morning ride along the riverbank.

Riding to within easy talking distance, Rab greeted the young poacher. "Hello laddie," he said. "I see you have a fish in your bag; is it a good one?"

"Not bad, mister, but a bit thin for a salmon." "Oh aye, can I see it?" Rab replied.

As Rab dismounted, the boy drew forth the fish from the makeshift bag he carried and laid it on the grass. It had been a good fish once, Rab thought, perhaps ten pounds weight or thereabouts, but he could see it was a kelt[xvii]—a spent fish, and not fit for the table. "Aye, I can see what you mean about it being a bit thin; do you know why that is lad?" "No mister, I just thought it was a bit thin, that's all." "Where are you from son?" Rab asked. "Dingwall, mister."

"Oh, come on now, Dingwall is a long way from here, and you didn't come all that way this morning to fish here," Rab said kindly. "No, mister, I am from Dingwall but I am staying in the Strath with my granny. Grandpa died two weeks ago and my ma sent me down to stay with granny till they decide how best to care for her." "Two weeks ago, you said, then your grandpa would have been old Jamie McPherson then?"

"That's right, mister; did you know him?" "Aye, that I did son, and a more decent man never lived in these parts. Let me tell you a story about your grandpa. It was he who was with my father on the day he was killed in the forest. He escaped, but my father didn't, and the pile of logs killed him when they slipped. He and your granny Margaret came to our house not long after and I remember them bringing some milk and bread and potatoes. My mother never forgot that lad, and neither did I. I was just a child myself then but I remember it well for all that. Your grandpa must have been in his nineties then when he died?"

"He was in his ninety-third year." "How is your granny Margaret now, then?" "She is able to get about, but I carry the water and firewood for her, and if she is laid up, I can make her the porridge in the mornings. I can cook too, mister, but mostly granny cooks and bakes the bread."

"The fish is for her then, is it?" "No mister; big Frankie said if I caught a good fish he would give me ten shillings for it, so I would buy granny something with the ten shillings." "That would be big Frankie Fraser?" "How do you know all this, mister?" the child asked wonderingly.

Rab laughed at this, and at the child's innocent expression. "Sure, I was born around here lad, and the Strath is a small place; everybody knows everybody else. I thought big Frankie was in jail."

 "Well, "He was, but he is out again now and has started doing the markets round about. Fruit and vegetables mostly. He gets me to help him sometimes and gives me a few coppers for it." "I wouldn't have thought that a small market stall could afford two workers."

Well, it's not actually work I do mister; just messages now and then when he needs something and doesn't want to leave the stall. Maybe a slice of haggis for his lunch, or going to the shop to see if his tobacco has been sent up from Glasgow, or telling his wife something or other."

"Never knew big Frankie to smoke a pipe, but he must if he gets a supply of tobacco for it," Rab replied.

"Oh it's not a pipe, mister. Frankie makes his own cigarettes. He rolls the tobacco in special paper and smokes it just like a cigarette. No one else in the village uses that make, so he gets it sent up from Glasgow. It has a lovely scented smell too—not like other tobacco. Big Frankie likes it best, he says."

The mention of the rolled cigarettes was not lost on Rab, but he kept the conversation general and commonplace, for it would never do to involve the boy in this poaching problem, especially with Frankie Fraser as a suspect. Frankie was bad news and had few scruples about how to make a living.

"I take it that Frankie told you of this fishing place then lad?" "Aye, mister. He said if I come up near the old bridge here, nobody would bother me, for fishermen don't come this far up on account of the weeds and very shallow flow. He said that even Strathmore ghillies never come up here, so I would be safe from them too."

"Did he now?" Rab chuckled. "Big Frankie has it all worked out, hasn't he? Ten shillings, he said he would give you. What would he do with a salmon on a vegetable stall?" "Oh, he sells fish too mister. Every Monday or Tuesday he has them, but not on other days. He keeps them under the table, for he says the sunlight dries them out. He always knows who wants a bit of salmon, so he doesn't need to put them on the stall." The innocence and naivety of this lad was a joy to behold, but a well-brought-up child under the influence of Frankie Fraser was a sore point with Rab, for sooner or later such an arrangement would lead to mischief and criminality.

"Listen, son, I have a few things to say and I want you to note them well. Can you take a little advice from a friend of your granny, and of your now-dead grandfather?" "Sure, mister, and I know my granny will be pleased that I have met you."

"Well, son, that fish is no good for the table, and big Frankie will not want it. Take a good look at those fins; note how they are frayed and worn. See how those gills are not red and healthy-looking; they are pale and not a good colour. The shape of the fish is not right either. It is too long and thin for a healthy salmon, with no depth or firmness to the body. This is what is known as a kelt.

A kelt is a fish that has entered the river perhaps months before and, having not eaten since it came from the Atlantic, spawned here in the Ringhorne where it was once spawned itself a few years ago. Now, having spawned, it might have survived to return to the ocean if you had not caught it. Unlike American species of salmon, the Atlantic salmon survives the spawning cycle to return again to the river of its birth. We sometimes call them spent fish, for that is what they are. Throw that fish to the crows and magpies and I will give you ten shillings to buy your granny something fit for the table; how's that for an offer?"

The boy could hardly process all this information and good news, all coming so quickly from the lips of this kindly stranger, and his face showed his wonderment and puzzlement. "How do you know all about fish, mister? Will you really give me ten shillings for my granny? What will I tell big Frankie if he asks me if I caught a fish today?"

The questions were brought to an end by Rab placing a kindly hand on his shoulder. "What's your name laddie?" "Ian McHenry." "Well Ian, I want you to tell your granny everything that you can remember of our conversation here today, but not a single word to Frankie Fraser. Tell him you did catch a fish but it looked sick and thin, so you left it on the riverbank. He will know immediately what it was and never question you, and you will have told him no lies. Do you understand what I am saying here? Frankie is not to be told of our meeting."

"Granny has warned me too, mister, to be careful of Frankie." "There you are then boy, I am glad of that, very glad of that. Do you know who I am, Ian?" "No mister, I don't, I just thought you were someone riding by." "No Ian, I am not just someone riding by, I am Rab MacKenzie, ghillie of Strathmore estate, and I am on the lookout for any sign of poaching up here on the river. But you were not expecting a ghillie on a horse, were you? That is why you were not alarmed when I came in sight."

The child was taken aback by this revelation from the lips of his new-found friend, and Rab, who would not have scared him or hurt him for all the fish in the Ringhorne, quickly put the lad at ease.

"Ian, not to worry. Let me explain to you. This is all private ground on both sides of this river, and the taking of fish without permission is poaching. Big Frankie knows this, but he sent you here anyway, for he has no regard for the rules and regulations of society. To fish on this river a permit is needed and permission from the estate.

Today you are poaching and are breaking the law. But I have a plan to fix that for you. The management of this estate can give a visitor a permit that covers all the legalities with the law, and since you are now my visitor, I am sure Lady Eleanor would not object to giving you one; indeed, I am sure she would be delighted to do so for your granny's sake.

Now, Ian, there is one very important thing that goes with the fishing permit. You must not tell Frankie Fraser you have it, and you must not tell him of our conversation here today. Do you understand this Ian?" "Yes sir, I do, and I will never mention it to him." "Good; now if anyone approaches you while you are fishing, just show them the little paper you will get today. Call for it on your way home, and the ten shillings too, and remember—tell your granny everything, but Big Frankie nothing. Take care lad, and watch out for an undercut bank. Sometimes they give way and leave you in the water." "I will sir, and thank you for everything. I'll tell my granny the whole story, and I know she will be very pleased to hear it."

As Rab lay that night, sleep forsook him. He could hardly believe his good fortune in meeting old Jamie McPherson's grandson, and the information the lad gave, quite unknowingly. He was sure now in his own mind concerning the poachers' methods, and he was sure exactly where they would strike next. He knew now for a near certainty that Sunday night would be the next time they would appear, and he knew their route to the very spot. Without the knowledge he gained from young Ian McPherson, Rab knew he would have been hard put to put an effective plan into action, but now he had, as it were, a blueprint of their next excursion. Could he ask for more?

With this knowledge of the poaching gang well and truly implanted in his mind, Rab allowed his thoughts to travel to the damage poachers of this calibre do. If it were only a man sneaking a salmon now and then, it would hardly be worth the effort to catch him. But Rab knew that a gang using a gill net was far removed from stealing a fish or two. The old Colonel had introduced Rab to the miraculous breeding cycle of Atlantic salmon. Unlike other species that died after spawning, the Atlantic salmon survived the breeding cycle and were able to return to the sea from whence they came. Every salmon egg that was spawned on the upper reaches of the Ringhorne River, if it survived to adulthood, would one day return to the same spot to repeat the spawning cycle. Large numbers of hen fish therefore, bursting with eggs to deposit on the Ringhorne redds[xviii], if netted and killed by poachers, would leave a significant gap in the numbers of fish returning to the Ringhorne in the returning migration three or four years later, for the success of a good salmon river depended on a good hatch on its redds. Large-scale poaching therefore, was not something that could be neglected.

Rab was sure he had the gang identified, for the Strath was a small place and only a local would know the most isolated beat on the river, and have the knowledge that Sunday was off limits, and therefore the most opportune time to trespass without detection.

Although poaching was not an actual hanging offence, and therefore low down on the scale of priorities, the police had now an ongoing murder investigation since the death of the gamekeeper, and Rab was sure they would be very interested in the information he had, and more than willing to assist in any plan he had that would apprehend the potential culprits!

Rab had a plan, and it was a simple one. He had seen the forestry trail where the poachers had driven to within half a mile of the river. If he could get as many uniformed constables as police resources would allow, he could muster a dozen men to assist them. If just a couple of constables, waiting and hidden on the forestry track where the gang parked, they could arrest the driver, or whoever was left to mind the vehicle, after the others made off to the river. The remainder of the police and volunteers would already be at the river, and when the gang retrieved the net and were making ready for the night's poaching, Rab himself would spring the trap.

The Colonel too, would have a part to play in this exercise, even though he had been dead for a few years, and the thought made Rab smile. In the estate gun room, there was a cabinet that only Rab had access to. It was the Colonel's private cabinet, but Rab had been in it enough times to know exactly what it contained. Cartridges for the Mannlicher, and boxes of ammunition for the estate Lee-Metfords.

Some fuse wire and detonators left over from a blasting job years ago were there also, and Rab remembered it well when a very large boulder had to be removed to allow a carriage path to the river. There was also an almost new German C-96 semi-automatic pistol that the Colonel had 'captured' from a Boer commander. It was a prized possession to the Colonel, for a young Winston Churchill had told him a similar weapon had saved his life in the last cavalry charge against the dervishes of the Sudan. Churchill had changed from sabre to pistol mid-charge owing to a long-standing shoulder injury, and but for that change, he would have perished like so many more of his comrades. The Colonel loved to recall the merits of the pistol that day, and, of course, in later years Churchill's fame only added to the tale.

But it was not the pistol that Rab had in mind. Lying deep inside the cabinet was a cardboard box not much bigger than a chocolate box, and within that little box was Rab's secret weapon, and he was confident that if all went to plan, it would instil fear and awe into the hearts of the most determined of poachers.

With the full cooperation of the local police, the next Sunday night saw the men in place, well hidden, and with a very stern directive that there would be no noise and no smoking.

Rab himself was directly across the river from the trees where the net was hidden, not forty feet from where the arrests would take place. As fortune had it, it was a moonless night, and the gang, confident of their mission, walked quite boldly to where their net was concealed. The low murmur of their voices was the first indication that they were near. In a few more moments, the glow of a small torch they carried was a giveaway to the waiting Rab, an indication that they had indeed retrieved the illegal net and were now readied for the work in hand. This was Rab's cue to bring to bear the plan they had so meticulously put together with the police. Reaching into a gunny sack, Rab produced the Colonel's old Very Pistol and, pointing it to the sky, pulled the trigger. A starburst flare made a curving arc heavenward and a blinding light lit the scene in graphic detail, the police inspector at the same time giving voice through a loudhailer for the gang to surrender.

It was all over in seconds. The gang were transfixed like a deer in a spotlight, and, without the slightest move toward violence from the gang, the constables moved in to cuff them and take over. As the light from the flare faded and spluttered to extinction, the volunteers disappeared quietly, and the gang never knew who was in the raid that captured them. It was a good result, and Rab's fears for the apprehension were unfounded after all; no one was hurt in the process. The suddenness of the blinding light and the loudhailer did the trick, and the criminals knew that resistance was futile.

As Rab lay awake that night in his little cottage, his thoughts went back to the dead keeper and the little children he left behind. They had just arrested a poaching gang, and a poaching gang had killed an honest man in cold blood. Was it within the bounds of possibility that two poaching gangs were operating in the Strath, or was it one and the same, and was the murderer of Alec Grant now in police custody? Time alone would tell.

Chapter 15

Frankie Fraser was a dangerous man, and known to be so. A violent and sadistic individual with a long record of criminality to his credit. Even jail time did not deter Frankie. He was not known as 'Mad' Frankie for nothing. He was heavily involved in black-marketeering, when so many of his countrymen were giving their lives far away on foreign soil for freedom and liberty. Frankie was the kingpin for criminality in the Highlands and had recruited many young and impressionable lads to do his bidding. Heavily built and with a temper that could pass for insanity, he was feared by his underlings and given a wide berth by the law-abiding community.

If Frankie was now operating a market stall, there was an angle to it; Rab was certain of that. It did not signify a change of heart on his part. Rab was convinced it was a cover for something else more lucrative, and making a friendship with the young Ian McHenry was part of a plan to appear as Mr. 'Nice', and to deflect suspicion from him when things went missing in the neighbourhood, or when a house was entered in the dead of night and valuables stolen.

Frankie was sure to do jail time for the salmon poaching business, but what were a few months' imprisonment for a man who had left a gamekeeper dead and a little family without a husband and father? Rab had no proof of this of course, but he knew in his heart that Fraser was responsible, and he determined in his heart to do his utmost to bring him to justice. It was autumn now, and the Christmas season was the next big national event, but in his own small community a widow and five children would feel the unimaginable pain of loss and grief, and it did not sit well with Rab MacKenzie that such a situation should go unchallenged, while a vicious perpetrator could continue flouting the law with impunity.

It was this settled conviction that had prompted Rab to arrange a meeting with the investigating detective on the murder case, and on the morning after the arrest they met. As the two men sat in the privacy of the Lodge annexe, Rab immediately came to the point of his concern.

After outlining the main features of the poacher's arrest the night before, he enlightened the detective about what he knew about Frankie Fraser. He told the listening investigator that he felt that if a little time were given to focusing on Fraser as a suspect, as the main suspect, it would pay off, for there were so many things, little things, pointing to Fraser as the perpetrator. The detective listened carefully and respectfully to his host, and when Rab concluded, he shook his head sympathetically.

"Mr. Mackenzie, I do not doubt your sincerity, and your assessment of the situation is very possibly correct; I might even share your views, but I have absolutely nothing to connect the two events—the murder and the poaching. I learned a long time ago that suspicion cannot get a conviction, and neither your suspicion nor mine will carry in a court of law. We have nothing tangible to strengthen our suspicions, and unless one of these men confesses, which I fear is highly unlikely, we are at a standstill on the matter.

I fully understand your frustration, but let us concentrate on what we do have and press home the poaching case to its full imprisonment potential. In the meantime, if something does transpire that could help us with this murder investigation, it can be reopened, even though time has passed."

Rab however, was not deterred by the detective's words; in fact, he was pleased. Here was a man who would pursue the case if at all possible, and so he pressed on with his argument even more earnestly now.

"Well, sir, allow me to share what little I have on the matter. I have done a little investigation this past week; indeed, since last Monday morning, I have been pursuing this." Pulling out a matchbox from his pocket, Rab emptied its few contents on the table before them. A cigarette stub, the hand-rolled variety, and two broken, spent matches. "Now, sir, we have an old man working at the Lodge; he brings in the deadfalls and keeps the estate in firewood. He is a smoker of fifty-odd years; I had him look at this cigarette stub and he assures me that the brand of tobacco used is Old Holborn, a sweetly scented variety.

I got a tip that Frankie Fraser is the only man in these parts who smokes that variety of tobacco, and I followed it up. The shopkeeper on the Aviemore road has a special order sent up from Glasgow for Frankie Fraser, for he never knew anyone else to use it in these parts as long as he has been working there."

Rab stopped at this, for the detective had ceased to look at him, his eyes fixed on the contents of the matchbox before them. He never spoke a word for a long moment or two, so much so that Rab began to feel he had gone too far with a fanciful theory and the detective was embarrassed by it. Then the suspense was broken as the police investigator lifted his eyes to meet Rab's, and spoke in low and earnest tones. "Mr. MacKenzie, could I take you into my confidence in something—very strictest confidence?" "Certainly, sir."

Pointing to the contents of the matchbox on the table, the detective then said, "I have identical items in my locker at the station. I picked them up when I visited the scene. If these items, yours and mine, can be proven beyond a reasonable doubt to have been Fraser's, we will have a case. I also found vehicle tracks in the roadside mud, and now that Fraser's van has been seized, we can compare them to it. Mr. MacKenzie, we have made a breakthrough, and may I thank you for your own efforts in this—you have done well, and you have my utmost appreciation. My only problem now is to match our evidence with Frankie. I need him to roll a cigarette for me and break another match so we can compare them. Let us keep our progress absolutely in the strictest confidence. Even criminals have sympathisers, and a police uniform is no guarantee of fidelity, sad to say."

It was a thoughtful and appreciative Detective Sergeant McGivern who made his way back to the station. Men like Rab MacKenzie were few and far between and very hard to find in any investigation, and, as the police depended in great measure on public and community support, it was a sad observation that community support was not always so forthcoming.

The next morning, McGivern put his plan into action. He had spoken to his superiors about an interview with Fraser and, violence alone excepted, he was free to have a discussion with him! Having chosen two constables to be part of the plan, he arrived in the interview room to see a handcuffed Fraser sitting at a table, and the two burly constables standing inside the door in a pose reminiscent of a US death-row security detail.

McGivern himself was something of a hard nut and was committed to law enforcement as a moral duty rather than just an employment choice. Appearing nonchalant and wearied with repetitive police work, he addressed Fraser, who was eying him suspiciously. "As a matter of courtesy, Fraser, I have come to see you before your transfer to Barlinnie on a charge of murder. Even criminals ought to be given a chance to speak for themselves. If you have anything to say therefore, that could be looked upon favourably by the jury, now would be a good time to say it." "What's all this about, McGivern? Transfer? Murder charge? I am in for poaching and will get bail today."

"No, Frankie, sorry to disappoint you, but the others will be out by lunchtime; after all, we can't keep men in jail for the sake of a few fish, even if we wanted to, but you are being charged with the murder of Alec Grant, the gamekeeper of the Strachan estate two months ago." "Never heard of it," growled Fraser. "Well, you must have heard about it Frankie, for it was in all the local papers and the village was abuzz with it." "Oh that," he sneered, "yes, I saw that but beyond that, I took no heed of it."

"Well, you had better take heed now Frankie, for your mates from the Ringhorne poaching trip have been very cooperative and helpful, and it has all fallen on you now. They will be free and you will face the judge for murder." "You have no proof of this, McGivern; I wasn't even there, and if anyone told you different they were lying, more than likely to save themselves too."

"I have proof, Frankie; I have the plaster cast of your tyre tracks, and another one from your hobnailed boot; I have all the proof I need, otherwise I wouldn't be in here now wasting my time trying to help you. Barlinnie is not a nice place, and the hangman's rope is always successful. But it's your choice Fraser, not mine." With this, McGivern reached into his pocket and pulled out a well-worn tobacco tin and took out a ready-rolled cigarette. Lighting up, he blew a cloud of fragrant smoke across the table, while Fraser eyed the tobacco tin longingly. "I don't suppose you could spare a smoke, could you, McGivern?" "I don't have another made up, but if you can manage the procedure, you are welcome to the makings." The police investigator pushed his tobacco tin across the table and half-turned to engage the two constables in conversation. He could not afford Fraser to notice the interest he was taking in the rolling procedure, and so he kept his eyes diverted as much as he could in conversation with the constables. Fraser took his time in preparing his cigarette, and when it was rolled, he took a match and carefully pushed the protruding tobacco strands well into the paper before lighting it. McGivern felt the tension rising within him as he watched the man before him draw deeply on the cigarette, but it was not done yet. The match was still in his fingers, where he twiddled with it a moment before finally snapping it in two and dropping it into the ashtray, conveniently placed before the interview began.

In the next few minutes, Fraser rambled on about how he was going straight now. He had a market stall and was doing well at it. He regretted he had made a mistake over a few salmon, but when the poaching case was settled and done, he would make good on his freedom. McGivern kept him in such small talk until the cigarette was finished, and when Fraser dropped it in the ashtray, he said, "Well, Frank, you are on your own now. It's entirely up to you, but I advise you to think very carefully about what you do in this case. This is not about a few salmon anymore; this is about Alec Grant, and he was murdered." With this, the detective stood and, lifting the ashtray, walked out. If Fraser realised what had just taken place, he gave no sign of it.

Chapter 16

The court was hushed and still, and the noise of the Edinburgh traffic barely penetrated the thick walls. Many had travelled down from the little village in the Highlands to where the final scene in its latest tragedy was being acted out—the trial of Frankie Fraser.

Mrs Grant was there early, her two eldest children accompanying her—a boy of fifteen years and the firstborn, a girl of seventeen. They sat quietly and respectfully, taking in all that was happening around them. Rab MacKenzie was there also, but since he was a witness, he could not become a mere spectator until he gave his evidence; therefore, he was waiting in another room adjacent to the courtroom. Mrs Grant knew Rab was there, for he had told her by way of encouragement that she would not feel isolated in such a strange environment, and in consideration of the tragic circumstances that brought her there in the first place.

As Fraser was being led in, the court went even quieter; every eye was upon him, taking in every detail. Frankie had a reputation, and that added to the public interest in him. They wanted to see this 'hard man' in the flesh, and they took their opportunity to the full.

There was a sneer on Fraser's face this morning as he entered the court, and the trademark swagger was not lost on the gathered crowd. The solemnity of the situation had not yet penetrated the mind of the criminal, and his face showed the unconcerned callousness of his character. The choice of court guards may have had a bearing on Frankie's demeanour that morning, for, big as Frankie was, the guards were a full head taller, unsmiling, and imposing. As he stood somewhat dwarfed between them, he must have felt the psychological impact such a choice was sure to make, but he brazened it out, looking intently round the crowded courtroom, as if to memorise who had come to witness his downfall.

As the judge called the court to order and the proceedings got underway, the prosecution outlined the case in brief.

"Your Honour, ladies and gentlemen of the jury, we bring to your attention today a crime of tragic proportions—needless, wicked, and cowardly. Alec Grant, a gamekeeper on the Strachan estate in Ross-shire, a husband, a father, a hardworking and respected man, was brutally killed in the execution of his duty on the first of September of this year. It is my task today to lay before you first of all the broad facts of the case, and to show, beyond all reasonable doubt—far beyond all reasonable doubt, I may add—that Frank Fraser, also known as 'Mad' Frankie, the man now in the dock, perpetrated that crime and, as fate would have it, it was while engaging in another crime one month later, that his involvement in the former murder came to light.

The prosecution will show that on the said evening, September the first, 1941, Mr Fraser's vehicle was parked near a pheasant roost within the Strachan estate, with Mr Fraser and two other men present. At some time around midnight, on that moonless night, Alec Grant came upon the thieves, and as a result was bludgeoned to death with this weapon—a cudgel or cosh—Mr Fraser's cosh, and one which he carried on his person regularly. It was on his person on the night of the first of October, a month after the murder, when he was arrested while poaching salmon on another estate that neighboured Strachan. This weapon, although not very big, is indeed a most fearsome instrument.

Turned from hardwood, smoothed and tapered to fit the hand, and with a raised lip on the end grip to give a sure hold, I can guarantee you that just one head blow from this will immediately disable any man, no matter how brave or strong he may be.

A cigarette end and a broken match, plus a tyre track and a right boot track, were also found at the murder scene, all of which I can prove belonged to Mr Fraser. The tyre track gave a perfect plaster cast, and even showed a flaw in the tyre that made it, while Mr Fraser's right boot imprint showed three nails missing and the iron heel guard badly worn. The boot was a hobnailed boot, such as is used and distributed by the military.

One month after the murder, a similar cigarette end and a broken match were found at the poaching scene, and on a forestry track close to the river, there was evidence also of vehicle tracks identical to those at the murder scene. It is quite clear that the same vehicle that was used in the poaching was also the same that was at the murder scene—Frank Fraser's vehicle. That, ladies and gentlemen, forms the basis of the prosecution's case.

"Mr McCleod, defence?"

"Thank you, Your Honour, although I don't rightly know just where to begin to rebut such piffle as I have just heard. Members of the jury, am I to suppose that we are here today to try a man for his life on the strength of a couple of matches and two cigarette ends? Surely we have progressed much further than that in our judicial system. Scotland may be a poor country, but I like to think that the members of our jury are representative of the nation—a nation that has a proud heritage, and takes a rightful pride in being fair and just in matters of such great moment. Even our great and revered Bard, for all his shortcomings, understood and wrote of the finality of death.

*'Oh thou unknown Almighty cause of all my
hope and fear, in whose dread presence, ere an
hour, perhaps I must, appear.'*

Ladies and gentlemen of the jury, let us not be the ones to besmirch our sacred record, writ in blood upon the hills of our fair land, wherein our forefathers gladly gave their lives for justice and freedom. Will we renounce our glorious past by taking this man's life on the strength of two cigarette stubs and a couple of matches? How many men do you know who roll their own cigarettes? It is a common thing among us. How many men do you know who wear army surplus clothing, let alone boots, including the hobnails!" With this, a ripple of mirth went around the court as the aged veteran continued.

"Men and women, it would not be the first time I have heard of a vehicle being stolen for criminality and being left behind by next morning, and the rightful owner knowing nothing about it. Members of the jury, this is 1941, not the Middle Ages, or the Salem witch trials. My client, Mr Fraser, was nowhere near the Strachan estate on the night of September the first. He was at home with his loving wife and children. If he has erred in succumbing to a little salmon poaching, then let him face the courts and take his punishment, but for this heinous murder, on the strength of a few missing nails in a boot, a couple of matches, and two cigarette ends, we must acquit or forever bear the shame of our own weakness and cowardice. I wish to call Mr Fraser to the stand, if I may."

As Fraser stepped into the witness box, he glared around the court with a venomous look and took up a defensive air and bearing. He was arrogant and he showed it, as he did in answering the first question put to him.

"Mr Fraser, where were you on the evening of September the first of this year?"

"I was where I told you I was, and I told the police too, but they didn't want to hear."

At this point the judge, Peregrine L. Kavanagh, intervened. "Mr Fraser, I feel it my duty to make you aware that this is no light matter, and will not be settled by bandying words with counsel, or by using belligerent and sarcastic remarks in reply to questions put to you. You are being tried for your life today, sir, and this is not a time to be making enemies. Please answer the questions put to you in a civil and proper manner."

"Mr Fraser, I put the question again. Where were you on September the first this year?"

"I was at home with my wife all evening before we both went to bed around half-ten or so." "Thank you, Mr Fraser; you are quite sure of that then?"

"I am absolutely sure of that." "No more questions, Your Honour," and McCleod took his seat. Gillespie then rose to cross-examine the man in the witness box.

"Mr Fraser, where were you on the evening of the thirty-first day of August?" "I could not answer that; it was three months ago." "Come, come, Mr Fraser, you should be able to remember that quite easily," Gillespie said softly. "Think on it; where were you on the thirty-first of August?"

"Am I to be expected to recall where I was on a night three months ago? I guarantee there is not a man in this court who could do that if asked. It is not a fair question. I don't keep a note of where I am each night."

"Very well then; can you tell me of any notable events in the whole month of August that strike you today as memorable, and that you could share with us?"

"I cannot answer questions like that, and it's unfair to use them against me. What relevance does it have to the case today? Let's stick to that."

"Very well, Mr Fraser; let's stick to the relevance of today's case. I am sure the jury may find it interesting that, since you don't keep a record of your daily business—few of us do, by the way—why, since you cannot account for the thirty-first of August or indeed the whole month of August, you are absolutely sure about the first of September. Strange circumstance, I must say.

Is that your cosh on the table, Mr Fraser?" Gillespie switched tactics. "It looks like it, but they all look similar." "Well, your initials are scratched into the handgrip." "Well, then it is mine if that's the case."

"Why do you carry a cosh, Mr Fraser?" "Why does anybody carry a cosh? For protection in my work, that's why." "What protection did you think you would need on that poaching evening, when it was found in your pocket?" "It just happened that I forgot to take it out of my pocket that night, that's all; no other reason." "Did you ever use your cosh on a person, Mr Fraser?" "Never; it is not for that at all; it is for biting dogs and thieves when I am carrying cash from my little business." "Are you sure, sir, you never used your cosh on a person?" "I am quite sure." "Thank you, Mr Fraser; no more questions."

"Mr McCleod, have you any more witnesses for the defence?" "I would like to call Mrs Fraser to the stand, Your Honour."

Frankie Fraser's wife was a pitiful sight to behold as she shuffled to the witness box and took the oath. Shabbily dressed in an old blue dress, and a pair of shoes that had seen better days, with a shawl pulled much too tightly around her shoulders, as if to draw comfort from the very constriction of the fabric, it was apparent to all that she was not here out of choice or marital loyalty. These things did not go unnoticed by the judge, and he spoke to the unfortunate woman in a kindly way. "Mrs Fraser, are you aware that taking an oath to tell the truth is a serious thing, and not just a protocol of the court? Those who take such an oath are obliged by law to speak the truth, and if not, then they can be punished. Are you aware of this?" "Yes, sir," the woman answered tearfully.

"Very well then; you may proceed, Mr McCleod.

Mrs Fraser, where was your husband on the night of September the first of this year?" "In the house, sir." "What house, Mrs Fraser?" "In our own house, sir, with our children." "Did he leave the house at all during that evening?" "No, sir, he did not." "Thank you, Mrs Fraser; you may step down now."

"Just a moment, Mrs Fraser," the judge interrupted; "it seems to have escaped Mr McCleod that Mr Gillespie may wish to cross-examine his witness. Apologies, Your Honour." "Accepted, Mr McCleod. Mr Gillespie?"

"Thank you, Your Honour. Mrs Fraser, how long have you been married?" "About twenty years, sir." "Have you had a happy marriage, Mrs Fraser?" "Objection." McCleod was on his feet now, clearly desirous that Mrs Fraser would not have to answer that question.

"Your Honour, what relevance has Mrs Fraser's marital happiness got to do with whether or not her husband was in the home or not on September the first? Mrs Fraser has answered that question already. Are we to add the necessity of marital harmony now to the cigarette ends and matches? Have we not seen and heard enough of this nonsensical house of cards?"

To give him his due, old as he now was, McCleod's vigour and courage in pursuing his goal were undiminished. He may not have much to bring to the defence, but he would see it through nevertheless—an old warrior to the last.

"Mr McCleod, I feel it is of the utmost importance for the court to know the validity of this witness. A man is dead—a good man—and the only person in all the world to give us cast-iron clarity as to Frank Fraser's whereabouts on that night is here before us. We must ascertain the whereabouts of Mr Fraser on that night, for his life may very well depend on it. Objection overruled."

"Mrs Fraser, let me put the question again. Have you had a happy marriage?" "Yes, sir." "Are you quite sure of that answer, Mrs Fraser?" "Well, sir, like everyone else, we sometimes have had our ups and downs." "Including a time of separation, Mrs Fraser?" "Yes, sir." "How long was the separation for, Mrs Fraser?" "About two years, sir." "Hmm, two years, you say; quite a long time then. Can you tell me what brought the separation about?" "We had a row, sir." "Yes, but very many people have rows and do not separate; is that not true, Mrs Fraser?" "Yes, sir." "Let me ask you again, then; why did you separate after that row?" "Well, sir, I was in the hospital for a time." "Indeed, and why were you in hospital?" "Frankie hit me." "Don't you mean that he beat you, Mrs Fraser, and beat you so badly that you spent eleven days in hospital, and that he got twelve months in jail for GBH? Is that not the whole truth, Mrs Fraser?" "Yes, sir." "Did you have broken bones, Mrs Fraser?" "Yes, sir." "What bones were broken?" "My fingers, sir." "And how did that happen, Mrs Fraser?" "Frankie hit me with his cosh." "So you were trying to protect yourself and you put your hand up to do so; is that right?" "No, sir; Frankie held my hand on the table and hit it with the cosh." By this time the woman was trembling and sobbing to such a degree that Gillespie asked for and got a short recess that she might recover her composure. When they recommenced, Gillespie once again addressed her.

"Mrs Fraser, you said that your husband never left the house on that night; is that correct?" "Yes, sir." "Did you leave the house on that night?" "Just to put Mother to bed, sir." "Is she ill?" "She needs help, sir, in getting ready for bed, and I go each night to help her." "Where does your mother live, Mrs Fraser?" "Just ten minutes away, sir; it is not far." "If it were daylight, could you see your house from your mother's house?" "Oh, no, sir; there are too many streets and houses in between." "How did you find your mother that evening?" "She was badly upset, for she had fallen from her chair at the window and was lying on the floor when I arrived." "What time did you arrive?" "About ten o'clock, sir." "And what time did you leave?" "It was late, sir; about one o'clock in the morning. My mother was upset and I had to stay longer." "I see; so if you left your house to see your mother, and you were gone for three hours, you couldn't really say with all certainty that your husband didn't leave the house. Is that correct?" "I suppose it is, sir." "Indeed it is, Mrs Fraser; there is no supposing about it.

Do you know how far it is from your house to the Strachan estate?" "Not very far, sir." "Perhaps ten minutes by vehicle?" "Yes, sir." "So it is very possible that your husband could have been out of your house and returned again by the time you got back—possible, I say, for three hours is quite an adequate time for that to happen." "Yes, sir." "Thank you, Mrs Fraser; I have no more questions."

"Mr McCleod, do you have any more witnesses?" "I have no more witnesses, Your Honour."

"Mr Gillespie, I think you have other witnesses to call." "Thank you, Your Honour; I call Mr Rab MacKenzie to the stand."

<h1 style="text-align:center">Chapter 17</h1>

"M r MacKenzie, you are head ghillie on the McNabb estate, more commonly known as Strathmore Lodge, is that correct?" "Yes sir, it is." "Good. Can you tell the court how you came to be involved in a murder enquiry involving the Strachan estate?"

"I was on my weekly patrol duty on Monday the first of October last, on our salmon beats on the Ringhorne River. It was around eleven o'clock that morning that I saw fresh disturbance in the grass and undergrowth near the riverbank. As I dismounted to take a closer look, I found a net hidden in the undergrowth among the trees, and the footprints in the grass of several persons. On the ground beside the net and to the fringe of the trampled area, I saw a hand-rolled cigarette end and a broken match. Out of curiosity I picked them up and wrapped them in a handkerchief. After the successful arrest of the poachers the following Sunday night, it was found that one of them, Mr Fraser, used tobacco, and he also rolled his own. I later showed my items to Sergeant Gillespie and he informed me that he had found very similar items at the murder scene. That's all I can say sir, concerning my involvement in this case."

"Defence, do you wish to cross-examine?" "Thank you, Your Honour," McCleod replied.

"Mr MacKenzie, can you tell me what prompted you, a mere ghillie, to pick up a cigarette end and a broken match and put them in a handkerchief? I would have thought a man of your career status and calling would be more interested in magpie nests and fox droppings than forensic examples such as a cigarette end and a broken match." It was a put-down, an insult, calculated to influence the jury against giving credibility to this tweed-clothed countryman. If Gillespie was afraid that it would cause Rab to rise to the insult, he need not have worried.

"Yes sir," Rab replied. "Indeed I do take a close interest in those things too, for vermin control is vital to my work, as I am sure you are aware. Salmon beats are also a very important aspect of the Lodge, and any sign at all of illegal activity is considered more important than magpies and fox droppings. When I saw the cigarette end and the match, I picked them up, if only because they were the only personal items left by the thieves, and for that reason I kept them."

"Thank you, Mr MacKenzie. That will be all." McCleod was not used to being on the receiving end of an exchange, and his intended purpose, not being realised, made him reluctant to pursue the issue.

"Mr Gillespie, your other witness!" "I call Detective Sergeant Cole to the stand. Sergeant Cole, can you outline to the court what you have uncovered concerning this case, please?"

"Well sir, we already had an ongoing investigation into the murder of Mr Grant, but until I saw the items Mr MacKenzie had, we were at a loss to focus on any particular suspect. It was when I saw those items retrieved from the poaching scene that I knew that those at the murder scene were one and the same as those at the salmon poaching, for I had identical items in my locker at the station. I then proceeded to make more direct enquiries concerning the tyre and boot imprints I had, and found they both pointed to the same person—Mr Fraser. The plaster casts are pristine, sir, and in the case of the tyre print, even show a small flaw in the tyre. The right boot print is likewise clear.

Three nails are missing and the steel heel guard is very badly worn. We also found the garage that identified the tyres as the brand he sold, and he had just recently advised Mr Fraser that he needed a new tyre on the front offside wheel.

The cigarette ends were very helpful. We had them examined by a veteran smoker of fifty years, and he identified the tobacco as being 'Old Holborn', a very sweetly scented brand. We visited the only shop that sells tobacco in the Strath, and he immediately told us that there is only one person in all of Ross-shire, that he knows, who smokes that brand of tobacco, and that person is Mr Frank Fraser. It is a special order from Glasgow for him alone." "Thank you, Sergeant Cole; I have no more questions."

McCleod rose slowly and deliberately to cross-question the detective.

"So a cigarette stub and a broken match gave you the knowledge you needed to point the finger at Mr Fraser. And a damaged tyre and three missing nails in an army boot are the final proof you require to send a man to the gallows. Am I correct, Mr Cole?"

"Yes sir; considering all the evidence, you are correct in every detail except one." "And what might that be, Mr Cole? Enlighten me." "You have underestimated the importance of circumstantial evidence. In our enquiry we have found a very strong example of circumstantial evidence, and we are sure it will prove to be sufficient. We have the physical evidence in the form of the cigarette ends, tobacco brand, matches, and plaster casts. In the method used in hand-rolling these cigarettes, we have the evidence of the repetition of human behaviour, and we have independent witness testimony that Mr Fraser is the sole purchaser of that particular tobacco brand in the whole area."

The old man, hair whitened with years, wire-framed spectacles perched precariously on the end of his nose, bravely countered this with, "Do you really believe, or think it reasonable to believe, that a man whose hands were covered with fish scales and slime would stop to roll a cigarette in the middle of his crime?"

"A smoker who hand-rolls will always carry a few ready-rolled cigarettes for those occasions when rolling is impossible, but that was not the case with Mr Fraser. Mr Fraser did not get involved in the hands-on work; he always had plenty of young, impressionable lads to do the work."

"You seem to know a lot about my client, Mr Cole; is it first-hand knowledge or common village gossip and hearsay?"

"When Mr Fraser was arrested, he had companions with him; I have statements from them to that effect."

"We will leave the jury to decide the validity of the evidence you say you have, Mr Cole. That will be all; thank you."

Before the sergeant left the witness box, Gillespie got to his feet and addressed the judge. "May I recall this witness, Your Honour?" "You may do so, Mr Gillespie, if you feel his former testimony has not sufficiently covered the facts." "Thank you, Your Honour. Mr Cole, much has been said in a derogatory way about the evidence of the cigarette ends. Could you be more specific for the jury's benefit concerning the importance they have in this case?"

"Certainly sir; I will do my best. As in many other habits men and women have, they have personal preferences and tastes. Whether it be drinking a pint in a pub or rolling a cigarette, every man will have a custom, a method, a ritual, if you like. This ritual is part of his enjoyment of the habit. The hand-rolling of a cigarette is a very clear example of what I am saying. From the taking out of the pouch or tobacco tin, to the drawing forth of the rolling paper and laying the tobacco in it, the same method will be followed, whether consciously or unconsciously. Some roll a very thin cigarette; some prefer a fuller roll. Some men nip off the protruding tobacco strands with their fingers, while others take a match and pack the end back into the paper. It is not too much to say that every man leaves his signature in the product he produces.

Mr Fraser had a very pronounced signature in this regard. The two cigarette stubs that were found, one at each crime scene, matched in every way with the cigarette he rolled in the station interview room in the presence of myself and two police constables. I brought those three items, with the broken matches and plaster casts, in the evidence bag I have today. The cosh is here also." "Thank you, Sergeant Cole. That will be all."

When the detective mentioned the interview room, Fraser's head went into his hands. He knew then the game they had played, and the significance of the detective walking out with the ashtray. It was a bitter blow, and he now knew in his heart this was not going well for him.

The judge, who had listened intently to Detective Cole, called now for a recess, saying that when they returned, they would listen to the closing arguments. He also warned each member of the jury to wait until the court resumed before giving their verdict!

Chapter 18

It was to an eager and expectant crowd that the afternoon court session commenced. Every seat was taken, and Mrs Grant and her two children were back in their seats, bravely determined to see justice done for their loved one if at all possible. When all shuffling and seating procedures had settled, the judge called for the defence to give its closing address. The old man, slightly stooped and giving the overall appearance of learning and wisdom, rose slowly, a sheaf of papers in his right hand, which he would use freely as a means of emphasis or effect.

Gillespie smiled inwardly, wondering where McCleod would go with this, as he had already been quite vociferous concerning the items of evidence, and could hardly repeat himself without appearing beaten or outclassed in the exchanges.

McCleod addressed the jury quietly and sincerely, holding direct eye contact as he began his speech, and from the opening line, he had the jury's full attention.

"Ladies and gentlemen of the jury, you may think that I am an opponent of the death penalty, or that I am too lenient on those who err grievously against their fellow man. If any here think that, then they are very wide of the mark indeed. I am fully committed, both in law and in my conscience, that the death penalty is just and necessary, and for very good reasons too.

Unlike so many in this present modern age, I believe that the one who gave us life itself, and a beautiful planet to live on, also laid down social laws and markers whereby His creation could live out their lives in peace and harmony. Let me give you an illustration.

Who among you today would have the temerity to deny the validity of the Ten Commandments? I venture to say not one of you. And why not? Because each one of you knows very well that the very weave, fabric, and stability of our society is based on them. They are our societal norms, and without them, we would have chaos, anarchy, and utter confusion.

Why then are so very many people opposed to the death penalty, when it has been given from the same hand as the Ten Commandments? A command, ladies and gentlemen, not given to individuals, but to society as a whole, many centuries before the Ten Commandments were given, and many centuries before the Jewish race was named! A command, given to Noah upon his emergence from the ark, that wherever he and his offspring would travel, they would carry this with them to the uttermost corners of this earth.

I am called today to deliver Frank Fraser from this right and proper responsibility and requirement. Not because I do not believe in it, but because I do not believe that the evidence against him warrants it! It matters not what I think of Mr Fraser, but it does matter what I think of the evidence! That, ladies and gentlemen, is the heart and soul of my defence of Mr Fraser.

Waving his sheaf of papers vigorously in his right hand, McCleod paced the floor much as a lecturer would before his class, and the ruse was certainly getting him attention! Gillespie had noted the jury's reaction to this unorthodox but very evidently successful approach, and he felt the first fleeting thoughts of alarm and consternation. McCleod was no newcomer to the justice system. He had had an eminently successful career, and his benign manner, coupled with his innocent and fatherly appearance, had been the downfall of many in the cut and thrust of courtroom drama.

Gillespie knew too just how fickle juries can be, and how easily swayed by the emotion of the hour, or the fear of making a mistake in judgement. He wondered too just how this was going to play out for Frankie Fraser, who sat in the dock hanging on McCleod's every word.

Suddenly McCleod changed tack, calculated to bring the jury to a personal rejection of a death sentence, as being too solemn and final for ordinary people to decide.

"Ladies and gentlemen of the jury, when I was a young man starting out on my career in law, I had a conscience crisis concerning this very penalty. Could I, my heart reasoned, if called upon to do so, use my skills, learning, and knowledge to send a man to his death? I struggled all through law school with this, so much so that I was moved at last to apply to the authorities to attend a hanging. I had heard so much of the so-called barbarism of the execution method we use in this country that I had to see for myself, and I would then decide as to my attitude to the outworking of this penalty in our justice system.

The hanging that I gained permission to attend was of a man who had brutally murdered his young wife, for no other reason than that he had a wicked and uncontrollable temper. One evening, when his supper was not immediately on the table, he beat her so badly that she expired there and then on the kitchen floor. What was his dinner on that night, ladies and gentlemen? Just this—turnips and potatoes, neeps and tatties. A very common meal, yet that poor woman was beaten to death because it was a few moments late in her wicked husband's time schedule.

This is what happens when there is no respect for law or life, and I was there to witness the final part in that tragic drama. The official witnesses, including myself, were already in the execution chamber when the sad procession came through from the adjoining cell. It was only six or seven paces from one cell through to the other, and the speed at which the whole was accomplished was almost as big a shock as the execution itself. I had a pocket watch—I have it with me today; my father gave it to me when I passed the Bar exam—and when I heard the activity next door, I glanced down at my watch.

The executioner came through first, followed by the condemned man and the assistant executioner. The condemned man's hands were already secured behind him with a short leather strap, and as he reached the chalk mark on the gallows trapdoor, the executioner stopped him, and both men followed a well-practised routine. Pulling a cotton hood from his breast pocket, he swiftly placed it over the head of the condemned. The noose followed immediately, gently yet firmly tightened just under the angle of the left jaw. The assistant executioner, meanwhile, was fastening a leather strap around his ankles and quickly got off the trapdoor, while the executioner ran to the lever and, first pulling out the safety pin, pushed the lever forward.

Ladies and gentlemen, it took all of twelve seconds for all that to happen, including walking from the condemned cell to the execution chamber. The now taut rope, suspending the dead miscreant below us, and the silence of the aftermath, was indeed a salutary lesson to us all of the suddenness and finality of death. There was not a man in that cell who was not shocked and moved by what happened in those twelve seconds—visibly shocked too.

Why do I tell you this today? I'll tell you why, ladies and gentlemen— to impress upon you the awful solemnity of an execution, and to call attention to the terrible and irreversible consequences if a mistake is made, when an innocent man is declared guilty. There was no brutality in that execution, men and women of the jury. The murderer received more consideration than he had shown his poor wife. The state had fulfilled its responsibility, and did so with dignity. Humanely, swiftly, and finally—the state brought again to the public's attention the preciousness God puts on life, and the sacred manner in which we ought to regard it. Mark my words— whatever day the death penalty is abolished, murder will become commonplace. The man who murdered Alec Grant deserves that same penalty—deserves it, I say, with all the sincerity my heart and mind can express—but I do not believe the evidence produced here warrants that penalty for Frank Fraser.

A few cigarette stubs and matches—three as a matter of fact. A cosh found in his pocket, and three nails missing from one of his boots. Really, men and women, can we in all seriousness consider these as evidence in a murder trial? Will you put a hangman's rope around this man's neck for such common trifles?

It was a masterly performance, and Gillespie knew it—brilliant, genius. Playing the horror of the gallows against the trivia of a few matches and cigarette stubs. A piece of courtroom drama one only reads about in novels, but here today in Edinburgh it was being enacted before the eyes of fifteen men and women who held the power of life and death, and in an hour or so would give their decision. But McCleod had not yet finished.

"Finally, members of the jury, are we to believe that because a man carries a cosh that he is a murderer? I know postmen who carry such means of defence—not for any other reason than vicious dogs that may need chastising. I know milkmen who do the same on the day they take the milk debts. Rent men also do the same thing on their rounds. Is Mr Fraser not entitled to do the same as he pursues his lawful business, and fulfils his deliveries?

Is it beyond reasonable doubt that the three nails missing from Mr Fraser's boot are unique in all of Scotland? Since war began, half the population is shod with army footwear. How many other examples of missing boot nails has the prosecution looked for?

A tyre print from his van! There are literally tens of thousands of such tyres in circulation; it is the most common brand. Are we to suppose that in the mixing or pouring of the plaster cast there was no possibility of an error? Or that there is not another tyre in all the land with a similar blemish? If I were to send a man to the gallows, I would hope I would have more to go on than a plaster cast print taken from a muddy roadside verge, or three non-existent nails from an army boot.

Ladies and gentlemen, put aside all preconceived notions about Frank Fraser. None of us is perfect, after all. We all have our ups and downs. Let the evidence guide you today, and the evidence only. Set the evidence, such as it is, against a man's life, and do your duty by setting this man free to return to his wife and family. Thank you."

The court was hushed and still as McCleod took his seat. He had made his mark; there was no mistaking that, and as Gillespie rose to his feet to bring his own closure, he knew he had a task before him. Gathering a few papers together, he rose slowly and deliberately. He did not want to disturb or otherwise take away from the solemnity of the atmosphere generated by the defence, for he planned to use it now in his own final address.

Walking forward slowly and deliberately, he came to a stop before the fifteen expectant and waiting men and women, in whose hands lay the life or death of Frank Fraser. When he spoke, it was in hushed and reverent tones.

"I too am a firm believer in the ultimate penalty for the ultimate crime, ladies and gentlemen. My learned friend Mr McCleod has spoken of his own deep-seated convictions, and he has spoken well. When a man speaks from his heart, he will always speak well, and Mr McCleod has evidenced that today. We cannot blame a man who speaks from his heart, even though we may not agree with his argument.

The prosecution's evidence has come under great scrutiny today in this court, so much so that I feel I must clarify exactly what such evidence entails and how much credence we can put upon it. It is a common misconception that circumstantial evidence is somehow inferior to direct evidence. But that is not the case, ladies and gentlemen. Sometimes it can be stronger and more reliable.

May I give you just two examples? A person may give what purports to be an eyewitness account of a very serious crime. This would be direct evidence. But they may do so for a variety of reasons. They may do it through perjury and falsehood—sadly an all-too-common practice. They may do it sincerely, but mistakenly. Indeed, all too often, eyewitness testimony is found wholly unreliable! Poor eyesight, colour blindness, memory problems, and mistaken identity, to name but a few.

Circumstantial evidence has none of these drawbacks. When several items of evidence, from different sources, each reinforcing and corroborating one another, and each pointing to the same conclusion, they cannot lie. Together they provide an unshakeable testimony to the validity of the conclusion they point to. When we then apply inference and reasoning to what such circumstantial evidence has to say, we can reach a moral certainty as to guilt or innocence, and from a reliable and more trustworthy source than many eyewitness recollections.

A fingerprint alone is circumstantial evidence, ladies and gentlemen— evidence that a person touched an object. Direct evidence is someone actually seeing that person touch that object.

Can I give you an instance? A man is seen to enter a house. Angry words are heard. A shot is fired, and the man is seen to leave. The homeowner is later found dead. All circumstantial evidence, ladies and gentlemen. But, we infer, we reason, from those same circumstances, that the man seen entering and leaving the house did indeed fire the shot that killed the homeowner. Circumstantial evidence allows us to infer, to reason, and indeed calls for our reasoning, that beyond all reasonable doubt, a fact exists. The circumstances bring us to the conclusion of that fact.

Reasonable doubt therefore, is the highest standard of truth when considering circumstantial evidence.

Let us now apply these principles to our case today.

We will begin with the cigarette ends and matches. We have witnessed a demonstration of Mr Fraser rolling a cigarette and discarding the spent and broken match in the interview room of the police station. He was unaware of the importance of that incident; therefore, he was quite natural in his actions. We then compare an identical cigarette end and broken match found at the poaching site, and another identical one at the murder site, where Alec Grant was brutally done to death. Identical in every respect, ladies and gentlemen, including the tobacco brand—a brand that no one else is known to smoke but Mr Frank Fraser.

The discarded and broken matches were likewise identical. Would honest reasoning and inference point us to any other person than Mr Fraser, and can there be reasonable doubt when we consider that this is a three-fold witness?

If we take the plaster casts, we have a similar certainty that they belong to Mr Fraser. Can we have a reasonable doubt that in all of Scotland, there is another vehicle with a peculiar and distinctive offside front tyre defect, and that the owner of that same vehicle has three nails missing from his right boot?

All I ask is your honest reasoning. You must ask yourselves what the chances are of all these circumstances happening by random chance, and let your reasoning rule it out as the impossibility that it is.

To put it another way—if Alec Grant was your son, your husband, your loved one, would you reject the weight of this combined circumstantial evidence, and let the accused walk free?

The cosh, ladies and gentlemen? We know, of course, that some men, in the exercise of their duties, do carry necessary protection such as a short baton or cudgel; that is not a crime. But we also know that Mr Fraser did not carry it for protection against vicious dogs or thieves. He had already used it to break his poor wife's fingers while he held her hand outspread on the kitchen table, leaving her hospitalised, and for which he got twelve months' jail. I put it to you today that the same cosh was used to murder Alec Grant when he came upon the pheasant thieves on September the first this year.

But more than all these things—why did Mr Fraser lie concerning the evening of September the first, when he swore on oath that he never left the house, and both he and his wife retired to bed around ten-thirty? Why lie about that particular night? Would an honourable reason move a man to do so? You all know the answer to that. Only a guilty secret would cause a man to tell a lie as to his whereabouts on a night when murder was committed. When a man is confronted with an accusation, and he either remains silent or tells a lie, he has a guilty secret he dares not reveal.

I put it to you today, ladies and gentlemen, that when all is said and done, and every avenue is fully explored in this sad case, and all the inferences and reasonings considered, they all point, without a shadow of reasonable doubt, to the guilt of Frank Fraser as the murderer of Alec Grant.

You have three verdicts open to you today in Scottish law. You can bring in a not guilty verdict, or you can bring in a not proven verdict, which is essentially an acquittal, or you can bring in a guilty verdict. I ask you, therefore, to take the evidence we have presented here today and see which of these verdicts it unmistakably points to—the only verdict it points to—and bring it to us.

Thank you."

Lord Justice Kavanagh waited until Gillespie had taken his seat, and the released tension and court bustle had settled before he spoke.

"Men and women of the jury, you have heard strong appeals today from both defence and prosecution. Both men are adamant in their beliefs as to the guilt or innocence of the accused. However, I want you to consider well the evidence presented today, the evidence - and only the evidence. If I may borrow a thought from the Good Book itself, *'separate the precious from the vile'*, or, to further clarify the metaphor, *'separate the wheat from the chaff.'*

The case is not a complicated one, and counsel has set forth the issues at hand. Apply, therefore, what you have heard to the guilt or innocence of Mr Fraser. Eight persons are all that is needed to bring in a verdict. You may now go and deliberate."

It was late in the afternoon when the court officer made it known that the jury had reached a verdict. Hurriedly entering the building again, those who had been waiting close at hand made sure of their seats. They had been patient throughout the trial, and they did not want to miss the outcome. As the jury filed to their seats, each member sought to avert their eyes from the watchful and expectant crowd who now thronged the building. It had been an ordeal for each member—ordinary folk as they were—and the strain showed on their faces.

"Foreman of the jury, have you reached a verdict?" "We have, Your Honour."

"Do you find Mr Frank Fraser guilty or not guilty of the crime of murder?" "We find the defendant guilty." It was inevitable that there would be a court reaction to this long-awaited decision, and the reaction swept over the crowd in an audible wave. Using his gavel, the judge called for silence and asked, "Can we have the voting numbers, Mr Foreman?" "It was twelve to three, Your Honour." "Thank you, Mr Foreman."

Arranging some papers before him, the judge, Peregrine L. Kavanagh, slowly raised his eyes to meet those of the condemned man. "Do you have anything to say before I pass sentence, Mr Fraser?"

"It was an accident, Your Honour. I didn't mean to hurt him badly; it was an accident." If Fraser thought his last-minute explanation would somehow help him, he was sadly mistaken. The judge never commented on the confession, but after the court attendant placed the black cloth upon his head, he began his address to the prisoner.

"Mr Fraser, you have been found guilty by a jury of your peers of the murder of Alec Grant, and it is a decision I wholeheartedly concur with. There is only one sentence in the law for such a crime. You will be taken from this court to a place of lawful execution where, on the twenty-third of December, you will be hanged by the neck until you are dead. You, by your own admission just now, have committed the dastardliest crime, and now you must pay the forfeit. May it be a lesson to those who have any inclination to follow in the example you have set.

You have the regulation three Sundays before execution, and two weeks within that time to reflect on your evil deed. I would strongly suggest you make good use of the remaining time available to you and avail yourself of whatever spiritual comfort your opportunity may bring.

Take him down."

Thus ended one of the most trying periods in Rab MacKenzie's life.

Chapter 19

Frankie Fraser was dead, but Rab could find no satisfaction in his death. Fraser had taken the life of a good man and had paid the price. It was, in his opinion, just and proper that it should be so, but there was no satisfaction beyond that.

As he lay awake at nights in the silence of his little cottage, mulling over in his mind all these things, and the issues and ongoing needs of Strathmore, Rab never thought the Colonel's funeral would become such a turning point in their fortunes, or that the life he had enjoyed for so long would suddenly lose its appeal. The vivid images of that day, and the effect upon the neighbourhood, had stayed with him, and he often recalled in his private moments those scenes, as they made their way to the churchyard and open grave.

As the four black horses stepped out in practised unison, plumes nodding and harness shining, pulling the hearse which contained a plain deal coffin—the Colonel's request—it was a grand sight to be sure. A fitting reminder to all who watched that day that they were saying a last goodbye to a true gentleman, a friend of the friendless, and an old soldier of a bygone age. The Colonel himself would have been impressed at the detail.

His own riding mount, groomed to perfection, was the centrepiece of the procession. Hooves blacked and shining, saddle and bridle oiled and rubbed to a dull, rich gleam, with the riding crop tied neatly to the pommel ring. The riderless steed, with the stirrups holding reversed riding boots, a stable boy leading it behind the coffin, brought a tear to many an eye as people realised the Colonel was indeed gone, the riderless horse seeming to convey the message more poignantly than the coffin.

A fitting tribute, yes, but, unknown to them, also a harbinger of worse to come, for things were never quite the same after they laid the Colonel to rest.

After the funeral, Rab had thrown himself into the work in a whole-hearted endeavour to succeed, and to keep up the standards that had made Strathmore the envy of many estates round about. They may have been bigger, and had a higher guest list each season, but they had not the personal and homely reputation that had made Strathmore a firm favourite with many, and who, by their annual visits, had enabled the Lodge to function comfortably and without the pressures that so often attend those who are always striving for the future, without savouring the enjoyment their present privileges life had brought them.

In the immediate aftermath of the Colonel's death, Rab brought to the Lodge a complete programme of new amenities in the hope of creating a renewed interest in it, and, with the permission of Lady Eleanor, had implemented them, giving each area his attention, and bringing in new, energetic, and interested young hopefuls to carry on the programme daily.

He began with a deer park. The estate had around three hundred acres of lowland, interspersed here and there with mature deciduous forestry, and bordered with a broad band of tall conifers which made a very natural and effective windbreak in winter. On the Colonel's Day, the land had been used—and still was—for a small flock of imported Damara sheep, with a Merino ram for cross-breeding, and a few Highland cattle. These had little monetary value to the estate, for the Colonel kept them as more or less a commodity, and could often be seen driving his vehicle through them and dropping off swedes or some other titbit or treat.

Now and again, he butchered a few just to keep the numbers in control, but mainly they were his pastime, another nostalgic reminder of his earlier days on the bushveld. The larger part was mostly rented to local farmers for hay or grazing, and the land was in prime condition on account of this husbandry. It was not wasteland by any means, and he could see a future for it that could be very profitable for very little expenditure or effort.

Rab had considered the existing livestock in his plans and deliberations for the lowland acreage, and had come to the conclusion that even with the livestock, it could be of greater use by introducing deer to it, and with the numbers he had in mind, there was more than enough room for both to coexist without detriment to either.

There was one other issue, however, that he was led to consider very carefully before he brought his new programme to the Lady of the Manor. Since her husband's death, Lady Eleanor had withdrawn somewhat from the everyday Lodge life and was not seen among the staff as before. She rarely visited the open courtyard and took no interest in the day-to-day procedures, or in the many guests that came and went through the gates.

There was one place, however, that she could be seen each morning, and unless a downpour was either taking place or about to take place, she would be at the stables, grooming and saddling her favourite horse. It was a black Irish Draught, strong-boned but not heavy, and with a sturdy, broad chest that spoke well of its wind and stamina. The Colonel had it shipped from the Curragh, Ireland, and he was assured of its temperament and pedigree. A four-year-old gelding, broken and jumping, it was the Colonel's last gift to her, just months before his tragic death. Since the Colonel's death, Lady Eleanor had thrown herself into her outdoor love of riding and would be gone for hours each day if the weather permitted.

Rab had spoken to her about her long absences, and she had graciously consented to follow the hill-stalking protocol of writing her planned route on a chalkboard, nailed on an inner door of the tack room. Rab knew the inner grief she bore, and was concerned lest her grief make her careless, reckless, or indifferent, and end in tragedy in some lonely out-of-the-way corrie, or at the foot of one of the many crags that edged the estate's bridle paths.

Since Lady Eleanor herself used the lowland meadows for a gallop, Rab was desirous of coming to an arrangement that would allow her to continue with her custom, for the combination of sheep and cattle had kept the greensward short, and it made for safe footing.

He knew the meadow was where she could give rein to her mount and feel the wind in her hair, knowing, as only those who indulge in it, the exhilaration of such. The inner well-being that the combined smell of warm leather and a lathered horse can bring to a jaded soul can only be experienced. Words cannot adequately convey the feeling, Lady Eleanor had once told him, so Rab knew he could never propose something that would rob her of this simple outlet, and so he had given long thought to it beforehand.

Quite apart from the employment aspect, Rab and the staff greatly admired her Ladyship. She had taken a while to recover from her fall that day on the moors, so long ago now, and since that time could no longer ride side-saddle, owing to her injuries, but rode astride, cutting a fine figure indeed as she urged her black steed down the meadow at full tilt. Sometimes, if she felt like it, she would jump a deadfall that lay at the lower end of the gallop. She was fearless on horseback and was the envy of not a few for being so.

Much of the gallop was in view of the Lodge courtyard, and on the days when Lady Eleanor made for the meadow, she didn't know she had an audience. The staff, if working near at hand, made it their aim to catch a glimpse of the lone rider, the ribbons from her bonnet flying in the wind, and from a distance, her blonde hair, pulled back in a ponytail, a mere ripple of motion against her black riding coat. Each member of staff secretly grieved for the lonely figure, but the sight of her on the gallop, leaning forward, half-seated and well-poised, driving her mount on, made them feel proud that she was their mistress. Whatever future use could be gained from the lowland acres, therefore, must not interfere with the gallop.

The deer park was a success from the very beginning. Having sent to Kent, England, for a few sika and fallow deer, Rab advertised a young shots programme.

He had found it unsuitable to take children to the hill. It was much too arduous—cold, sometimes bitterly so, and always physically demanding, not to mention an extra person to be aware of and the safety problems the situation called for. Then there was the stalk itself, sometimes taking hours, and the quiet approach so vital to success was not something that would be relished by a child. Although some guns did ask for it, he always declined on the grounds that the nature of the hill ruled it out.

A deer park, however, was an entirely different scenario, and the programme opened the way for the young shot to enter a sport that also required stealth, discipline, expertise, and determination, yet in more amenable circumstances. There was all the difference in the world between lowland stalking and hill stalking, and the workload on the ghillie was greatly reduced.

Rab had even allowed himself the thought that he might take on the lowland young shots programme, for a quiet walk through the park at dawn or dusk, or sitting in a high seat in the forest, was nothing to the rigours of the hill, and the guests seldom failed to be presented with an opportunity to test their skills on a live target. Rab also commenced a systematic series of heather burning, seeking to improve the success of the grouse hatch on the moors by providing new heather shoots that were so vital in the grouse food chain.

He did away with the estate pheasant rearing in favour of bringing in already hatched pheasant chicks, and did what he could to prevent foxes or pine martens[xx] from wreaking havoc if once they gained entrance to a pen or house. All this took time and effort, and in just two years they began to see the work flourish and establish itself in every aspect of the new projects. Things were looking good, and the record books told the story of the financial benefits the new programmes had brought.

The new year promised more of the same, and Hogmanay with the staff and neighbours was a happy and joyous occasion. Then came the accident, and brought to an end all that they had known from the history of the estate.

Chapter 20

Like most accidents, it was preventable, but the human element in the affairs of life makes even the preventable inevitable. There are never any winners when tragedy occurs. Guilt or innocence is rarely given proper consideration when the trauma of great grief and loss overtakes a human heart. So it was with the Symington tragedy, and Strathmore bore the brunt of the responsibility.

Richard Symington came from East Anglia, the son of a wealthy banking executive. He was a young man just born for the wild open spaces, and the vast expanse of the Fens supplied plenty of the same. By the time he was twelve years old, he was an accomplished punt gunner. He took great pride in the 'market hunting' that was then common, following the great rafts of duck and geese that gathered in their thousands on the Wash and the drainage system that flowed into it. Twice, he had bagged a hundred birds with the customised gun he had mounted on his punt. With a barrel over nine feet long and a two-inch bore, the gun carried a pound of shot and was devastating on a mass of birds within a hundred-yard range. The young Symington had his method of taking advantage of the roosting birds.

In the dark of the very early morning, quietly poling or rowing his punt into line with the raft of waterfowl, he got as close as he could without alarming them. Then, simultaneously, he struck the side of his punt with a piece of wood while pulling the lanyard on the trigger. The rising mass of birds, now on the wing and presenting a much larger target, fell prey to the pound of shot propelled towards them by 340 grams of black powder. To the onlooker, it seemed as though a large hole had appeared in the flock, while the dead and dying birds littered the water over an area the size of a playing field. A shotgun, carried in the punt, dispatched the 'flappers', and the young hunter was well rewarded for his skill and ingenuity when he took his morning's work to the dealers.

The Symington family home was halfway between Cromer and Spalding, and so the young man was well placed to avail himself of the wildfowling opportunities the Fens and Wash presented, and he spent every spare moment in pursuit of the winged prize. It was inevitable, therefore, that a young man such as he looked to fresher fields as he grew older, and the Highlands beckoned him with an allure he could not resist.

Thus it was that he came to Strathmore, bringing his own rifle and fitted out with the very best customary hill-walking equipment. He came for a week on the hill, and Rab was obliged to bring in another guide to cater for the young man's expectations. Richard, or Rick as he preferred to be called, was filled with enthusiasm. A trophy head to take back home was his sole objective, and he had set aside a whole week to fulfil it. Danger never entered his head; he was too young to think of death—life was for living, and he was living for life. It would be a fatal mistake!

On the very best of days, the hill can be a capricious lady. Those who fail to recognise the warning signs, the subtle hints, those little markers that can turn pleasure into peril in a few moments, are like the blind, walking on the edge of a precipice without knowing it is there. It was a bitterly cold morning as Ian Forsythe and Rick Symington set out on the first morning of the week-long booking. They carried the usual necessities for such weather, and before he left, Ian went to the tack room and wrote just three words on the chalkboard there—Loch Shannagh. Forsythe.

This was one rule every man had to abide by, and a crucial one at that. In the event of an incident, the rescue party would have a head start in knowing where to begin the search. Not only so, but another stalker or ghillie would know not to overlap boundaries, and so put himself or Symington at risk from a stray bullet.

The short January day came to a close, as guests and ghillies trickled in, exhausted and hungry from the salmon beats or the hill, but of Symington and Ian Forsythe there was no sign. Suppertime came and went and still no sign of the pair, and Rab knew in his heart that there was something greatly amiss that had prevented them from returning. There was little he or anyone could do until first light, but he did go to the tack room and check the board. Sure enough, Ian's scrawl was there, and they would know where to look tomorrow.

Although he did not raise an alarm, Rab himself took a vehicle and drove as far as he could in the direction of the loch, and at the highest point he alighted and glassed the mountainside for over an hour in the hope of seeing a light or some sign of the missing hunters. When he had satisfied himself that there was no sign of any activity, he returned to the Lodge to prepare for tomorrow's search.

It was with heavy hearts that the four men set out the following day. It was still dark, but by daylight they would be well on the way to the loch. Well provisioned, they again drove as far as possible and then set off on foot; with a stiff breeze against them, they began the climb to where the loch nestled in a secluded valley just beyond the ridge above. When they reached the snowline, they saw the evidence that they were on the right path—footprints, both human and deer, and a blood trail leading straight on to the top. None of the men spoke, but every man had his thoughts nevertheless.

About an hour later, now on the ridge top, they came to where the trail led directly into the trees that went down to the water's edge.

Consternation gripped all four as they began to fear the worst, but as they broke out of the trees, they came upon a sight that shocked every man to the core, seasoned as they were to life's experiences.

Ian Forsythe sat at a small fire on the loch shore, and he was crying. As the men approached, he looked up with reddened eyes and ashen features, gaunt with grief, his misery accentuated by the dark stubble against the whiteness of his skin. Seeing Rab, he cried out loudly and pitifully, "I knew you'd come, Rab; I knew you'd come—I couldn't leave him, Rab, until you came."

"Where is Rick, Ian?" Rab said in a voice strained and low. "He's gone, Rab; he's gone—out there under the ice. I couldn't save him, Rab; I couldn't save him. He wouldn't listen to me. All I could do was watch him drown and listen to his last cries for help. I'm sorry, Rab, but I couldn't stop him." With that, Ian Forsythe broke down and cried like a child—loud and long he cried, until it became such a wail as prompted Rab to intervene and kneel beside him, holding him in his arms and gently encouraging him. "It's not your fault, Ian; it's not your fault. What could you have done to stop him? We can only advise on the hill. If a grown man chooses to disobey, he must bear the consequences for that, not the ghillie. Tell me what happened, Ian; how did this come about?"

"He got a shot, Rab—a mile or so back. It was a long shot at a good beast. We could have got closer, and I wanted to, but he was afraid of losing the opportunity. I told him we had a whole week ahead of us, and that we would get another opportunity, and a much surer shot, but he was adamant that he could pull it off with the Remington he had brought, and the new American ammunition that was specially made for long-range kills. Since the shot was well within reason, I relented, and he took it. The stag was hit, Rab, and well hit too, but as sometimes happens, the bullet missed the vitals, and it passed through, leaving enough energy and vigour in the beast to allow it to run, and run it did. We watched as it made for the high ground, and the blood trail from the snowline was easy enough to follow. When it came to the loch, it did not turn along either shoreline, but made off across the ice and fell dead just a hundred yards out.

Rick wouldn't leave it, Rab. He said he could easily drag it off the ice. I warned him the ice wouldn't hold him, but he laughed at me and said, 'Just watch.' He had no sooner reached the beach when the whole area round about him began to sink; finally, the ice broke and he disappeared. The ice could have borne him, for it bore the weight of the stag, but it couldn't bear the weight of both. I should have stopped him, Rab; I should have stopped him—it's my fault for letting him go."

"How could you have stopped him, Ian? It's a nonsense to even think so. Would you have hit him, knocked him out, pointed the rifle at him and threatened him? Don't think it was your fault, Ian—far from it. Rick was young, and he paid the price of being young in a situation that called for maturity and wisdom. I am sorry it happened, and truly sorry this young man lost his life in these circumstances, but this can never be said to be your fault. Grieve if you must, Ian—no one will ever blame you for that—but it is not your fault, nor Strathmore's when it comes to that. We are guides, not gods, and the guests must realise that and act and decide accordingly.

You have done well, Ian. Last night was one of the coldest in twenty-five years, and you stayed with your charge. You risked your own life without shelter for the sake of your dead stalker. We are going home now to report the incident and notify the family. Your wife and children are waiting for you; they are your responsibility—don't let them down over another man's mistake, something that is done and cannot be changed."

The other three men stood gazing at the dark spot on the ice—all that remained visible of a terrible event. It was a salutary lesson for all concerned, and the lesson was not lost on them. Finally, gathering the rifle and equipment together, they began the journey back, knowing in their hearts that this was not the end of the matter.

Chapter 21

Strathmore was never to be the same after the Loch Shannagh tragedy. Try as he might, Rab just could not summon the needed enthusiasm to plan ahead and to carry on as before.

When the party returned that day without Richard Symington, the weight of responsibility was very squarely laid upon the Lodge, and on Ian Forsythe and Rab MacKenzie in particular. Strathmore was unprepared for what happened next. It was always a quiet village. People knew one another and, apart from the usual harmless village gossip, it was a homely place, friendly, and always ready with help where and when help was needed. Like thousands more in villages like theirs, the inhabitants were just simple Highland folk, making their way through life as best they could, and quite oblivious to the corporate corruption that was prevalent in the wider world.

It all began very subtly at first—an unexpected visit from a hygiene inspector. All routine, of course, but leaving no stone unturned from the kitchen to the cupboards! It was strange, Rab thought, for he couldn't remember it happening before, but after all, there must be someone to keep things in order, and so he put it to the back of his mind. Then he heard from a friendly shopkeeper that there was a stranger in town—well dressed and well spoken—and asking about the Colonel's death and that also of Stu McDonald.

Next, a letter arrived one morning announcing an inspection of the armoury and of the firearms registration books. This was a new scheme, it said, seeking to prevent gun crime and poaching in the area. When the gun room inspectors arrived the morning after the letter, the penny finally dropped. Someone was targeting Strathmore. There was already a date set for an enquiry into the death of Richard Symington, and all these visits and queries about Strathmore business were an attempt to gather evidence of carelessness and neglect on the part of the estate, and bring responsibility for the tragedy upon estate's negligence. Rab MacKenzie had been blindsided by Symington senior and blamed himself for the fact. He ought to have seen it coming. He was yet to learn that he was out of place among those who put money and power above morals and principles, and his openness to help the enquiry was as *pearls before swine*, after all.

Symington senior had travelled to the Lodge and had taken charge of the body retrieval. The police were of a mind to leave it until spring on account of the great risk to rescuers, but Symington would not hear of it. He marshalled a group of volunteers from an airbase in Lossiemouth and brought them to Loch Shannagh. With the aid of an inflatable dinghy, sledge hammers, and ice axes, they cut a path to where the stag had lain. The blood mark where it had expired was still visible, and the team had no difficulty identifying exactly where to begin the underwater trawl with the grappling irons.

Ernest Symington looked on with a stony glare at the proceedings, and although Rab and Ian Forsythe stood beside him, he never once looked their way or made any attempt to speak. That cold January day, on the highest moor of the estate, the volunteers were very fortunate indeed. Loch Shannagh was known to have strong currents on account of several water springs erupting from the loch floor, and because of this, Rab thought that it was highly unlikely they could recover the body from the area where it went down. But, by a dark twist of fate, because of the intense cold, the body of Richard Symington, and the carcass of the stag, had not bloated, and so they had remained directly under the hole in the ice where they had broken through, the stag's antlers no doubt having a part to play in anchoring the grisly load to the loch bottom. As a result of these factors, the grappling irons caught them on the second throw. As they hauled in their grim catch, another surprise awaited them. Richard Symington's hands still firmly grasped the stag's antlers, as if he were unwilling to lose it even in death. It was not a pleasant sight, and Rab was sorry that Richard's father should see him brought to shore in such a manner.

Strapping the body to a stretcher and collapsing the inflatable, the group set off for Strathmore again without as much as an acknowledgement to the Strathmore staff who had so readily shown sympathy in joining the recovery party. As Rab and Ian stood alone on the shore, Ian spoke. "They are out to get us, Rab." "Yes, it appears so, Ian, but let's wait and see how the whole thing comes together; there's no use jumping bridges before we come to them."

"What did McEwen say when you phoned him?" "Well, as you know, McEwen is no longer in the local police scene, so he cannot help us from that side, but he gave good advice for all that. He told me not to assume that Symington senior had the ear of the enquiry panel. He may have been influential in getting it set up, but they may not be our enemies on that score. He told me to speak the facts and nothing more, and not to allow any personal feelings to be shown or known while doing so. McEwen said this was very important. He said to remember that it is not what we know that will prevail for us, but what we can prove. Keep that in mind, Ian, when you come to speak—fact only, and spoken without rancour or personal prejudice.

Let them do their worst, Ian, and we will do our best. We have nothing to be ashamed of, and we have done nothing that can be used against us. Right will prevail in this, messy though it has become, but right will prevail—wait and see."

On the morning of the enquiry, all were gathered at the local school, where the large assembly hall was made available to them, and it was suitably seated for the occasion. The meeting began promptly at nine am, and the chairman, Ivor McCormack, a chief inspector from Aberdeen, made the opening remarks.

After thanking the school for the assistance given and welcoming all present, he outlined very clearly the primary purpose of the enquiry. It was, he said, to ascertain the facts concerning the death of a young man who came to Strathmore on the first of January for one week's hill stalking, and was dead on the second of January in shockingly tragic circumstances. The cause of death is without dispute—the post-mortem has revealed he was drowned—but it is the remit of this enquiry to find out how he came to be drowned. Was it an unfortunate accident, or was it gross negligence? The answer to these questions will have very serious repercussions on those responsible, so it is in the interests of all to give the utmost assistance to the panel, that the truth may be made known, and that innocent men are not punished for the sad death, or, on the other hand, guilty men are not allowed to go free.

McCormack went on to state the powers of the enquiry. It was a police enquiry, a preliminary enquiry, set up to find facts that may lead to prosecution, and therefore anyone found prevaricating, or hiding vital testimony, or in any way misleading the panel, will themselves be open to prosecution in the event of criminal proceedings.

With the panel's remit now firmly entrenched in people's minds, McCormack then offered deepest sympathy to Ernest Symington, Richard's father, and any other relatives who might be present. He did warn them, however, about the proceedings—that they may hear things today that were distressing or unpleasant—but in such an event they were not to interrupt. The enquiry would hear the evidence and would take its course, and any decision would be based on whatever evidence they heard. The whole affair was distressing enough already, and in the interests of fairness and justice, it was important that all testimony be heard respectfully and responsibly. Having thus set the scene, the chairman then called the first witness.

"Could Mr Rab MacKenzie come forward? Rab slowly made his way to the chair provided at the front of the hall, just to one side of the panel. He had not specifically dressed for this occasion, except to wear newly washed and clean clothing, and as he sat down, he looked every inch the Highland ghillie—three-piece estate tweeds, waistcoat, jacket, and trousers, a warm check shirt, and soft green tie. Gaiters and stout boots finished off his striking attire.

"You are Mr Rab MacKenzie, are you not—ghillie and manager of Strathmore estate?" "Yes, sir; that is my name and occupation, and since the Colonel died, I have taken over the managerial duties of the business." "Can you tell us how you first came to be acquainted with the deceased, Mr Richard Symington, and what was your participation in his visit to Strathmore Lodge?" "My first meeting with Mr Symington was when I was asked to settle a dispute between him and the cabin maid assigned to his cabin. Mr Symington had complained that his cabin was cold on arrival and scolded the maid, threatening to report her to management for laziness. The maid, who is here today, tried to tell him that the procedure at the Lodge was to meet the guest and take his luggage, and then escort him to the kitchen where he could have breakfast. It was while he was there that his room would be made comfortable, the fire lit, and anything else attended to."

"And what was your decision when you were asked to intervene?" "I simply explained to the guest the usual procedure as already spoken by the maid, but told him we were sorry for any misunderstanding, and I hoped his stay would be an enjoyable one, notwithstanding the cabin fire issue."

"What was your opinion of Mr Symington?" "I do not express opinions of the guests, sir; my job is to welcome them and see that they have a pleasant time with us at Strathmore."

"Well, I must remind you, Mr MacKenzie, that you are obliged to answer any reasonable question put to you, and so I ask you again—what was your opinion of Mr Symington?"

"He was a well-spoken lad and a very good shot, but he appeared to me to be accustomed to having his own way." "Thank you; now, after the incident with the cabin maid, what did you do then?" "We went first to the kitchen and had a cup of tea and a chat; that was where I learned of the punt gunning he had been engaged in, and the opportunities the Wash offered if I ever had the notion to come down that way. We didn't stay long in the kitchen, and then we went directly to the range where I introduced him to Ian Forsythe, the man I had appointed to be his guide for the duration of his stay." "On what basis did you appoint Mr Forsythe? What special qualifications did he have to fulfil that role for a complete newcomer to hill stalking? In other words, why did you choose him?"

"His age, his character, and his experience put him ahead of many in the locality. Mr Forsythe is a man of fifty years of age; he is not a novice by any means. He has been employed by a local quarry as blasting master for the past twenty-five years and is a trusted employee. As far as the hill is concerned, he has been with Strathmore for around twenty years as a regular on the annual cull, and ghillie when needed, and has shot hundreds of deer in that time."

"Well, Mr MacKenzie, I am willing to accept your last point, but I find that just because a man is fifty years old and blasts in a local quarry is hardly a recommendation for entrusting him with a young man who needed guidance in a new and strange environment. Do you get my point?"

"With all due respect, Mr McCormack, I cannot agree with your assessment of what I have just related concerning Mr Forsythe. His fifty years have been spent in the Highlands. His employment at Strathmore has always been in times of pressing need, and he has been found to be most reliable in all that he has ever been asked to do. Fifty years in any environment will mark any man, and in those years here with us, he has gained a very well-deserved reputation. If the enquiry knew a little of his quarry employment, they might see him in an even better light from that which I have just expressed."

"Perhaps you can tell us of Mr Forsythe's quarry work, and we will let the enquiry make of it what they will."

Chapter 22

"Just two years ago sir, Mr Forsythe gained a commendation for bravery from his employer. The circumstances of that incident concerned saving the life of the employer's son, risking his own life while doing so.

He was training the young man in blasting technique and he gave him the task of priming the last two blast holes and fixing their leads to the main line that ran the length of the blast area for that day. The detonation itself would be initiated by a blasting cap or detonator joined to the main line and set off by lighting a fuse, and Mr Forsythe had this responsibility. The young man was out of sight behind some whin bushes when Mr Forsythe heard him give the all-clear. He gave it twice, as already agreed, and thereupon Mr Forsythe lit the fuse and made for the safe area. When he got to the safe area, the lad was not there, and his calls to him received no reply. Fearing something was greatly amiss, he ran to where he knew the boy was working and saw him lying unconscious over the last charge he had just laid.

He knew the fuse had only seconds left to burn, but Mr Forsythe ran to the stricken man and, putting him on his shoulder, carried him to safety, even as the detonation went off behind them. Just a few seconds more and they both would have gone down with the rock face in the explosion. The quarry owner had seen it all from the office window, but was powerless to do anything about it. The young man had broken a cardinal rule—when a charge is set, walk away to safety;

do not run. In the excitement of the moment, the lad had tried to run and had slipped, his head hitting the bare rock surface.

Mr Forsythe risked his own life that day, sir, and it was a witnessed fact. So, yes, I chose him particularly as a guide to Mr Symington, for I knew he would be in good hands."

There was a hush that fell on the meeting as Rab ended his description of Ian Forsythe's trustworthiness. Men fiddled with their pens or moved papers and documents as they waited for the uncomfortable quiet to pass. Finally the chairman spoke.

"Thank you, Mr MacKenzie. What you have just said will be invaluable to us as we come to deliberate on our findings. May we have Mr Ian Forsythe come forward now, please?" Ian Forsythe walked forward slowly and sat down on the now-empty chair. He did not appear a well man—pale and gaunt, his eyes were sunken and black-ringed, and his shoulders, once broad and straight, had a stoop they never had before.

The chairman looked hard at him before speaking, and when he did speak, he spoke softly. "Mr Forsythe, we are here today for one thing only, and that is to establish the events that led to this young man's sudden and unexpected death. I realise it must have been a terrible sight for you to behold, and that even today, as you relive those moments, it will be difficult and a great trial for you. I would encourage you, however, to hold up as best you can and tell us of the hours spent with the guest, and especially of the decision he took to go after the stag when it was lying on the ice. If there is anything you do not understand, any question you have difficulty with, just tell me, and I will do my best to help you with it."

"Thank you, sir; I will do my best to answer your questions." As Rab looked at his friend sitting there, a broken man, he felt very keenly for him. Ian Forsythe was a quiet man, a decent man who would go out of his way to help a stranger in a time of need. Now here he was, through no fault of his own, and by the malice of another, before an enquiry that may destroy all that he had been, and all that he may yet be. In his heart, Rab felt the injustice of it and directed a prayer to the Lord, praying that He would give him wisdom and strength to answer and that right would prevail for him that day.

"Mr Forsythe, could you just recall what took place that day between you and young Richard? Please begin from when you first were introduced to him."

"When I was introduced to him that morning, I took him to breakfast, although it was nearer lunchtime. We then made our way to the gun room, where I showed him our rifles, and I offered him his choice, even though they were all identical. He declined to use an estate rifle, saying he had just bought a new Remington and had special ammunition that was highly recommended for large animals. He smiled at our gun rack and said I would hardly expect him to use antiques when he had the very best from America. I was happy to have him use his rifle, for I understood what that meant to a young lad. There was no issue there, although privately, I viewed the new rifle as a little more than what was needed on our stalking ground. I then spoke a little of the shot itself, making clear that the outer limit was two hundred yards in good conditions, and there were to be no head shots attempted."

"Excuse me, Mr Forsythe, but Mr MacKenzie has stated that the young man was an excellent shot, yet you forbade a head shot, which I can only assume would be the most humane and instantaneous death in such a blood sport. Have I missed something here?"

The speaker was a small, bespectacled man who himself was engaged in banking at some level, and by the sarcasm in his voice, did not appear too friendly or sympathetic to the matter under discussion.

"We do not allow head shots unless three things are very evident. The first is the competence of the shooter, the second is the prevailing weather conditions, and the third is the distance to the target. Since Mr Symington was never on the hill before, and had never shot a stag before, we do not take the chance of head shots for novices. Even with a proficient shooter, the distance is crucial. It must not be more than a hundred yards.

A headshot is a very small target. The brain lies slightly to the front and between the antlers, and is not a large organ. At long range, there are so many variables to can deflect a bullet from a true trajectory. If lateral drift occurs due to cross-wind, then the bullet may strike to either side, in the eye area, and the result of that doesn't bear thinking about. Or if, due to factory error, a round is faulty and loses velocity— or if a shooter 'pulls' a shot, then it may strike low in the nose or jaw area and condemn a fine animal to a very long, lingering, and painful death. There is no trophy worth that risk, sir, and so we have our rule."

The bespectacled gentleman was by this time cleaning his glasses, purely in pretence, for he did not want to meet the eyes of those who had witnessed his former sarcasm, and his embarrassment now at being too clever with those who knew the subject best!

"When you got to the range, how did that go, Mr Forsythe?" McCormack seemed somewhat disgruntled at the interruption by the banker, for it had broken his train of thought for no good purpose. "Can you tell us of your time on the range?"

"At first the young man did not want to shoot. He said he had zeroed his rifle before he left home and it had taken no knocks or abuse in transit. He was happy that it was accurate. Moreover, he told me he was a very competent shot and he would show me when we got to the hill. I informed him that I needed to know before we got to the hill, for if I was to choose a shot for him, I needed to know he was capable of it. Eventually I did get him to fire five rounds at the plate, and he did extremely well indeed. After he had shot, I told him of our last rule—no alcohol—and that a packed lunch would be provided. That in the main concluded the day's preparation, and we then agreed to meet early next morning in the kitchen for an early breakfast."

Chapter 23

"The next morning was cold and clear, and a frost had settled even on the lowlands. We set out at first light, heading for Loch Shannagh, for I had noted some good beasts on the slopes there shortly before. About two miles from the summit, we spotted a nice animal, and after a successful stalk, we came within two hundred yards or so of it. I wanted to get closer, and we could have done so, but the guest wanted the shot from where we were. I saw the strike myself, but the beast hardly flinched; it just took off at a fast run for the summit. We followed it by sight, marking where it entered the trees that bordered the loch, and when we reached the snowline, the blood trail told us it could not run much further."

"How did you know it could not run much further?" another panel member, unused to the hunt, asked. "It was easy enough, sir; the tracks in the snow showed the animal was now staggering, and it had fallen twice. When we got to the shoreline, we saw the stag had walked out on the ice and had fallen about a hundred yards out."

"Tell us, Mr Forsythe, what you know and can remember of those moments immediately after you both saw the stag on the ice." "Mr Symington was very excited and laid his rifle down in preparation for retrieving the animal. I said, 'No, it can't be done; the ice is too dangerous.' He replied, 'The stag did it, so why not me too?' I told him that the weight of the stag was spread over a greater area, but the ice cannot bear you both. I took a large stone and broke the ice beside us to show him how thin it was. It was barely an inch thick, but he wouldn't listen."

"Excuse me, may I clarify something here, Mr Forsythe?" an older man at the end of the table enquired. "I have been told by the volunteers who retrieved the body that the ice could have borne a vehicle, yet you say it was only an inch thick. Which is true?" "Both are true, sir. The difference is that there was a time factor between these estimations. The cold weather came just the day before Mr Symington came to Strathmore. The ice on the loch was new; it had not had time to reach safety thickness. The volunteers who retrieved the body saw ice that was a week old, and that made all the difference."

"What exactly happened in those last few moments, Mr Forsythe? It might be difficult for you, but please try." The chairman's conciliatory tone had a calming effect on Ian Forsythe, and he began to explain in detail the trauma of that day. "I can remember thinking that beyond physical intervention, I could not stop the lad from going after that beast. It was so near—just a hundred yards, perhaps even a little less—and it was very tempting to a beginner. He was sure he could drag it in, and despite my pleadings, he went out on the ice. All went well until he reached the carcass. As he stooped to grab hold of the antlers, I saw the whole area around him begin to sink; then the ice under him broke and he went under. He came up almost immediately and grabbed for the antlers, hoping, I suppose, to pull himself back on the ice, but instead the stag itself went into the hole and both disappeared."

At this, Ian Forsythe broke down and began to sob uncontrollably, the chairman having to call for a recess to deal with the grief-stricken ghillie. It was a harrowing tale just to listen to, let alone see it happening, and the unfortunate man had the sympathy of many in the room that day.

After the recess, the chairman called again for Rab MacKenzie. "Mr MacKenzie, we have heard how this young man was an excellent shot, and Mr Forsythe has testified that he saw the strike. Why then would an animal run for almost two miles if it was hit so well? I must confess I am more than a little perplexed at this."

"It has to do with the velocity, the type of bullet used, and just blind chance, sir. Not being a ballistics expert, I can only describe what I know happens sometimes, and give my opinion of this particular shot, speaking of what I know, little though it may be. At Strathmore, we use rifles that are not nearly so powerful as the one young Mr Symington brought with him. We also use a bullet that is round-nosed as opposed to the more modern spire point. I have used these older rifles for twenty years and never saw this circumstance before, although I know a few men who have.

With a lower velocity blunt-nosed bullet, the likelihood of it passing through the beast is greatly reduced. Moreover, sir, such a bullet has a greater tendency to deform upon impact, thereby causing greater damage to the inner organs and bringing about major blood loss as a consequence. When a bullet stops within the target beast, all its energy is expended on the animal, and this can have a significant bearing on the result, which is, of course, to bring the beast down humanely.

Some ammunition is spire-pointed and sharp, streamlined for greater velocity. Given this much greater velocity, combined with the shape, they are prone to pass through and expend much of their energy in the heather beyond, rather than on the target.

Mr Symington was using a very heavy calibre with a high velocity rating and a spire-pointed copper-cased bullet. It is my opinion only, sir, that the bullet, in passing right through, and although causing fatal damage, yet missed a vital organ. Hitting a vital organ, with whatever bullet is used will cause immediate and fatal blood loss, and collapse is inevitable. Mr Symington's shot, while very well placed, and for the reasons given, allowed the animal to run. These things sometimes happen and defy all our expectations."

"Thank you for that, Mr MacKenzie; now could you tell us exactly what you found when you eventually found Mr Forsythe at Loch Shannagh?"

"I found a friend in such a state of distress that I feared for his sanity. He was crying uncontrollably and trembling with cold, having nothing but a light rain cape against the mountain chill. He kept repeating the same sentences and phrases over and over again." "What was he saying?" "He kept repeating, 'I couldn't save him, Rab; I couldn't save him. He wouldn't listen and I couldn't stop him. I'm sorry, Rab; I'm sorry.'

Just that, sir—over and over again." "What did you do, Mr MacKenzie?"

"I went to him and gave him a nip or two of restorative from a flask I carried for that purpose; then I put my arms around him and comforted him. I told him he was not to blame, that Mr Symington was an adult and ought to have taken heed of the warning given. I kept repeating this until he settled down; then we made the journey back to Strathmore. He had not eaten from the day before, and he was in a bad way physically and mentally."

"Hmm, I see. Does anyone else have a question relevant to this issue? This is the most harrowing business I have ever been engaged in, and I want to make it perfectly clear that the cause of this young man's death will be pursued to the end, whatever that end may be. Now is your chance to speak if you have any query or any matter you are not clear on." The chairman waited patiently, and finally an aged gentleman, a retired magistrate, cleared his throat in a manner calculated to draw attention to the importance of his query.

"Could I have more clarification on the issue of the ammunition used? It seems to me that the ammunition, such as Mr Symington brought with him, was most suitable for his rifle—ammunition that had passed the highest clearance, no doubt from the factory. Are we to suppose then, that such ammunition is unsuitable for Strathmore deer and that their antique rifles are superior? And what about this fanciful statement about bullets passing through without hitting a major organ? Quite frankly, I find such testimony a little bizarre.

Perhaps Mr MacKenzie may wish to retract the statement upon reflection, and we will understand that people can get a little carried away in the crisis of the moment, and, of course, we will not hold it against him."

It was not only a direct attack on the credibility of Rab MacKenzie, but also a negation of the moving and heartfelt testimony of Ian Forsythe. Rab knew in his heart it would come from somewhere, but he didn't expect it to come so late in the proceedings. He had thought things were going well for them, but this man had shown that there were those on the panel who were hostile still, and as such needed careful handling lest they lose what ground they had already won.

"I did not use the word unsuitable, sir; I merely stated that Mr Symington's rifle and ammunition were over and above the needs for killing red deer—far over and above—and that the calibre and velocity may have had a part to play in the fact that the stag ran for nearly two miles after being hit."

"Well, I have been reading Remington's own manual on both Mr Symington's rifle and ammunition, and it specifically states that it has been extensively field-tested and has proven far superior to comparable ammunition when used on elk, moose, and buffalo. Do your qualifications exceed Remington's, Mr MacKenzie?" The question was so pointed and insulting that all in the room were in no doubt where this man's sympathy lay, and waited with interest for Rab's reply—some of them wondering just how he could reply!

"But you have just confirmed my point, sir. A bull elk is twice as heavy as a red deer stag; a mature bull moose weighs about a ton and a large buffalo something similar. Mr Symington's ammunition was specially designed for such large beasts, but we do not have elk and moose and buffalo at Strathmore, sir; therefore, Mr Symington's ammunition was greatly excessive for his needs. May I ask you a question, sir?"

"I am not here to answer questions; I am here to ask questions." "But the chairman said anyone could ask for clarification. Mr Chairman, am I entitled to ask a question that might better enable me to state my case?" "I cannot see how we can deny that request, Mr MacKenzie, without the risk of being partisan in this matter, and we cannot afford to appear biased. Yes, you may ask whatever you will, provided it forms part of your argument and leads to a conclusion in that argument."

Chapter 24

"Thank you, sir. I would like to ask the gentleman a few questions concerning his objection to my opinion on the ammunition and the fact that I stated a bullet passing through an animal without striking a major organ. Have you ever shot a deer, sir?" "I have no interest in blood sports, Mr MacKenzie; I never had."

"Very well then; I take it you have never dressed out a deer carcass?" "You have it right—never." "That being the case, sir, how can you describe as fanciful the fact of a bullet's trajectory passing through an animal without hitting a major organ, when you have never seen the positioning of an anatomy[xxi] that would allow it to do so?

As far as the Remington booklet is concerned, it likewise has demonstrated today that it is you and not I who do not have the qualifications for such a discussion. In my twenty-eight years here, I have shot hundreds of deer, all with black powder and round-nosed bullets, and I have never lost one or seen such a runner as Mr Symington's stag. Time and time again, I have seen how a bullet reacts upon impact and how it deforms to make the strike even more lethal. Booklets don't kill deer, sir. A proper combination of rifle and bullet kills deer in the hands of a competent shot. Even then, the unthinkable can happen, as happened in the Symington case. His shot was right on target, but for the reasons given, his beast ran for over a mile. Strathmore may not be the most modern establishment in the Highlands, but we pride ourselves on guest safety and proven practices on the hill, and we use only the best and most trustworthy guides to make it happen for them.

You have quoted from a leaflet printed by a manufacturer promoting his product to an open market—a factory production.

My book, sir, is a volume that took over thirty years to put together. Every page of that book is a real-life experience—hill experience, success experience. Nothing in the world of theory or ballistics can match that. Do you have any more questions, sir?

Rab's scathing put-down brought the room to silence. His argument, logic, and conclusions struck home forcibly to all in the room, and if any other had frivolous or mischievous questions to ask, they must have thought the better of asking, for none were forthcoming. This ghillie of Strathmore, when roused, had proved himself a formidable adversary and a staunch and loyal defender of the unjustly accused. It was Hamish McCormack, chief inspector of police, who finally broke the impasse, and he did so in a most admirable manner.

"Mr MacKenzie, I have listened to both you and Mr Forsythe speak of the art—if I may call it that—the art of hill stalking, and the humane dispatch of Scotland's most majestic of beasts, the red deer. As meat consumers, we as a nation kill millions of domestic animals and fowl each year, many of them reared in quite appalling conditions, and I know from experience that the killing of such leaves a lot to be desired sometimes. Yet we as a nation allow those things to happen. We do so because the love of meat or fowl far outweighs the knowledge we have of the cruelty involved in such mass production of our favourite food.

I have been educated today by the knowledgeable descriptions given of the means used to kill deer on the hill stalk—also of the ammunition and the rifle, and most of all the humane instant dispatch of a target animal ninety-five per cent of the time, and at least a very quick dispatch all of the time. I will never have negative views on hill stalking again, for I see in you men a consideration and respect for the animal rather than the trophy, and that has impressed me greatly. Thank you for enlightening me on a pursuit I had only heard of before.

The panel will deliberate on what we have heard later, and in the morning, if we all assemble here promptly by nine o'clock, we should be finished by lunchtime. Thank you for coming today, and although it has not been pleasant for any of us, I think we all have a much clearer picture in our minds as to that terrible day's events, when that young man lost his life most shockingly and tragically. Until tomorrow, then."

Before Rab went to give his daily report to Lady Eleanor, he and Ian Forsythe went to the kitchen and pulled chairs close to the fire. The fireplace was not used for cooking purposes, but it played a vital role nevertheless. Guests found camaraderie there and could relax and discuss things of mutual interest with one another. "Thanks, Rab; thanks a lot for those kind words you spoke on my behalf. I really appreciate that and will not forget it." "They were not kind words, Ian; I spoke nothing more than the truth. The things I said are what you are, Ian. Don't let this tragedy take that away from you. I want you to go from this enquiry with the confidence that you did the right thing, and that Richard Symington did the wrong thing, and lost his life by doing so.

Let no man judge you on this tragedy, Ian. Stand firm on the facts of the case as regards your decisions and advice, and do not yield to false guilt, or allow an attitude of failure to overcome you." "How do you think it went today Rab? What will tomorrow bring for us?" "Well, my reading of today's proceedings is a favourable one. Only three men asked a question, and two of them would have been better off remaining quiet. The last question was a gift, for it gave opportunity for us to cover areas that will be beneficial to us in the summing up.

I think the police who are attending are more centred than the rest; and although they are not saying much, they will be the deciding influence when it comes to assessing the findings. It is a sure thing that McCormack's speech was a nail in the coffin of the naysayers to stalking, and that can only do good as they come to deliberate. I am hopeful, Ian, and I only hope that old man Symington does not cause a scene at the end."

The next morning, punctually at nine o'clock, all were gathered again in the school's assembly hall. Mr Ernest Symington, the dead boy's father, was also there. He was not an old man by any means, and at fifty years or so it was evident that he kept himself in fair shape. Tanned and fit, he spent most of his spare time on his sea-going yacht, and was known to be highly competitive and a bad loser!

To date, he had not recognised Rab or any of the Strathmore staff, and it had been quite apparent to all that he was out to avenge his son's death by whatever means possible. In the proceedings the day before, he had taken a seat by himself, and today he did the same. In his opening remarks, Hamish McCormack could not have been more conciliatory and sensitive.

"It grieves us all today to be met again to conclude this dreadful business. To Mr Symington senior, who has so bravely attended this enquiry, I offer again my deepest sympathy. There can be nothing so heart-breaking to a parent as to lose a child, and a child of exceptional abilities is an even more tragic loss.

However, my colleagues and I have looked very carefully at every aspect of this case; although Richard's time at Strathmore was brief, a picture has emerged of that brief visit, and that picture became quite clear to us in our summing up.

The Strathmore testimony and the quarry testimony, given by men who have been eminently successful in their chosen profession and who have the utmost respect of their employers and community, cannot be lightly ignored. Moreover, I have found no animosity directed towards Richard, even though he appeared to treat this sport and those engaged in it in a manner somewhat indifferent. It would have been very easy for these men to fabricate a story, a narrative that favoured themselves, but they have not done that. Rather, they have given the lad credit where credit was due, while simply stating those areas where Richard differed from them. I find this an honourable attitude, and commend them for it.

This is a preliminary enquiry only, set in motion by Richard's father with a view to a possible prosecution if gross negligence was found. As far as Mr Rab MacKenzie is concerned, we find that he did indeed bring in a most trustworthy man to be a guide to the young Richard. As far as Mr Forsythe is concerned, we find that a man who would risk his life at a high-altitude loch shore in freezing conditions, out of loyalty to a corpse, must be believed as to his testimony. Richard was young; let us not blame him for that, but likewise, let us not blame those awful consequences on these innocent men who went out of their way to make his visit enjoyable and successful.

We therefore find that neither the Strathmore estate nor its ghillies are in any way to blame for this tragedy. Richard Symington died as a result of reckless disregard for a heartfelt and legitimate warning of great danger."

The panel sat immobile, waiting for the expected outburst from Symington senior. No one spoke, and, as the moments wore on, the chairman himself seemed a little apprehensive as to what might happen. Finally, there was a stir at the back of the room as a chair scraped the floor, and Ernest Symington stood to speak. "Mr Chairman, may I have an opportunity to share with you all that is on my heart today?"

McCormack, for a very brief second or two, seemed to hesitate, no doubt unwilling to open up an opportunity for a grief-stricken harangue from the father, but something in the softness of Symington's tone moved him to grant the request. "I don't see why not, sir; after all, the departed is your son, and I am sure you will want to honour his memory by speaking on his behalf. What father would not want to do that? By all means, Mr Symington, feel free to unburden your heart to us."

Chapter 25

Unexpectedly, Symington walked forward and took the now-empty chair at the front, where he could be seen and heard by all. He looked aged from the day before, and no longer walked in his usual upright and square-shouldered manner. As he turned to face the room, he sat with his hands on his knees and leaning slightly forward, as if nervous of a situation he had never experienced before.

"Gentlemen," he began, "it is true what Mr McCormack said. I did indeed instigate this preliminary enquiry. Richard was all I had. His mother died when he was six years old, and I must confess to my shame today that I left the child and his needs to nannies and friends. I was too busy chasing after my own dreams to consider an innocent child in his grief—a grief that he had to bear alone. I failed to see that the well-being of my child was more important by far than finance and banks together. I substituted love and affection with money and gifts, and it was a fatal mistake. It is my fault alone that Richard grew up indulged, and as a consequence, became indulgent himself.

We lived separate lives—I on my yacht and Richard in the Fens and the Wash. That became his passion, gentlemen—a solitary passion pursued with passion. It was that passion that brought him to Strathmore, and it was that passion that led him out onto the ice. Even had I been with him, I could not have stopped him from going after that stag. I have been greatly moved by what I have heard and witnessed since I came to Strathmore. There is a deep respect in the community for the Lady of the Manor, and I understand the Lodge is and has been a benefactor to many. This is so different from the world I move in that it has come as a great surprise to find it so.

I, too, have listened very carefully to the testimony of these two ghillies, and I find no fault with them. To my utter shame, I find that Mr Forsythe gave more loyalty to my son's corpse than I ever gave him in his lifetime. I must live with that, gentlemen, and I know I will never forgive myself for the neglect that ultimately led to Richard's death. I was told in the village that there is a strong religious or Christian ethos in Strathmore, and always has been. I scoffed at that, for in the world I live in, corporate corruption pervades every aspect of the nation's life, and God and His influence are treated as unwanted commodities. Gentlemen, I have found another world here at Strathmore—a better world—and I am only sorry that I did not find it sooner.

Richard's death will forever live in my heart and conscience, and I must accept the pain that it will bring, but these two ghillies and the estate they work for will also remain in my heart, as a testimony to their integrity and transparency, their faith and practice—a faith I have seen proven in the face of great trial and false accusation. May it please God to bring me to this faith one day, for I have seen something more enduring than riches, more precious than anything this world can offer.

Please pass on my sincere regards to the Lady of Strathmore Lodge, for she, and her late husband, seem to be central to all that I have witnessed here."

After he had spoken, Symington senior rose very slowly and walked the length of the room to where the exit was. He looked neither left nor right, but his empty and sorrowful gaze told its own story. He was a broken man, and it showed, not only on his face but on his physical frame. As he made his way out the door, many hearts in the room went with him, and many were the silent tears that wet weathered cheeks that day in Strathmore's schoolroom.

Thus ended one of the most trying and troubling episodes in the history of the estate, and one which had far-reaching consequences for Rab MacKenzie. He had not spoken of this to anyone, but that day on the shore of Loch Shannagh, he reached a Rubicon in his own life. A line had been well and truly crossed, a decision made, a new beginning contemplated. Try as he might, he could not shake off the intent conceived that day, and so forcibly planted in his mind and heart. He would leave Strathmore.

The strain of the Fraser trial, and the subsequent hanging, had never left the ghillie. Now the Symington tragedy was another memory to add to the trauma of these past couple of years. Rab was suddenly tired of it all. The constant pressure, the physical and mental burden, the weight of responsibility had become too much for him, and he no longer looked at his work as he did before. There was only one other thing that he had to settle, and then he would be gone, and he determined to settle it, tonight!

Leaving Strathmore would not be easy, for his life had become entwined with the Lodge and the couple who had so graciously cared for him for these past forty years, almost, but the deed was already done in his heart, and he could never continue now that he had experienced this heart-change. Like the *'turtle-dove, swallow, and the crane'* he had often read of in the book of Jeremiah—birds of passage who knew instinctively the time of departure to better climes—Rab knew this was his time, and there was no mistake about it. He could now see that the past events of the last few years had merely been as life's seasonal changes—prescient reminders of the fact that his time at Strathmore must sooner or later come to an end.

Rab often pondered his life experience from that day on the moor fifty long years ago. He had spent thirty-five years all told at the Lodge, and it had been two years now since the Colonel's death. Yes, it was indeed his time.

Chapter 26

He had gone over the estate books very carefully, and they showed well. But apart from what the records stated, things were never the same since the Colonel died. It was as if a light had gone out, a door had been closed, an era had passed. While the Colonel was alive, things had a future, a purpose, an aim. All that had now gone. There was no future, for there was no heir, and what was the point of all the labour when there was no hope of a successor? Even Lady Eleanor herself had lost her former lustre, and the staff were aware of it too. Rab's endeavours since the Colonel died had paid off handsomely, but there had been no enjoyment with the increase. The estate was functioning very well as to turnover, but it was a hollow victory, and the emptiness left by the Colonel's loss could never again be filled. It was over, and Rab could not see any reason in prolonging the inevitable.

It was early moonlight when he made his way to give his report, and he knocked and waited. It had been his practice since the Colonel had been killed to bring a full report of each day's proceedings, good or bad. It was the least he could do, he thought. It is one thing to lose one's partner, but quite another thing to be left out of the estate affairs, and although he was never specifically asked to do so, Rab had been meticulous in this duty of reporting daily.

The door opened and Lady Eleanor bade her ghillie enter. The first thing Rab noticed was the Colonel's rifle. It had been mounted on the wall above the fireplace, and an ammunition pouch hung beside it. Rab walked to where he could better see the display and stood gazing at it in silence, seemingly oblivious to all else in the room. He was brought from his reverie by the voice of Lady Eleanor:

"What's in your mind, Rab?" "Just thinking of the Colonel, M'Lady." "What is it you are thinking then?" "Oh, just a few lines that came to me when I saw the rifle on the wall." "Would you care to think them out loud, so that I may share them too?"

"M'Lady will know the epitaph[xxii], but I will be happy to repeat it as a tribute to your husband:

'Under the wide and starry sky, Dig the grave and let me lie.
Glad did I live and gladly die, And I laid me down with a will.
This be the verse that you grave for me: Here he lies where he longed to be
Home is the sailor, home from the sea, And the hunter home from the hill.'

Going quietly to her desk, Lady Eleanor sat down and had tea brought by a maid. There was a silence that neither of them wished to break, as memories filled their minds, and strong emotions filled their hearts. Finally she spoke. Her voice was subdued and had more than an air of tired resignation about it.

"Well, Rab, what have you brought me tonight? What has the day brought to Strathmore?" "Everything is much the same, M'Lady, and yet not the same at all. The drowning of young Symington has upset us all, as I am sure you already know, and we are grateful for the fact that we have been exonerated from any blame in the matter. Yet the damage has been done, M'Lady. I feel different now concerning Strathmore, and I am feeling the onset of years on the hill. As well as all that, it becomes more difficult to find the inner drive or motivation to train a successor.

A ghillie could be found, but a manager is something different. It's not just myself, M'Lady, but the atmosphere has changed in the whole estate management. When the Colonel was alive, he brought confidence to us all. He was the mainstay of our daily labours, and with him among us, we felt secure and happy. But that has all gone now, and while we are doing well financially, there are some things money cannot buy. The staff all feel for you, M'Lady, as I do myself, and we all wonder what will become of you when change comes, as come it must, for as you know very well, nothing stays the same for long.

I have come tonight to discuss the future with you, and to ask you to consider selling up and moving to a more amenable lifestyle, for the burdens of estate management are not easy to carry as you have done until now. These things are not easy for a ghillie to speak of, M'Lady, but I feel I would be disloyal if I failed to draw your attention to them, and ask you to consider them very carefully."

"I know you would not be disloyal to me, Rab, and I must confess I have thought of very similar things of late, for I too am getting on, and the burden does not get any lighter with the passing years. But on the other hand, I am at a loss to know which way to turn, or the best way forward. I am undecided, Rab—fearful of change, yet knowing I must change. I have known nothing but Strathmore since I was a young bride of twenty years old, and change does not come easily in those circumstances. I will consider what you have said tonight, and give it my utmost attention, and I thank you for your faithfulness in speaking to me as you have just done. There is a verse, in Proverbs I think it is, that tells us, *'Faithful are the wounds of a friend.'* Now, I know you have not wounded me, Rab, but the lesson holds just the same. You have been very faithful to me, and I thank God in my prayers each day for it. Is there anything more, Rab, or is that enough for one day?"

"Well, there is something else, M'Lady, if I may speak of it." "Certainly, Rab; you are free to speak of whatever is on your mind, and it has always been so, has it not?"

"That it has, M'Lady, but this concerns a very personal matter"

A secret, Rab?"

"Until tonight, yes." "I love a good secret; tell me, Rab."

"I wish to be married."

"Married, Rab?" Lady Eleanor exclaimed in genuine surprise. "I didn't know you had a girl."

"There are many things you don't know about me, M'Lady." Lady Eleanor laughed at this. "So it appears, Rab; so it appears. Who is the very fortunate girl then, and where does she live?"

"Not very far away at all, M'Lady."

"Oh, a local girl; that's nice, Rab, and I wish you every blessing, for you deserve a good girl." "Do you think so, M'Lady?" "I know so, Rab. You will make a fine and loyal husband and make someone very happy; of that I am convinced. How did you come to meet your girl, Rab? For you don't do much socialising—was it recently or a while ago?" "It was quite a while ago, M'Lady—forty years or thereabouts."

"Goodness, Rab; that's a very long time to keep a girl waiting. What has caused you to delay until now, or is it a big secret?" She was gently teasing him, enjoying his hesitancy and bashful attempt to break this news, but at the same time her curiosity had been well and truly awakened by this news.

When he didn't immediately respond, she continued. "Tell me about her Rab; what was it that brought you together?" "I met her on the moors one day, M'Lady, and she spoke to me, and from that moment onwards I have carried her in my heart until now." "Why, that's just beautiful, Rab—a real love story, and how sweetly described even after forty-odd years. What was it she said that formed that bond so immediately and so lasting, Rab?"

" Oh, just two or three words M'Lady, just two or three words."

"Well, aren't you going to tell me, Rab? You have me intrigued now, really intrigued; tell me," she said, a smile playing around the corners of her mouth.

"She said M'Lady, in the Gaelic, " Cuidich mi."[1]

Lady Eleanor looked stunned, as if she couldn't comprehend what she had heard. The colour drained from her face, and the pen she had been holding fell from her fingers and clattered across the floor. Rab never spoke, and both looked at each other for long moments in absolute silence—Rab, expecting a reply, and Lady Eleanor still trying to process what she heard. Only the deep rise and fall of her bosom gave an inkling of what was going on in her pounding heart.

Satisfied now that Rab was serious, and she had heard right, she rose up and walked around the desk towards the man she had spoken to every evening since the Colonel was killed.

"Rab, Rab, what are you saying? I was a married woman that day, and you were a child of ten. Surely this cannot be as you think it is. Surely you must be mistaken as to your feelings."

---

[1] Help me Please'. Answer, 'I will help you'.

The gentle kindness of the woman standing before him only emboldened the humble ghillie, and he poured forth his heart as never before.

"Dearest Eleanor, it is true what you are saying. I was but a child that day, and knew nothing of the married state or those things that belong to it. All I knew was that I loved you from the very moment I saw you lying injured and bleeding.

I could not help it when such a strong emotion took hold of me, so I just carried it within my heart as a secret. When I grew older and began to understand what marriage entailed, my first thoughts did not differ or change. I still loved you the same; I had no conflict.

For me to see you and the Colonel happy together made me happy too. I can truly say I served the Colonel faithfully throughout these years without ever coveting what belonged to him, but he is dead now—two years—and I think a respectable and reasonable period of time has elapsed for me to reveal my heart to you.

I have watched as the light has gradually gone from your eyes, and the joy gone from your heart. I cannot longer bear it. It has not been easy for me to come here tonight and reveal my heart unto you, but circumstances have brought me to this moment.

Eleanor, will you have me as your husband? I must know. I have prayed about this moment, and sought the face of God for wisdom in it, and I have made my position as clear as I can find words to do."

Lady Eleanor raised a hand and gently touched Rab on his cheek. "How old are you, Rab?" "Coming fifty-two very soon."

"Do you know how old I am, Rab?" "Coming sixty-two, I suppose." "That's right, Rab; I am coming sixty-two. Don't you think we are a little too old for marriage? We are not young anymore, are we?"

"If it's a marriage based on youth and all the things that come with youth, we cannot have that. But is that what we want? Can we not have something better? A marriage based on proven mutual respect and mature love—a marriage not threatened by the temptations and pitfalls that we see all around us, and which bring the best-laid plans to nought in the marriages of much younger people.

I want the joy and comfort of each other's company for as long as the Lord gives us time on earth—the heart contentment that only a companion, a soul mate, a trusted and proven confidante brings. Someone I can care for and look after, and who might one day come to care for me in the same way.

I have my own money, Eleanor, and enough for you too. Sell this place and come away with me. You can have Rachel for a companion or a maid of your choice. I don't want you to be in hardship, or to be tied to the duties of housekeeping. I want us to have time to spend together.

Picnics on the moors, visits to the capital city, even Europe, entertaining old friends and acquaintances, too long neglected. We can move away from here, or remain if you choose. I just want you to be happy, for us to be happy, as man and wife."

With this, Eleanor put her forefinger on Rab's lips to silence him. "Say no more, Rab," she said. "I have a secret too. I have lived with it for forty years, and I must speak of it now.

When you began to come to our home after my fall on the moor, I was more pleased than I dared to confess. I was deeply grateful for your timely appearance and help to this stranger, when you could have so easily run off and hidden yourself away for fear of the consequences of being caught poaching. But you didn't, Rab, and that touched a chord in my heart ever after. That day on the moor, I felt so ill I thought I would die. The pain in my back I could hardly bear, but I had another pain in my heart that seemed worse, for I was three months pregnant, and I feared greatly for my child. As it happened, I did miscarry, and the nurse who attended me told me the baby was a little boy.

I was heartbroken, Rab, and the news I received afterwards brought a wound that has not healed to this day. I was told I could never carry another child, and if we attempted another pregnancy, it could well be fatal for me. The Colonel, too was greatly upset, but, being the man he was, he made the best of the situation. I never told him the baby was a boy, for I did not want to add to his sense of loss. We were extremely careful, Rab, for the Colonel said I was more precious to him than a dozen children, and as long as he had me, he would be happy.

When you came into the picture, I looked upon you as a gift of God—a replacement for my lost child. Your visits were the highlight of my week, and your questions and innocent outlook on life uplifted my heart and impressed me greatly. Although I did not tell the Colonel, I began to look upon you as my son, and consequently, I grew to love you as such. When you grew to be a man, my love never changed towards you. You were still my son in a sense—a son now grown to be a man that I was proud and privileged to know. Although I can say before God that there was nothing sinful in that love, I kept it to myself, for I found it hard to express the nature of it, and feared it might be misunderstood.

Since the Colonel's death, I had resigned myself to widowhood and have never once thought of remarriage, but you have tonight revealed a door I have never seen before, and which gives me hope that I might find happiness again.

Could it be possible that what you have said tonight has brought to pass that verse for me*: 'No good thing will he withhold from them that walk uprightly?'"*

With this, Lady Eleanor moved closer to her ghillie and put her arms around him. As she felt the coarse tweeds against her cheek, smelling of the moors and heather, and with Rab's strong arms encircling her, she experienced a long-forgotten emotion. She knew again what it was to be a woman, to belong to someone, to be whole again, and to be fulfilled in the presence and company of a man who loved her, and who would cherish her.

"I will, Rab; I will. I will be your wife," she whispered. "On one condition." "Oh, and what would that be, M'Lady?" "No more secrets!" And with that, she kissed him into silence. There was nothing more to be said.

The End

APPENDIX

With welcome additional comments indented.

[i]Cull

Thinning out a population of deer by selective slaughter. This is a necessity when the numbers become too many for the habitat that sustains them. Older animals, or the sick and weak, are the first to be taken. This helps ensure a sustainable food source and provides a healthy gene pool for future breeding.

> Nature, left to her own devices in our modern landscape, cannot cope when man's intervention has irreversibly altered the balance that once existed.

> Older animals, or the sick and weak, are the first to be taken out of the herd, just as any apex predator would naturally select. This is not sentiment; it is sound management based on observation and experience. The stalker becomes nature's agent, applying the same principles that wolves once did, but with precision and purpose.

> Such selective culling ensures a sustainable food source and provides a healthy gene pool for future breeding. Without this intervention, the alternative is far more brutal—wholesale starvation, disease outbreaks, and the inevitable collapse of the population. I have witnessed overpopulated herds, and the sight is not a pleasant one. Emaciated animals, stunted growth, barren does—this is the reality of unmanaged populations.

> The cull, properly executed, is conservation in its truest sense. Those who oppose it on emotional grounds have never stood in a wood where deer have stripped every piece of vegetation within reach, where saplings stand like skeletal fingers, where regeneration has ceased to exist.

ii Cuidich mi, please

Help me, please

iii Cuidichidh mi thu

I will help

iv Croup

The top line of a horse's hindquarters, from the hip to the base of the tail.

This is fundamental anatomy that any horseman worth his salt should know instinctively, yet I have witnessed supposed experts who cannot properly identify this crucial area.

The croup tells you everything about a horse's conformation and breeding. A well-muscled, slightly rounded croup indicates power and athleticism—the mark of a horse bred for performance. A steep, angular croup suggests speed but perhaps less endurance, whilst a flat, poorly muscled croup often betrays inferior breeding or inadequate conditioning.

When assessing a horse, I always examine the croup carefully. The slope, the muscle development, the way it flows into the tail-set— these details reveal the animal's capabilities and limitations. A hunter needs substance here; a racehorse requires different qualities entirely.

Many modern riders, obsessed with pretty heads and flashy movement, ignore this fundamental area. They purchase on emotion rather than sound judgement, then wonder why their horse lacks the power or stamina they expected. The croup doesn't lie—it tells the truth about what lies beneath the surface, if you know how to read it.

This is knowledge gained through years of handling horses, not from textbooks or weekend courses. The croup speaks to those who have learned to listen.

^v Royal

A Red deer stag with twelve points or tines on its antlers.

This is the crown prince of the Scottish Highlands, a magnificent beast that has earned his title through years of survival, cunning, and dominance. To encounter a true Royal is to witness nature's aristocracy in its finest form—an animal that has outlived his contemporaries, outfought his rivals, and claimed his place at the apex of the herd.

I have stalked these monarchs for decades, and each one teaches you something new about patience, fieldcraft, and respect. A Royal doesn't achieve his status by accident—he has learned to read the wind, to use ground that would confound lesser beasts, and to vanish into a landscape that seems to offer no concealment whatsoever.

The antlers themselves tell a story of genetics, nutrition, and age that only the experienced eye can properly read. Six points to each beam, perfectly balanced, swept back in that distinctive curve that marks true nobility. Yet I have seen so-called experts miscount tines, confusing brow points with bez points, or failing to distinguish between a true Royal and a heavy-headed beast with irregular growth.

The uninitiated often assume that any large stag qualifies for the title, but they are gravely mistaken. A Royal must carry exactly twelve points—no more, no less—and those points must be clearly defined, not mere bumps or malformed growths that the hopeful might claim as tines.

To take a Royal is the pinnacle of the stalker's art, but to encounter one and choose restraint—that, perhaps, is the mark of true wisdom.

^{vi} Glassed

To view the area to be hunted with binoculars or a telescope.

This is where stalking truly begins—not with the shot, but with the patient, methodical examination of every fold of ground, every shadow, every potential lie where a beast might rest unseen. The amateur rushes forward, trusting to luck and keen eyesight. The experienced stalker knows that proper glassing can make the difference between success and returning empty-handed.

I have spent entire mornings glassing a single corrie, watching light change the landscape, revealing what was invisible moments before. A patch of bracken becomes the flank of a hind; a boulder transforms into a resting stag. The eye, unaided, sees what it expects to see. Good glass shows you what is actually there.

The quality of your optics matters more than most sportsmen realise. I have watched stalkers struggle with inferior binoculars, squinting through fogged lenses and poor resolution, missing opportunities that proper glass would have revealed instantly. A deer at eight hundred yards is invisible to the naked eye, a mere speck through poor binoculars, but crystal clear through quality optics.

The art lies not just in looking, but in knowing how to look. Systematic sweeps, overlapping fields of view, and patience to examine each suspicious shadow twice, thrice if necessary. Movement catches the eye, but it is often the perfectly still animal that provides the finest sport.

Modern stalkers, obsessed with technology and range-finding, often forget this fundamental skill. They rely on thermal imaging and laser range-finders when what they truly need is the patience to glass properly—a skill that cannot be bought, only learned through long experience in the hills.

[vii] Gralloch

Gaelic for intestines. Still used today in the deerstalking community. To gralloch a deer simply means to remove the intestines. This is sometimes done in two stages after a kill. The first gralloch removes the stomach and intestines only (the heavy part), leaving the liver, heart, and lungs to be removed in the game larder.

This is where the real work begins—where the romantic notion of stalking meets the bloody reality of field craft. The gralloch is not a task for the squeamish or the inexperienced, yet it is essential if the venison is to be worth eating.

I have watched novice stalkers turn green at their first gralloch, yet within minutes they understand the fundamental truth: this is not butchery, but respect for the animal you have taken. Done properly, it is swift, clean, and purposeful—the final act in a drama that began with the first glimpse of antler through the morning mist.

The Gaelic term has endured because it captures something the English language cannot—the practical necessity wrapped in ancient tradition. When a Highland ghillie speaks of the gralloch, he is invoking centuries of knowledge passed down through generations who understood that every part of the process matters.

The two-stage approach is born of hard experience. Remove the heavy gut immediately in the field, and you save yourself the burden of carrying unnecessary weight across rough terrain. Leave the organs that provide the finest eating—the liver, heart, and lungs—for careful removal in controlled conditions where they can be properly preserved.

Modern hunters, obsessed with trophy photography and social media glory, often rush this crucial stage or delegate it to others. They miss the point entirely: the gralloch is where you truly earn your venison.

^{viii} Cup

The last three or more tines on the antler top, usually in a cluster.

This is where a stag's true magnificence reveals itself—not in the length of beam or sweep of antler, but in the complexity and formation of his crown. The cup is nature's final flourish, the culmination of years of growth and development that transforms a good head into something truly exceptional.

I have examined countless stag heads in my time, and the cup tells you everything about the animal's maturity and breeding. A young stag may carry impressive length, but it is the old monarch who develops that distinctive clustering of points at the antlers' terminus—nature's own coronation.

The uninformed often overlook this crucial feature, fixated instead on overall spread or beam thickness. They fail to understand that a proper cup formation indicates not just age, but superior genetics and optimal nutrition throughout the animal's life. It is the hallmark of a beast that has reached its prime and established its dominance.

I have witnessed stalkers pass up magnificent specimens simply because they lacked the beam length they desired, yet those same men would have given anything to possess a head with a well-formed cup. Such is the ignorance that pervades modern hunting— all flash and little substance.

A true cup formation is becoming increasingly rare in our overhunted Highland glens. When you encounter a stag carrying such a crown, you are looking at something approaching perfection—the product of generations of nature's unfailing magnificence.

[ix] **Pulled the shot**

Simply a movement at the crucial moment of squeezing the trigger, causing the shot to go wide of the intended mark. It may be an involuntary movement, a flinch, or too-early pressure on a light trigger before the shooter is properly set to shoot.

This is the stalker's nightmare—the moment when everything that could go right goes catastrophically wrong. I have witnessed it countless times, and experienced it myself on occasions I prefer not to dwell upon. One instant of lost concentration, one fractional movement at the critical moment, and a clean kill becomes a wounded animal disappearing into dense cover.

The pulled shot is often the mark of the inexperienced shooter who has not yet learned to control his breathing, his heartbeat, his very thoughts in that crucial second when finger meets trigger. But it can equally betray the veteran who has grown overconfident, who assumes that experience alone will guarantee success.

I have seen men who could place five shots through a sixpenny piece at the range yet pull their shot when faced with a Royal stag at two hundred yards. The difference between target shooting and stalking is the difference between theory and reality—when that magnificent beast stands before you, knowing that you may never see his like again, the pressure can overwhelm even the steadiest hand.

The light trigger that feels so precise on the bench becomes a liability in the field, responding to pressure applied before the shooter has properly settled his sight picture. The flinch that never troubles the range shooter suddenly manifests when the stakes are real.

There is no excuse for the pulled shot, yet every honest stalker will admit to at least one in his career. It is a humbling reminder that perfection remains forever just beyond our grasp.

[x] Concentration Camps

One of the most controversial policies of the South African invasion, that the British public was outraged when they became aware of it. The Boers suffered cruelly from this Kitchener strategy. People died by their thousands from disease and hunger.

This was no accident of war—it was deliberate policy, conceived in the comfortable offices of Whitehall and executed with ruthless efficiency in the African veld. Lord Kitchener's solution to Boer resistance was as simple as it was brutal: remove the civilian population that sustained the commandos, and the war would end.

I have studied the records, visited the sites, and spoken to descendants who still carry the scars of this shameful chapter. The statistics tell only part of the story—over 26,000 Boer women and children died, along with thousands of black Africans whose suffering has been largely forgotten by history.

The camps were not built for comfort or care. Overcrowded, under-supplied, and administered by men who viewed their inmates as obstacles to victory rather than human beings deserving of basic dignity. Disease spread like wildfire through canvas tents and corrugated iron barracks. Children wasted away before their mothers' eyes.

When Emily Hobhouse exposed these conditions to the British public, the outcry was immediate and fierce. Yet the policy continued, justified by military necessity and imperial ambition. This is what happens when war is fought without honour, when the ends are deemed to justify any means.

The concentration camp was Britain's contribution to twentieth-century warfare—a legacy we should remember with shame, not pride.

[xi] Isandlwana

Fought on 22nd January 1879, when approximately 1,800 British, Colonial, and native troops and civilians were overwhelmed by 20,000 Zulu warriors. 1,300 perished. The Zulus had won their first victory against the English invader.

This was no glorious defeat—it was a catastrophic failure of leadership, arrogance, and military incompetence that cost over a thousand men their lives. Lord Chelmsford had divided his forces, leaving the camp at Isandlwana woefully undermanned and inadequately defended whilst he chased shadows elsewhere.

The British had grown complacent, drunk on their own superiority and the supposed invincibility of the Martini-Henry rifle. They failed to understand that they were facing one of the finest military machines in Africa—warriors who had perfected the art of war over generations, led by commanders who understood tactics that would not have disgraced Napoleon himself.

I have walked that battlefield many times, seen the white cairns that mark where redcoats fell, and stood where the Zulu impis swept down like a black tide. The horror of those final moments is etched into the very landscape—men fighting desperately with bayonets when their ammunition ran low, the terrible efficiency of the assegai and knobkerrie against increasingly desperate soldiers.

The Zulus fought for their homeland against foreign invaders who had come to steal their independence. They showed no quarter because none had been offered to them. Cetshwayo's warriors proved that day that courage, tactical brilliance, and righteous fury could triumph over modern weapons and imperial arrogance.

It was a lesson the British establishment would prefer to forget— but one that deserves to be remembered with honesty, not the sanitised heroics of Victorian mythology.

xii Rorke's Drift

The troops at the nearby Rorke's Drift, six miles away from where the massacre of Isandlwana was taking place, had more success in their encounter later in the same day and into the next. This victory was largely due to the fact that the attacking force at Rorke's Drift was much smaller than the force at Isandlwana, which was estimated at 20,000 men.

The massacre at Isandlwana was not without military blunders. The force was not properly prepared—the commander didn't think entrenchment was necessary since it was a temporary camp. Their defensive perimeter was spread far too wide, and even the new Martini-Henry single-shot rifle could not compensate for military incompetence. Armed mostly with spears and cowhide shields, the sustained ferocity of the Zulu advance could not be stopped. Bravery alone could not save "the lions that were being led by donkeys."

Even at Rorke's Drift, where 150 troops defeated a force of 4,000

Zulus, divine intervention cannot be ruled out. At the last, they were reduced to using bayonets and revolvers—hand-to-hand combat became their desperate reality. In this engagement, 19,000 rounds were fired. Eleven Victoria Crosses were awarded, the highest number of VCs given for a single action by a single unit in the history of the British Army.

I am certain that among the brave men now lying in mass graves at Isandlwana, many more could have been justly recognised with medals. But the dead tell no tales, and history is written by those who survive to tell it. The real tragedy is not just that good men died, but that their sacrifice was made necessary by the arrogance and incompetence of those who should have known better.

[xiii] Martini-Henry

A new breech-loading, single-shot rifle that was used by the British Army in the Zulu Wars. It used a very heavy calibre bullet; the cartridge was encased in brass. The rifle was a major development, but the early ammunition proved a disaster. Encased in rolled brass, it was much too thin to withstand the pressure of cartridge ignition, and it proved to be a serious drawback, especially in a hot rifle, as the cartridge was difficult to eject, the brass often tearing and the breech (and rifle) becoming unusable. Bayonets and hand-to-hand fighting therefore were the cause of many deaths.

This was typical of British military procurement—a weapon designed by committee, tested in comfortable conditions, and deployed to men whose lives depended upon its reliability. The Martini-Henry looked impressive on paper: a .450 calibre round that could drop a charging warrior at considerable distance, a falling-block action that promised rapid reloading, and the prestige of being the Empire's latest technological marvel.

But I have examined the records, spoken to descendants of those who carried these rifles into battle, and the truth is far grimmer than the official histories suggest. When the action heated up—

literally and figuratively—the weapon became a liability rather than an asset.

Picture, if you will, a redcoat at Isandlwana, Zulu warriors bearing down upon him, desperately trying to extract a torn cartridge case from his rifle breech whilst the assegai-wielding impis close the distance. The finest rifle in the world becomes merely an expensive club when it cannot be reloaded.

The .450 round was indeed powerful—when it fired. But power means nothing when your weapon jams after a few shots, leaving you with eighteen inches of steel bayonet against warriors who had perfected close combat over generations.

How many good men died because the War Office chose the cheapest contractor rather than the most reliable? We shall never know—but their ghosts haunt every account of those desperate final stands.

[xiv] Ananias and Sapphira

A couple mentioned in the Book of Acts, chapter 5, who forfeited their lives because of a wicked deception.

[xv] Stomping

Deer will do this when they see something they don't fully recognise as imminent danger. A display of this nature involves walking towards the object with greatly exaggerated 'goose steps'—raising and planting the front feet down in a very purposeful manner.

This is where the inexperienced stalker often makes his fatal mistake. He sees the deer approaching and assumes he's been accepted, that his concealment has worked perfectly. Nothing could be further from the truth.

I have watched this performance countless times, and it never fails to fascinate. The deer knows something isn't quite right—some instinct is warning of danger—but curiosity compels it forward. Each step is deliberate, almost theatrical, designed to provoke a reaction from whatever has caught its attention.

The stomping is both a challenge and a test. The deer is saying, in effect: "I know you're there, now show yourself." It will advance to within surprisingly close range, sometimes mere yards, before making its decision to flee or investigate further.

The novice hunter, heart pounding with excitement at this apparent stroke of fortune, invariably moves at precisely the wrong moment. A slight shift to improve his shooting position, a barely perceptible adjustment of his rifle—and the spell is broken. The deer explodes into flight, leaving behind only the echo of its alarm bark and the stalker's bitter regret.

The experienced hand knows to remain absolutely motionless during this ritual. He understands that the deer's senses are heightened to an extraordinary degree, that the slightest movement will betray his presence. Patience becomes everything—the deer will either satisfy its curiosity and move on, or approach close enough for a clean shot.

To witness stomping is to see nature's intelligence at work—a creature balanced between caution and curiosity, survival and investigation.

xvi Sea Lice

Small parasitic crustaceans found on Atlantic salmon when they enter the rivers on their breeding migration from the sea. The fact of sea lice being found on a salmon simply means that the fish has just recently entered the river, as sea lice cannot survive long in freshwater. Since salmon do not feed during their river migration, sea lice also denote a salmon at its best—strong, healthy, and prime. In other words, a worthy fish to bring to the net.

This is the angler's equivalent of striking gold. When you see those grey, flattened parasites clinging to a fresh-run salmon, you know you've encountered something special—a fish that has just completed one of nature's most demanding journeys and arrived in perfect condition.

I have examined thousands of salmon over the years, and the presence of sea lice tells an immediate story. This fish was feeding in the rich waters of the North Atlantic perhaps days ago, building the strength and fat reserves needed for the ordeal ahead. Now it has answered the ancient call to return, swimming hundreds of miles through salt water to reach this very pool.

The inexperienced angler might recoil at the sight of these parasites, viewing them as something unclean or diseased. He fails to understand that he's looking at nature's own certificate of authenticity—proof that this salmon is the genuine article, not some tired fish that has been wallowing in freshwater for weeks.

Within days, those sea lice will drop away, leaving no trace of their presence. The salmon's silver flanks will begin to dull, its condition will deteriorate, and its value as both quarry and table fare will diminish accordingly.

To hook a fish still carrying sea lice is to connect with the ocean itself—to feel the power and vitality of a creature at the absolute peak of its magnificence. These are the salmon that test tackle to breaking point, that strip line from reels with contemptuous ease.

Such fish are becoming increasingly rare in our depleted rivers. When you encounter one, you're witnessing a small miracle.

xvii Kelt

A salmon that has spawned after migrating from the sea. Sometimes called a 'spent' fish.

This is a creature transformed—no longer the silver torpedo that fought its way upstream with single-minded determination, but a shadow of its former magnificence. The Kelt has completed nature's most demanding journey and paid the ultimate price for the privilege of reproduction.

I have witnessed these fish in the weeks following spawning, and the change is nothing short of dramatic. Where once gleamed bright silver flanks and powerful shoulders, now hangs loose, discoloured skin over a frame that seems barely capable of sustaining life. The hooked jaw that developed during the spawning run remains, giving the fish a predatory appearance that belies its weakened state.

Most anglers, encountering a Kelt, feel only disappointment—this is not the prize they sought. Yet there is something profoundly moving about these survivors. They have fulfilled their biological imperative at enormous personal cost, and now face the daunting prospect of returning to the sea to recover, if indeed they can manage such a feat.

Many will not survive the journey back. Disease, predation, and simple exhaustion claim the majority. Those few that do reach salt water again may, with luck and time, regain their strength and return once more to spawn—though they will be fewer still.

The kelt reminds us that in nature, success comes at a price. There is no glory without sacrifice, no continuation of the species without individual cost. It is a lesson worth remembering.

^{xviii} Redds

The shallow, stony-bottomed river headwaters where salmon lay their eggs.

This is the destination that has driven every salmon's epic journey—the ultimate purpose behind thousands of miles of oceanic wandering and the brutal upstream migration that follows. To witness a redd in active use is to observe one of nature's most fundamental rituals.

I have stood beside these gravel beds many times, watching the ancient drama unfold. The hen fish, heavy with roe, excavates the depression with powerful sweeps of her tail, each movement precisely calculated to create the perfect nursery. The cock fish hovers nearby, his hooked jaw and darkened livery testament to the hormonal changes that prepare him for this moment.

The casual observer might see only disturbed gravel and clouded water. The experienced eye recognises something far more significant—the continuation of a cycle that has persisted for millennia, unchanged despite man's interference with rivers and seas.

These shallow, oxygen-rich waters provide exactly what the developing alevin require. The gravel offers protection whilst allowing vital water flow, and the consistent temperature ensures proper development through the long winter months ahead.

The location of redds is no accident. Salmon return to the exact waters where they hatched, guided by an olfactory memory so precise it defies human understanding. They will excavate these beds in the same stretches their ancestors used, often to within yards of the same location.

To destroy a redd through careless wading or ignorance is to undo years of natural effort. Those seemingly insignificant patches of disturbed gravel represent the future of entire river systems.

The wise angler marks their locations and gives them the respect they deserve—the nurseries of tomorrow's kings.

^{xix} Hanging

In modern times, certainly since the 1950s, the procedure of hanging a person was over in astonishingly few seconds. This was due to the new execution suites that were purpose-built for the task. Before this, execution sheds were the norm, necessitating a sometimes-lengthy walk from the condemned cell. In the new suites, the condemned cell was immediately adjacent to the death chamber—a matter of only six or seven paces from the trap.

The actual procedure was simple and methodical. On the stroke of the hour appointed for death, the executioner and his assistant, with the sheriff and other designated officials, entered the condemned cell. The condemned, by prior arrangement with the prison warders who accompanied them, was seated with their back to the door. Upon entrance by the executioners, the warders stood and had the condemned stand with them.

The executioner then bared their neck and brought the unfortunate's hands behind their back, strapping them—not tightly, but firmly. Nothing was done in a violent manner or in any way that would unduly alarm the condemned. The executioner then turned and walked through the now-open door to the execution chamber, whilst his assistant and warders followed with the condemned.

On reaching the trap (the executioner there first and waiting), the condemned was positioned directly on the chalk mark where the doors of the trap met. Pulling a white cotton hood from his breast pocket, the hangman placed it over the condemned's head and followed with the noose, the eyelet of which was placed under the angle of the person's left jawbone. A rubber washer on the rope ensured it remained firmly in place.

In these few fleeting seconds, the assistant hangman strapped the condemned's legs and stepped off the trap, whilst the executioner moved swiftly to the lever, pulled out the safety pin, and pushed forward. It was a carefully rehearsed routine, and almost every condemned person was compliant, allowing the inevitable to take its course in the time I have outlined.

From when they stood to be pinioned until they were dead on the rope, the average time the condemned had left to live was between ten and twenty seconds, though eight to ten seconds was common. The speed of this whole unfortunate transaction shocked the designated witnesses and warders alike. Sometimes even the doctor, who had to be present, could hardly fulfil his duty to pronounce death as he placed his stethoscope on the chest of the suspended figure in the chamber below.

Although many of those who were put to death in this manner were wicked in the extreme, and had committed atrocities too inhuman to recount, there was never a hint of revenge or jubilation in their punishment. To stand in a very small room and witness a person, just a few feet away, drop to certain and immediate death in a matter of seconds was a sobering experience for all concerned.

It brought to mind, as nothing else could, the wickedness of murder and the value the Lord has placed on innocent human life.

xx Pine Marten

A small, cat-sized member of the weasel family. They are carnivorous and ferocious killers when opportunity permits. Killing for killing's sake.

This is nature's perfect assassin—a creature that embodies everything both beautiful and brutal about the natural world. Do not be deceived by its appealing appearance or the charming videos that appear on social media. The pine marten is a killer of extraordinary efficiency and, when circumstances allow, appalling excess.

I have witnessed the aftermath of a pine marten's visit to a gamekeeper's release pen, and the scene resembled nothing less than a battlefield. Dozens of young birds lay scattered across the enclosure, far more than any single predator could consume. This was not hunting for survival—this was slaughter for its own sake.

The pine marten possesses an intelligence that makes it particularly dangerous to ground-nesting birds and their broods. It will systematically work through a clutch of eggs or chicks with methodical precision, killing each one regardless of hunger. The surplus killing instinct runs so deep that it appears almost compulsive.

Yet watch one in its natural habitat and you cannot help but admire its grace and athleticism. It moves through the forest canopy with fluid ease, as comfortable fifty feet above ground as on the forest floor. Its golden throat patch catches the dappled sunlight as it flows from branch to branch like liquid mercury.

The conservationists who champion its return to former ranges rarely mention the devastation it brings to native species that have prospered well without this predator. They speak of ecological balance whilst ignoring the evidence of what happens when this particular balance is destroyed.

[xxi] Anatomy

The incident with Rick Symington's stag is not fanciful. Ballistics are a fascinating study, and the surprises they hold in store are many and varied. The impact and effect of a high velocity bullet cannot be overestimated, and must sometimes be seen to be believed. Unlike in years past, when a variety of firearms and ammunition were used to kill deer, specific ammunition for large game is now a legal requirement and must conform to rigidly set principles—for example, calibre, bullet weight, minimum velocity, and an expansion feature of the bullet.

The UK legal requirement for Red deer is a .243 calibre, 100 grain bullet weight, minimum muzzle velocity of 2,450 feet per second and a bullet with a 'soft' tip (lead) which allows it to mushroom on impact, thereby causing optimum damage and accelerating death by blood loss. In the interests of clarity and transparency, when so many are using 'cruelty' as an argument against blood sports, the following may be helpful.

The most common and widely used target area for deer stalkers is the chest area of whatever species they pursue. From where the neck incorporates the shoulders, to almost the end of the ribcage, the crucial main organs are central. The heart lies low in the channel of the breastbone, right behind the front shoulder. The lungs are above, closely hugging the spine. Behind these comes the liver, and finally the stomach, extending right back and filling the remainder of the intestinal cavity.

The chest area, therefore, is the classic kill zone—the heart-lung shot that is so often spoken of. The area for this successful shot is the size of a football, and gives the stalker a decided advantage for a clean and humane kill, as pinpoint accuracy is not essential.

So successful is this shot that in all my years deer stalking, with multiple kills recorded, using the example of calibre and bullet described above, I have never once had to despatch a downed animal. When I walked to them, they were already dead—a death that could be measured in seconds rather than in minutes, literally so.

An expanding bullet in the heart-lung area is devastatingly effective, as I have many times witnessed. However, very occasionally, we might even say rarely, even such a bullet as described above can travel through without the required expected result, missing a major organ in its trajectory. How much more then a high velocity full metal jacketed spire point!

xxii Epitaph

From the poem 'Requiem'. Written in 1880 by Edinburgh-born R.L. Stevenson. 1850-1894. Buried in Samoa, it was his personal choice for his gravestone inscription.

> Here lies a man who understood the weight of words and chose his final ones with characteristic precision. Robert Louis Stevenson, that restless spirit of Scottish letters, penned his own epitaph decades before his death—a rare act of foresight that speaks volumes about both his literary genius and his acceptance of mortality.

> I have stood beside that grave on Mount Vaea, high above the Pacific, where the Edinburgh-born writer chose to rest far from the grey stones of his homeland. The inscription he selected—"Here he lies where he longed to be; Home is the sailor, home from sea, And the hunter home from the hill"—captures something essential about the wandering soul who gave us Treasure Island and Jekyll and Hyde.

There is profound courage in writing one's own epitaph. Most men shrink from such contemplation, preferring to leave such matters to grieving relatives who may or may not capture the essence of the departed. Stevenson faced his mortality head-on and crafted words that would outlive bronze and marble.

The choice reveals much about the man himself—no grandiose claims to immortality, no listing of achievements or accolades. Simply the quiet satisfaction of a journey completed, a hunter returned from his final expedition. It speaks to anyone who has felt the pull of distant horizons and the deeper pull of home.

That such words should come from a man who spent his final years in exile, seeking health in foreign climes, makes them all the more poignant. Sometimes wisdom comes not from where we end, but from understanding where we truly belong.

WHERE TIDES RUN DEEP

A TALE OF FAITH AND THE UNBREAKABLE HIGHLAND SPIRIT

Alan Dunlop

Faith prevails over adversity in this complete short story.

"Wherever family or friendships prevent the proper course of justice and truth, no institution on earth will remain safe from pillage or piracy………"

Lord Chief Justice MacDonald, Edinburgh. 1760-1840

Where Tides Run Deep

CONTENTS

CHAPTER 1

The Cottage

I t was the year of our Lord 1776, and it was the coldest January he could remember. A strong easterly rattled the window frame as the old man instinctively pulled his coat closer to him and gazed with rheumy eyes as another day tried to break through the heavy cloud that scudded across the sky in dark and angry rafts.

This was the old man's daily ritual. Soon he would turn his attention to the still-smouldering turf of last night's fire and fan it again to life and warmth, but for now the tiny window had drawn him once again.

As he gazed wistfully across the Moray Firth, with its white caps curling and breaking like orderly rows of advancing horsemen, he once again lamented the changes life had brought him.

His once lithe and muscular frame, that had carried him aloft in storm and tempest, now failed him. Limbs refused to obey the still strong and wishful impulses of his heart and mind. The old man had been a sailor.

Tall ships once carried him to far shores and distant lands, and, under his grizzled beard, his face bore the marks of winter's biting gales and the soft tanning influence of salt-laden tropical winds. He had breathed the heavily scented air of an island paradise and heard palm fronds rustle and whisper as the ocean breezes played constantly through them.

He had slept where the soft wash of distant surf lulled him to sleep, as the waves broke with unending rhythm on the coral reef far out in the bay.

"Aye, my fortunes have certainly turned, of that there is no doubt," the old man mused as he turned the pages of life's book once again in his mind, and reminisced again today as he had done yesterday, and no doubt would do so tomorrow.

Even the rain, which now beat incessantly against the pane, could not dim the visions now conjured up in his mind. As the raindrops ran together in crooked little rivulets, the Cromarty headland was barely visible across the firth, but through the distorted blur, his inward visions were still sharp and vivid.

Cold water from the burn that ran just outside the cottage provided for his morning ablutions, after which he turned to the fire, raked together last night's embers and fanned them gently into life, the creaking bellows protesting once again at this early morning chore. Placing the pot in the hearth, he dragged some of the larger coals around it, and it soon began to warm the coarse oatmeal that he had steeped the evening before. It would provide his breakfast. It was a simple meal, but then the old sea dog was a simple man in many ways, and easily pleased as to food and shelter.

Indeed, although he could afford better, he had returned in his old age to his father's cottage, being able to lease it from the Laird when his father died. It was a basic dwelling, common in the highlands, but strong and durable for all that. Three large pairs of 'oaken couples' or kipples, planted in the ground at intervals, gently sloped inwards till they met at the top and were 'coupled', not with iron, but with great solid pins of oak.

Upon these, oaken wattles were laid, till about 12 feet off the ground.

A thick stone wall was then raised to meet them on the underside, allowing the wattles to overhang, the walls being pointed with sand and clay. Thatch was then twisted and woven upon and through these wattles, defying the fiercest winter storm, and making the little home cosy and warm.

The timbers, both kipples and wattles, were visible to those within and were japanned black and shining with the 'peat reek' of centuries, and so hard that an ordinary nail could not be driven into them.

The building was old and had long predated his father's tenure. The clay that filled the stone wall cavities had shrunk in places, allowing the wind to blow his candle in a westerly direction, but it was in good shape for all that, and walls and beams could do service for centuries more on the same terms.

The thatch needed attention now and then, and like the turf for his fire, needed a stronger hand to provide, but there were always plenty of the neighbouring lads glad of that work, and even gladder of the added shillings it provided.

Inside the cottage, the furnishings were sparse and simple. Apart from his well-used sea chest and a deal table, three battered chairs and a cupboard formed the bulk of his furnishings. He could have done without the cupboard but for the frequent visitation of small furry beasties that often sought shelter from the highland weather, and so his oats and other vittles' were kept secure.

Being used to the confines of a ship's small cabin, he saw no need to enlarge his living quarters beyond that which he had, and he slept on a single pallet bed in sight of the fire. Indeed, from where he slept, he could survey all that he owned, and the dying embers of a flickering turf were always a comforting last vision to weary eyes as they finally closed in deep repose.

CHAPTER 2

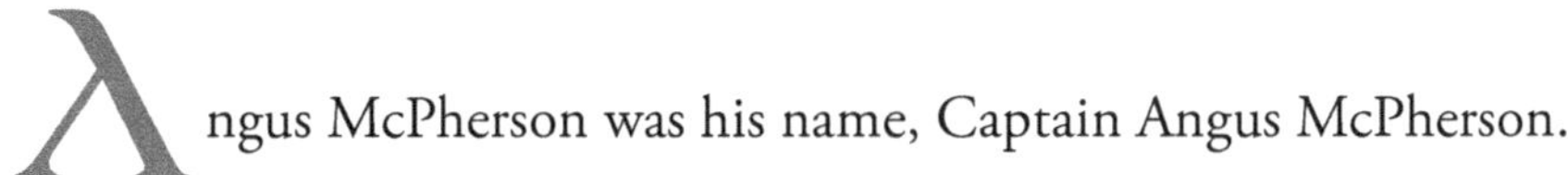

Angus McPherson was his name, Captain Angus McPherson.

In his many years as a young man before the mast, he had slowly but surely bettered himself where he could, and where others had given themselves to the coarseness of life at sea, the young Angus had determinedly steered by his own compass and avoided the same. He was a temperate man, careful and wise, and would not be brought under the bondage of excess to either gluttony, tobacco or rum. He often contemplated that since God had pronounced everything that He had made as "very good", how mankind had always somehow contrived to corrupt its way with it!

As a seaman, Angus was well known as an experienced hand. Sloops, schooners, windjammers or brigs. Clippers, square-riggers or cutters, he was at home with them all. He could 'hand, reef or steer' with the best, and was proud of the fact. But, try as he might, a crewman's wage on a merchantman did not extend to many luxuries, and certainly not to the purchasing of his own ship. This was a dream Angus had held since he was a lad, and his years at sea did nothing to diminish it.

Moreover, he found that the local and long-established shipping companies were very much closed to anything or anyone experienced enough to appear a threat to them. It would appear to him as jealousy, but why this would be so, the young man could not quite understand. They had their own contacts, their own methods of working, and their own handpicked crews, and most certainly, the field of trade was unlimited. It was well known, of course, that greed and favouritism were rife among them, and some even claimed distant shores as their own private trading ports! With such a tightly run business procedure, the young Angus found it impossible to get a berth with prospects, and such a berth with a well-established company would have given him the life and opportunities he sought on the open seas.

Then, as so often happens in life, fate took a turn. Time and chance fell to the young man. One bright spring day in April, between voyages, he was cutting turf for his father when he spied a figure striding purposefully across the moor towards him.

Tall and *braw (handsome), as he drew closer, the stranger reached into his sporran and drew forth a small package. It was not larger than a palm's length, and it was wrapped in an old piece of oiled sailcloth and tied securely with a length of tarred twine. Drawing near, the man first spoke in greeting and, beckoning to the distant cottage,* said in a broad dialect, "Your father said I should find you here—is it Angus McPherson I speak to?"

Angus looked at the man closely. There was something about him that kindled the thought that he had seen him before somewhere. It was a strong impression, but try as he might, he could not place him. His kilt and plaid he was not familiar with, but the dirk in his waistband bespoke a man that would brook no insult, and the deep scar on his left cheek reinforced the opinion Angus had of the dirk.

Laying down his spade, Angus answered the man. "It is indeed he you speak to, and what brings you to me, stranger?"

For answer, the man reached to his throat and snapped the string that hung there, and which held a small key. Placing the key with the package, the stranger reached both to Angus with the words:

"Murdo McPherson has trusted me to deliver this to your hands only. Now it is done, I have no more business here." With that, he turned abruptly and walked swiftly back across the moor.

There were a few hours of daylight left, and the weather was holding—Angus would cut what turf he could while he had the opportunity. Much as he was curious about the stranger and his errand, the package would wait till suppertime.

CHAPTER 3

The Killing Times

Murdo McPherson was the elder of twin sons born to Auld Rabbie McPherson, Angus's grandfather. They named the second Duncan. Rabbie and his wife Elizabeth had another child, a daughter, Ruth. They had reared the three children in a small crofter's cottage in a secluded glen on the shore of Loch Rannoch, in the very heart of the Highlands. Murdo had never married, Angus had been told, but Ruth had moved north to the Black Isle and had married there. From that union, Angus had a cousin, a girl called Elizabeth, after her grandmother, and she, with his own family, was his last living kin.

Born in 1664, the two lads, Duncan and Murdo, had been born into a world of bitter and bloody persecution under the Stuart monarchs, who were determined to rule over the Kirk as well as over the nation. The boys' first encounter with the evils of state-appointed worship and religious persecution was when the turncoat Kirk minister, Archbishop Sharp, the then appointed Archbishop of St Andrews, was killed at Magus Muir by those who were determined to oppose any other headship of the Kirk but Christ himself.

The lads were only 15 years old at that time, but the bloody reprisals and the hangings on a Christmas day of five men innocent of the deed left an indelible imprint on their young hearts. The following year, Richard Cameron, perhaps the most militant of those opposed to Stuart rule in the Kirk, was betrayed by a local Laird and overtaken by dragoons at Airds Moss in Ayrshire, where he was killed after a brief and fierce encounter with forces that heavily outnumbered him. The fact that his severed head and hands were taken to Edinburgh and shown to his aged father, before his head was paraded through the streets on a pole, shocked the young lads, and it affected them deeply when the news was brought to the family home.

How could Duncan's wedding day not be overshadowed by the report brought that two women had been tied to wooden stakes and drowned with the incoming tide at Wigtown? Margaret Wilson, 18 years, and Margaret McLachlan, an aged widow, both executed for refusing the oath of allegiance to a King intent on Kirk dominance.

Yes, the twins, Duncan and Murdo, had indeed been brought into the world in cruel and wicked times, and even through their young manhood had suffered much at the hands of Commander John Graham of Claverhouse, 1st Viscount Dundee. It was Claverhouse's dragoons that left the moors dotted with the graves of innocent men and women whose only crime was to deny the Stuart King's authority in the affairs of the Kirk. The Kirk had a King—there was no room for another, and for that, and that alone, many otherwise good men and true paid with their lives.

It was a desperate, cruel and uneven struggle, and many were the times the family fled from home to the heather as Claverhouse's forces closed in upon their dwelling, hoping to take them by surprise.

There were few tears shed when, in July 1689, Graham became the recipient of a musket ball and fell from his horse mortally wounded. Killiecrankie would be remembered for that one ball, among the many hundreds that were fired that day.

But times such as those 'Killing Times' do not always end with the last sabre thrust, or when the final shot is fired. Lives are changed by such events. Futures are forged, for good or ill, in the heat of such struggles. Families divided, severed asunder and destroyed forever by acts of such barbarity that would make angels weep.

The young Duncan and Murdo witnessed all too often the injustice of this carnage and atrocity, as decent folk were put to the sword, or shot out of hand like dogs. Well fed, well mounted and well-armed, the dragoons pursued their prey with a bloodthirsty relish and enthusiasm.

While the boys, being older, had remained at the croft, Ruth was sent away to an old couple in Applecross, a small village on the west coast. Difficult to access from the Highlands, barren and sparsely inhabited, the Bealach-na-Bà, that winding and dangerous drovers' path through the mountain passes, had in the providence of God proved an obstacle that even Claverhouse avoided, no doubt owing largely to the fact that from the head of the glen his dragoons could be seen from miles away. They would be in a single column on the narrow track, and had nowhere to run in the event of an ambush. Although a Jacobite stronghold, and now ruled by the Mackenzie clan, nevertheless the child Ruth found safety in Applecross. The fact that she too feared and fled Crown forces gave her a common bond of acceptance, and thus she was therefore largely shielded from the horrors of that time.

Of the two boys, Duncan remained with the Kirk, kept his faith and became a trusted and useful exhorter as those who escaped the slaughter sought to rebuild again shattered lives and broken hearts. He married, and he and his wife moved north to Nairn, where he lived frugally but thankfully, for he always put great store by two verses from Timothy: *"Godliness with contentment is great gain, for we brought nothing into this world, and it is certain we can carry nothing out."*

Murdo pursued another path. His childhood experience had affected him deeply. Murdo could not be tamed. Wherever he confronted injustice or cruelty, he took it upon himself to right the wrong, and he had little time for the niceties of reason or argument, preferring the immediate settlement with physical violence, be it fists, dirk or claymore. This wild abandon began early in his life, and it did not take long for him to take on the title of the 'Blacksheep' of the family. Trouble was never far away when Murdo was nearby, and it soon brought the lad into conflict with the authorities. After nearly killing a man in a senseless brawl, it was deemed advisable for Murdo to move away for a time to allow things to settle, and so, somewhat reluctantly, the young Murdo set out on what would become his life's pathway, for Murdo never came back. He kept in touch occasionally over the years but he never returned to Nairn, or the little crofter's cottage of his youth.

Angus had never met his uncle Murdo, but his name was still well enough known in the locality and the cottage. Till the day she died, old Elizabeth lamented the departure of her wayward son. At every opportunity, the old woman would keep reminding her only grandchild Angus, that there was another who belonged under the thatch, and her oft-repeated phrase, "My Murdo," were the last words to leave her lips as she lay dying.

It was an interesting history, of that there was no doubt, thought Angus, and as a boy he had often thought on it, and now, after all these years, there lay before him a package from this same prodigal and wayward son. But for the sight there before him, the young man would never have believed it. By this, Murdo had returned to the croft. Too late for the old woman, it was true, but return he had.

CHAPTER 4

A New Beginning

After a supper of venison broth and tatties, with a thick slice of coarse oatmeal bread spread with suet, Angus pushed his empty luggie (wooden bowl) from him and, reaching for the package, gave it a closer scrutiny. It was securely tied. Whoever wrapped and tied it did so with the intention of it remaining intact. His father, Duncan, sitting across the table, never spoke. He would wait with the patience and stoicism of his Highland breed, allowing his son the privacy and expectation that rightly belonged to him.

If Angus had anything to share by way of news, he would do so. Slowly lifting his knife, Angus cut the string that held it together and began to unwrap the covering. As he drew back the folds of sailcloth one by one, he finally uncovered a small wooden box, such as may be bought on a trinket stall in some far distant bazaar or souk. Taking the little key, Angus turned it carefully in the lock, and the lid sprang open and fell backwards.

Inside the box, there lay a soft leather pouch tightly bound at the neck with a thong, and enclosing something both hard and heavy. Slowly and deliberately, Angus untied the thong and emptied the pouch on the table before him. Now, tumbling heavily in a loose heap, and with the solid sound of authenticity, there fell 50 gold pieces. Bright, shining and new, they gleamed in the last fading light of sunset as only gold can gleam. Father and son were transfixed for a moment or two. They had never seen this amount of money before, let alone in gold, and the sight brought perplexity as well as wonderment. A neatly folded paper covered the bottom of the box, and Angus, reaching for it carefully, began to flatten it against the table with his open hand.

It was a short note in a well-presented but shaky script, written with quill and ink, dated and signed by Murdo McPherson, with an official stamp of approval from a law firm in Edinburgh.

Angus looked at his father. "It's from your brother, father—would you like to read it?" Angus offered, seeking to draw the old man into participating in this apparent windfall and good fortune. "Nay, laddie," the old man replied, "you read better than me, but if you were to read it aloud, I would be pleased to hear it." Tilting the note to the window, the better to catch the remaining light, Angus began to read.

> "To Angus McPherson, only son of Duncan McPherson, Nairn, Inverness-shire.
>
> This letter contains my express wishes toward the above-named beneficiary. Upon submitting this letter at the Faculty of Advocates, Advocates Close, Edinburgh, office of McLeod and Muirhead, a full explanation will be given.
>
> I have ceased the oversight of my business in the Carolinas owing to failing health, and it is now in good hands, but my ship and her trading lists I wish to gift to Angus.
>
> I have had many regrets, but I have made my peace with God, and I hope now I can make my peace with those I have wronged so many years ago.
>
> The gold pieces are for travel and any expenses you may need—all honestly earned, you have my word on that. Use them and welcome.

The vessel lies at anchor in Yarmouth, and I have taken my last moorings nearby. The port authorities already know of your entitlement to the ship.

I hope my brother is in good health. I never failed to honour his memory in all my dealings with my fellow man. Duncan was with me constantly in all these years, as were our father and mother.

God bless you both."

Murdo McPherson

Angus finished the letter and slowly laid it before him on the table. Neither man spoke for long moments. Then, in measured tones and carefully chosen words, it was old Duncan that broke the silence.

"I have not seen my brother in half a lifetime. Half a lifetime, I tell you. Our mother died with his name on her lips, and now this!" Angus could see that his father had yet something to say, so he held his peace till he finished.

Old Duncan then continued: "But if my brother wants to make peace, I cannot be the one to refuse such a clear and open request made in God's name. We cannot change the past, but we may yet shape the future. Take the ship, Angus—you have my blessing on it, and providence has brought her to you."

Angus waited a moment, then he answered: "Only if you are sure, father." Angus spoke softly.

"I am sure," Duncan replied. "Only one thing would make me happier at this moment, and that is if your grandmother were here to share it with us."

The last slanting rays of the fading light no longer fell upon the little window, and the room had fallen to semi-darkness. Had it been otherwise, old Duncan would have seen the tears that began to wet the bearded cheeks of the young man, as Angus gazed, first at his old father, and then at the contents of the little box that lay before him.

Thus it was that Captain Angus McPherson obtained his calling. He would rename the ship *The Endeavour*. That scene at the table seemed just like yesterday.

CHAPTER 5

Beyond the Highland Home

Two weeks passed before Angus made it to Edinburgh. He could not leave his father without some preparations, and he took great care to satisfy himself that his father would be well cared for in his absence. He had good neighbours, but the moors and Highland life did not lend themselves to frequent callers.

He had to ask directions to Advocates Close, but he found it eventually and knocked loudly on the stout outer door.

By and by, an ancient and bespectacled gentleman, bent over by years of toil, at last opened to him, peering up at him as Angus stood there in the bright morning sunlight. He was impeccably dressed in waistcoat, knee-hose and patent shoes, their buckles polished and shining brightly against the background of his shoes and black stockings. Snow-white hair caressed his collar as he led Angus down long and darkly-panelled corridors, before turning and bidding him to be seated till he enquired as to his purpose.

To Angus's great surprise, he was back in a few minutes with the message: "Mr McLeod will see you now." As Angus followed the old clerk, he felt that this world was so different from his own. The wind, the flapping sail, the curlew's call across the moors seemed now like a dream, but he was here now and he would see the business through, come what may, and would not be daunted by these strange surroundings.

He was ushered into a very large room where he was greeted by a florid-faced man seated behind a desk, whereon sat numerous piles of paperwork, and the usual accoutrements of his trade. An ashtray, made it appeared from the paw of some exotic animal, held a still-smoking cigar, and a well-filled spirits decanter sat nearby, with glasses beside it, presumably for use by those souls who worked and breathed in this strange new world.

Another man stood at the far end of the room, gazing out of the window. His back was to the desk, and he ignored the transactions that were taking place there. He was tall, broad-shouldered and well dressed, but above all he was silent. He did not turn, and he never spoke a word. The man behind the desk beckoned Angus to be seated and welcomed him by name.

Reaching for a sheaf of paperwork, McLeod fixed Angus with an earnest gaze and began the business of the day.

Murdo's Story

Murdo McPherson was dead, and as McLeod outlined the details to Angus, the full extent of Murdo's generosity became apparent. It was indeed a thoughtful and generous bequest, and Angus felt nothing but gratefulness as he listened carefully to what his uncle Murdo had planned for him, and wished now more than ever that he could have met the old man and thanked him personally.

But McLeod had more to tell than the details of Murdo's will, and with a glance to the tall figure by the window, addressed Angus directly. "Your uncle requested that, upon his death, I make known to you another matter." What McLeod had to say next held the young Angus in rapt attention, as he took in every word, the better to relay it to his old father back home in Nairn.

When Murdo left home that fateful January day so long ago, he travelled straight to Aberdeen. He knew it was a busy port, and although it was not sailing weather, yet he might better find his purpose there more quickly than anywhere else. As it happened, a ship was awaiting the next tide on her way to the Americas. It was a privately owned vessel, registered out of Aberdeen in the name of one Archie McGregor. He was travelling back to the Americas with his wife and daughter, but he had been beset with a grave difficulty on the eve of sailing. Some of his crew had succumbed to an outbreak of cholera, and he was dangerously short-handed for a voyage he now desperately wanted to make. He had put word out on the quay and in local taverns that he was prepared to pay a handsome bonus to any man who would sail with him on the next tide.

Even weary men will sometimes forgo hard-earned shore leave and risk all at the promise of gold, and thus it was with McGregor's offer, and Murdo found himself among them.

The hand of Providence was upon the wayward lad from Nairn. His mother's prayers availed even in his flight of extremity. At a time of year when shipwreck was always a close companion, it was an uneventful voyage. McGregor's ship had not only escaped the cholera, but the wind favoured their course, and in the long weeks of his ship-bound activity, hard work though it was, the young Murdo found himself greatly taken with Josephine, McGregor's 18-year-old daughter. She was a pleasant girl, a bonnie lass indeed, and not in any way given to the usual airs many of those of a privileged class often exhibit. Came the day therefore that Murdo stood before McGregor to ask for the hand of his daughter in marriage. The boldness of the approach took McGregor by surprise, for it is not every day a deckhand on a merchantman makes such a request.

McGregor was not high-born—he was a self-made man—but his early beginnings and humble birth never left him. While he enjoyed the obvious privileges his labours had brought him, he never forgot that a man's true character and virtue lie not in the things he possesses, but that common decency, honesty and integrity are the stamp that gives the coin its real value.

McGregor had observed Murdo daily for weeks now, as indeed he had all the hands, but it was Murdo that caught his eye. He was quick and lively, strong and ready for any task. Regardless of how menial the task was, this young man fulfilled it with dexterity and care. Not only so, but sailors had their own manner of speaking, and it was a manner that no young lady would wish to hear. Murdo, however, had kept apart from this coarseness, and it was clear that although a common lad from the Highlands, he had been well brought up, and had a manner and a deportment about him that was uncommon to the general character of the crew.

McGregor, therefore was greatly interested to hear what the man who had just entered his cabin had to say for himself, and so he allowed Murdo to put his case.

CHAPTER 6

Success!

After Murdo had made his request, there was a long silence. McGregor observed him closely. The young crewman did not beg, nor would he. He had spoken his mind, and that was that. McGregor liked that in him. He had prized honesty all his life, and when honesty is so boldly and clearly stated, it deserves consideration.

Here was a matter that required great care and tact, for he knew that Josephine had more than a passing interest in Murdo too, and so the knowledge of this led him to tread this path with great care.

Although the happiness of his daughter's marriage was certainly uppermost in his mind, McGregor was also a shrewd businessman, and he could see no harm in extending his proposition to include his plantation in the Carolinas.

He would need a trustworthy man to keep order in the daily running of his estate in a country where law and order very often stopped at the county line or township boundary.

"Very well, lad, McGregor said at length. "I promise nothing but an opportunity to prove your worth, both to my household and to my daughter. When we arrive, you will work for me for one year, after which we will all be in a better position to decide on Josephine's future. After we dock, and during that year, you may walk out with her, with a chaperone, and the proprieties will be observed at all times." He paused and waited a moment. "What say you to that, lad?"

"I shall count it an honour, sir, to obey your wishes regarding your daughter, and will endeavour to fulfil my obligations to the full on your plantation."

Thus it was that Murdo found his own life's calling on a shore far from his Highland home.

It was not long before the young man thus employed had the opportunity to prove himself to McGregor and to forge for himself a reputation that would remain with him for the rest of his life.

He was riding the labour lines one bright morning when he thought he heard a cry from within the standing crop in a remote corner of the field. Dismounting quickly, he entered the shaded gloom of the tall leafy growth and discovered the source of the cry. A male worker was struggling with a young girl with an evil purpose in mind. With a loud shout, Murdo sprang forward, and as he did so, the culprit swung round with his cutting tool and made to do murder.

That was his second mistake that day. Wresting the tool from him, Murdo cracked his skull with the iron-bound haft and left him senseless. Comforting the child first, for she was but a child, Murdo then threw the still unconscious figure over his saddle and made his way back to the house.

The sight coming through the courtyard gates that morning drew worker and owner alike. Josephine's eyes were wet with tears as she took the girl, while McGregor said little. But he took the miscreant in a wagon to the local jail and made sure he went before Judge Parker at the next assizes, where he got twenty years' hard labour for his misdeeds. Judge Parker told him that had not Murdo come along and saved the girl from defilement, he would have had him hanged, and felt his duty well done in doing so.

Murdo did not know it yet, but that morning in the courtyard, he became a made man in McGregor's eyes. In due course the marriage went ahead, and in the process of time a boy child was born.

But fate now extended a cruel hand to Murdo McPherson in this his happiest hour. As the tiny mite entered the world to the waiting hands of the midwife, the young mother departed this world to the waiting hands of angels. It was a grievous loss to all who had known the sweetness of the young mother's nature, and the gentleness of her affections to all those around her.

Murdo named and registered the child as Joseph, after his beloved Josephine, but called him Josie, the special term of endearment he had so often used in private to his now departed wife and sweetheart.

McLeod paused here—the office was hushed and expectant, and Angus waited in silence, for this was almost too much for one morning's business. McLeod then continued.

Nodding to the tall figure still standing at the window, he said, "This is Josie—you have a cousin, Angus." The tall stranger then turned slowly to face the room, and Angus saw again the figure he had first seen on the moors that day in April. Remembering how abruptly the stranger turned after he had delivered his message, Angus bridled at the knowledge now imparted to him.

Gripping the arms of his chair tightly in the tenseness of the moment, Angus said, "You might have told me, Josie. There were only the two of us on the moor that day, which would have been a good time to do so."

The stranger walked slowly across the room and laid his hand gently on Angus's shoulder. "I just found out myself, man—just a few moments before you came in. Neither you, your father, nor your grandparents were ever mentioned in our household. All I was told when we docked at Yarmouth a month ago was that there was an old man my father had known since childhood. He had a son, and father wanted to do something for them. I had only to deliver it to you and come away.

My father was a good man, and a good father, but his own family history was never spoken of. He brought me up himself after mother died, and I suppose I take my nature from him in that regard. I could wish it were different, but he meant neither you nor me any harm. His private thoughts were part of what he was, and so we leave it there."

CHAPTER 7

A Simple Life

The oats on the coals had sat long enough, and Angus rose and carried them to the table. Going to the cupboard, he fetched the last slice of cold haggis and laid it beside the bowl of cooked oatmeal. He did so absent-mindedly, for his thoughts that morning had run deeper than usual, and he had become almost oblivious to his hunger. Without salt, which he needed from the market, it would be somewhat tasteless, but they were vittles, and he had experienced enough hardship and want to make him thankful he had vittles before him.

Having spent so long at sea, he was glad that the necessity of eating salted meat, fish and ship's biscuit was over and done. Fresh food was the one luxury the old captain allowed himself, and, although he ate sparingly, he ate well. Nothing exotic, but plain and wholesome fare.

Kales, neeps and tatties (turnips and potatoes) were readily to hand from the market, as were breads, milk and cheeses. Living in near proximity to the shore meant that fresh fish were always available, and vegetables were plentiful.

His meat was sometimes drawn from the moors and glens around him. A brace of *moorfowl (grouse) from a friend, a saddle of venison from a poacher, or a salmon quietly netted from the pool while the Laird slept. All these were at hand,* and there was no scarcity. With the right contacts, and a closed eye sometimes to nocturnal activities in the Birks Shaws (beech woods) behind his cottage, they were always a welcome treat in their seasons, even though the seasons were sometimes extended if opportunity presented itself!

Although Angus had this welcome variety of foodstuffs, his main and regular meat provision came from the market, and it was the humble sheep. Be it mutton or lamb, rib, scrag (neck) or shank, it was never far from his table, and always on his list from the village butcher.

Made from what the more prosperous would throw to the dogs, the haggis was his favourite. Sometimes, if one already prepared were not to be had in the market, the butcher would be kind enough to send the whole sheep's pluck and some suet—heart, liver and lungs, and of course, the sheep's stomach to boil it in. Angus would then prepare and boil his own, and he often did, using from his own cupboard the oatmeal and seasoning. A good-sized haggis would last him a week if he was careful, as an addition to his other fare, and he never tired of it.

Old Angus was not a recluse, but he lived alone by choice. His wife was long since dead, and his family were scattered across the northlands, so that he rarely saw them, and he had never felt the need to marry again.

Because of his isolated dwelling, plus a deep scar that ran down his left cheek, the locals sometimes referred to him as 'Old McFearsome'. But it was an ill-founded sobriquet, for the old man liked nothing better than to help anyone in trouble, and he had a generous streak that was rare among old sea dogs of his day. The scar was from a shard of ice falling from a yard-arm in an Arctic storm. The same shard had killed the man beside him, and so Angus had always cause to be thankful that he was left with just the mark of the tragedy.

Like so many of his fellow Highlanders, Angus could be fiercely independent, and while he was still able, he kept to a regime of self-sufficiency. He did allow the help of the widow Ross, who lived not far over the moor, and she brought him his weekly table necessities from Auldean market, just three miles away.

He was happy with this arrangement, and had engaged with her to do so on the understanding that she take payment. Thus, for a guinea or two each month, Angus had his daily needs provided without the difficulty of going to town himself. Murdo's legacy had provided him with a comfortable living, and he could afford the benefit of the widow Ross and the transport she provided.

Angus greatly respected the widow Ross. She had five children, the youngest of which was just two years old. Her husband had been drowned in Inverness harbour two years earlier when an overhead sling on a Dutch East Indiaman slipped and carried him into the tide, and he never saw his last child. It was a hard blow for the young family, and Angus was glad he could help the woman in this manner.

Being a canny sort, the woman had invested the little compensation she received on her husband's death and bought a sturdy donkey cart and a sound animal to pull it. In a very short while, she had built up an acceptance in the neighbourhood, and by dint of hard work and honest dealings, she had now a strong respectability within the community, and the income from this ensured that her little ones never wanted food on the table or fire in the hearth.

Angus did his own washing, cooking and cleaning, such as it was, but the delivery of weekly foodstuffs had become a major difficulty, and surprisingly, the weekly sight of the little donkey cart cheered him!

CHAPTER 8

Regrets

A light knock on the door startled him, so deep was he in his musings. Since he rarely had visitors, it took him a moment or two to recover himself.

Opening the door cautiously, he saw a child of the widow Ross, sent from the roadway to get the old sailor's list for market. "Och, hello laddie," the old captain greeted the child, as he acknowledged his mother on the far path with a wave. Reaching into his pocket, he reached the child a tightly folded paper with the words:

"There's the list, and there is your mother's money—don't lose it now," Angus teased. The child suffered from a severe speech impediment since his father's death, and it made communication very difficult. But he was a bright and intelligent lad, and his understanding smile and the vigorous nodding of his blond curls were enough for Angus.

The rain had eased off somewhat, although the storm was far from over, and Angus stood for a moment and watched the boy skip lightly back across the moor. The scene brought another memory to his sometimes heavy heart.

His own family, now grown and scattered abroad through the islands and Highlands like spume in a gale, he rarely saw. What with his years at sea when they were young, and now each one having their own life to live, sometimes he felt as if he had missed those important times when familial ties and bonds were matured and fastened in the heart. This was to him a great, unspoken loss, and he felt that loss every day. He blamed himself for this, but, try as he might, he had as yet no satisfactory answer to it.

When his children were young, he was earning a living at an honest trade. He could not always be at home with them, and he had worked hard to provide what he could for them. Even as they grew older, each of them had known his willingness and generosity to assist in times of their need, and what else could he have done?

Perhaps more prayer and less remonstrance for their childish waywardness might have accomplished more, and he often thought of this aspect of their upbringing. But regrets can come too late, and such was this. An old deckhand's proverb came to his mind again, and its wisdom cut deep to his heart:

"The powder in the pan only gives you one shot—don't miss it!"

The Ross child running nimbly back across the moor reminded him again of just how wide he had missed his mark, and how he wished in his heart it could be different.

As he closed the door, he now gave attention to a letter the Ross lad had given him. The memory would still be there tomorrow, Angus thought, but today he had a letter.

Although rare were the times he had mail, his friend in the New World did keep in touch, not by the King's mail, but by the long-established network of trust in fellow mariners to carry and deliver—a trust that was strong and dependable, if sometimes a little slow. When his letters reached the Highland shore, the widow Ross ensured that they were safely delivered to his cottage.

This latest, now spread upon the table before him, was a welcome distraction.

As he read down the page, he was once again amused at his childhood friend's openness and candour. His plantation had done well this year, and profits were good. Angus allowed himself a little keckle (laugh) as he imagined his boyhood companion preparing the balance sheets on the season's harvest.

His family too were well as far as health was concerned, and his eldest daughter was soon to be married to the son of a wealthy landowner, a senator, and a Carolina Patriot. Preparations were underway, and the writer expressed the wish that Angus could join them in their happy prospects. As Angus read further, the news was more unsettling.

For a number of years now, the Carolina patriots had been deeply unhappy with the British Colonial administration, but now it had turned to the brink of civil war as Redcoats and supportive locals united against the Patriots. Under Cornwallis, the Redcoats had already begun a fierce and brutal campaign, and it had no sign yet of a conclusion. As Angus took in this latest news from the Carolinas, he could not help but think of Scotland's own struggles and the bloodshed past and gone: Bannockburn, Flodden Field, Solway Moss, and a host of other like slaughter fields. Culloden was still a recent memory, where the last hope of the Jacobite forces stained the heather red before seeping into the peat below. They were the enemy to freedom's cause, of that there was no doubt, but they were men for all that, and brave men too.

Even today, all those who passed by Drumossie Moor had cause to ponder the terrible human suffering that war brings, and the homes and hearths it destroys forever. Would it never end? Now it seems the New World was about to be shaped by the same means as the old: claymore, powder, ball, and bayonet. There was something to be said for a little cottage far away from it all.

It was ten by the clock when Angus finally rose from the table and put the letter on the high shelf above the fireplace. The little donkey cart bringing his market purchases would not arrive before four in the afternoon, and so Angus took his charts, papers, ship's logs, and manifests from his old sea chest and spread them out before him. He had done this many times before, but every now and then, he felt the need to refresh his memory as to what exactly was done and said in the matter of losing the ship he had so loved and appreciated.

CHAPTER 9

The Kirk

Angus McPherson was not an outwardly religious man. When he was a young boy, like all children before him, he had accepted the Kirk as it had appeared to him, and as he was taught by his parents, who were rigid in their Sabbath keeping and Kirk-taught observances. Did he not himself remember crossing the sea to North Antrim in Ireland to attend a communion service with those of like-minded precious faith? Those were exciting times for a young boy—the men labouring bravely at the oars as they rowed, and praying all the while that the weather would hold. But the passing of years sometimes changes a man, and so it was with Angus.

His years at sea and the long absences and isolation from the Kirk's social communion had whittled away his dependence on those common bonds that draw people together, and on which so many in the Kirk find essential to their religious lives. Sometimes enforced separation from the inherited habit of religious observances causes a man to read and think for himself, and in so doing, may sometimes find that all is not quite as it first appeared! So it was with Angus.

Over time, with the scriptures alone as his guide and counsellor, Angus's faith was no longer dependent, or in any way influenced by the Kirk, in matters of conscience, faith, or practice.

Nor was he ever tempted to boast of religious affiliation. To him it mattered not a whit where his fellow man worshipped. Angus received all men and accepted them on equal terms. They were all to him as sons of Adam's fallen race, and as such must be partakers of Christ's redemption if they were to see the Heavenly glory.

To Angus, to make tribal the simplicity of the gospel message, by forming so many earthly divisions, sects, and movements, so ardently defended by some, and boasted of by others, was a great stumbling block to Biblical evangelism, and a carnal vanity to be avoided at all costs. To him, when morality and justice were gone from any religious organisation, it mattered not what theology they claimed to hold.

The foundation of his own faith rested alone on the knowledge of his election to the redemptive work of the Cross of Christ. Believing very strongly in the absolute Sovereignty of God and the doctrine of Predestination, and being sure in his own mind that he had an abiding portion in it, he was content to claim the discipleship of Jesus Christ, and he cared for no man's opinion to the contrary.

The great stone on the path near Drumossie Moor marked the spot where, smitten with the inner conviction of his own sinfulness and lost condition before God, as a child he had found his personal peace. The memory was still fresh—how could it be otherwise? As his inner struggle led him to confess his sinful condition and receive by faith alone Christ's promise of acceptance and forgiveness, the burden he had carried for so long was lifted from him, as if by an unseen hand. He would not soon forget that day, or the change he had experienced there.

Moreover, as Angus read the scriptures in the long and lonely months and years at sea, he began to notice that what he found there was sometimes at variance with what was practised in the establishment of what some called the New Testament church.

Angus had nothing against the Kirk as a body. He knew very well that the words of Christ, as He sent forth His disciples to world evangelism, would not be accomplished without some attempt or expression of human organisation, for the age-old temptation of Babel is a deeply rooted one.

But try as he might, he could not reconcile what he saw of ornate, ostentatious church architecture, and equally ornate robes and various expensive vestments and accoutrements of religious ritual, with the example and teaching of the lowly Christ at the last supper, when in very plain surroundings, an upper room, He washed the feet of those who followed Him, and bade them have the same spirit of humility one towards another.

Therefore, as Angus looked at the page of Holy Writ, and compared what he saw there with the many additions in the various religions of men, he knew that both could not be true.

But quite apart from this very evident human elevation in things religious, Angus also realised the great danger of such in a more subtle form. A spoken unity of purpose, and a brotherly agreement on doctrine among those of *"like precious faith,"* he could understand as desirable and fruitful. But when that unity of purpose is formulated into something more substantial, and by binding articles of agreement becomes a matter of ecclesiastical law, the law of corporate or central control, thus taking unto itself the rights of the individual, and formulating rigid formalities and protocols that must be followed by the individual, then that becomes an evil thing.

Once such is allowed and established, an influence wielded by the power of a select few, yet binding on thousands, then that can only be an evil thing. Oh, Angus knew that decisions coming down from such a select few were portrayed as the result of an open and free consideration by all, but that was too often far from the truth. Men being men, those in power in religious establishments are the ones who are left to choose, to decide, to give judgement, and to impose punishments for non-conformity to their dictates.

Angus had come to realise that the more detailed and complex a religious organisation became, with its man-devised rules, policies, regulations, protocols, remits, committees, and suchlike, the less of Christ was too often evident. And the more human input that was imposed and carried to divine matters, the more vulnerable it became to corruption.

This was why Angus did not give himself unreservedly to the claims and oversight of the Kirk. He would give credit where credit was due, but he found it impossible to trust those who were more willing to preserve and protect the name and policies of their religious institution than to defend the poor widow, feed the hungry orphan child, give justice to the defrauded merchant, or aid the pauper in his extremity.

Nay, Angus thought, those who believe that the institution is in greater need of protection than the applicant with a genuine grievance, cannot be true to the Christ of the Book, nor serve Him in the best interest of justice and truth. Such then would not have his respect, nor would he accept their claims to authority, and the robes and garb of Kirk employment carried no weight with him whatsoever.

Was it not also well known that many entered the Kirk as a profession only? That their carrying out of divine duties was empty and void of the gentleness and humility of Christ's example?

Was it not true that there was often more honour and comradeship on a heaving deck in a gale, than in the many Kirk councils and conclaves so revered and lauded by men? Could a man therefore be the true servant of Christ who so demonstrably evidenced such a diverse character from the Master he claimed to serve?

Unlettered as he was, Angus didn't think so, and so man-made, man-named, and man-managed institutions, Kirks and religious movements therefore he viewed with great suspicion, and his soul was often stirred in anger at the hypocrisy and corruption so often found among them.

If he could find in scripture any evidence of such a detailed and organised religion, he would accept it. But Christ did not direct the twelve to form such as He sent them forth to preach. None of the sacred penmen ever addressed such in their letters and epistles, and even from Patmos, John was directed to write to seven individual churches, directing his inspired remarks to the overseer or bishop of each church.

Antiquity is no proof of authority, and it was clear to Angus that a full, unfettered freedom to worship God in spirit and in truth could never be experienced until the Spirit of the living God became the only influence allowed to be exercised upon the conscience, individuals being responsible for their own decisions of the heart, and being allowed the freedom to choose without the fear or favour of any man.

Was not this same principle at the very foundation of all Scotland's political and religious struggles? On the one hand, they had done battle with the Jacobite armies, with much blood being shed to prevent religious rule by a supreme Roman Pontiff, and on the other hand, had suffered great persecution and martyrdom to refuse the Stuart monarchy a similar authority. Why then build again the things they had destroyed by allowing their very own organised religious system, with a like ruling authority, to determine their conscience and practice in matters of great importance?

For the old man the answer was a simple one, and not difficult to defend. As far as he could determine throughout all the various religious divisions that prided themselves in their numbers and antiquity, when the weight of human influence outweighs divine requirement, or when morality is dismissed in favour of expediency and favouritism, Christ can no longer be in it. For a man who had a simple obedience to the Word, the matter was not complicated. He would call no man 'Father' as far as his faith was concerned, nor any organisation either.

However, his opinions were his own, gleaned through long years of study, and formulated from the plain teaching and example of God's book. That was his guiding star, and he sailed by that bearing. Others must be responsible for their own choices in such matters and chart their own course.

CHAPTER 10

A Full Sail

From the moment he unfurled 'The Endeavour's' sails, very many saw in her a more sure return for their financial outlay than the more established companies, who often had levies and penalties and were not always trustworthy in giving accurate reports to those who had signed up with them. Merchant shipping was rife with corruption, and a deep spirit of mistrust and jealousy prevailed among those whose interests lay in foreign ventures. Angus knew this and determined that with his new company, this would not be so. Transparency and customer satisfaction would be guaranteed, and seen to be so, even though it would bring opposition from others in a similar business.

The 'Endeavour' was everything Angus ever wanted in life, and for nigh on twenty years, the legacy that Murdo had left him was a fruitful venture. The best years of his life were thus spent on the high seas, doing the work he loved and cherished. Not every man has such a privilege. However, he had inherited the ship late in life—he had been nearly fifty years old—and now, owing to his advancing years and the rigours of seafaring life, he had grown weary. He had crossed the equator too many times, and been round the Horn more times than he could remember, and had begun to feel the need for assistance in his ventures.

It was in fulfilling this desire that McPhail was taken on board. He was young and inexperienced, had no qualifications or testimonials as to his fitness to serve, but Angus thought this could be to his advantage, for he could be taught.

A tall, thinnish individual, bearded, blind in one eye, and with a shock of fair hair, he was opposed privately from the beginning by the older crew. They said he was unreliable for such responsibility. Some of them felt he was not active enough for the demands of shipboard life, for he did not readily enter into the hard work involved, and was too prone to leave his work to others to do.

Others claimed the new first mate had once taken holy vows and then abandoned them; others differed, affirming that he had only had a fondness for religious service of some sort, but had never followed through with the attempts he made.

Whatever it was, Angus did not pursue it, for remembering the jealousy that had confronted him in his quest for employment, he dismissed the crew's opposition, and McPhail was given a berth as first mate on the 'Endeavour'.

Aaron Radnay McPhail was his given name, and from the moment he came on board, Angus treated him well, for above all things he wanted him to succeed. Although too young and without a natural ability to lead **a** seasoned crew, out of respect they called him Mr Radnay. This pleased him, for he felt somewhat disadvantaged by his lack of experience among the older hands. But despite his inexperience, he ate at the captain's own table and had privileges extended to him that no other ever shared.

Little did Angus realise that all his years of success would soon be stove in like a ship's planking on a reef—when his first mate decided to seize command and orchestrated a mutiny to achieve it!

Purely as a matter of personal habit, over the years, Angus had kept all his correspondence, logs, manifests, and muster rolls, so it was from these, and not hearsay or idle speculation, that the evidence of the first mate's eventual treachery was made apparent.

Angus looked closely once again at the papers, just in case he had missed anything or mistaken anything. But every paper was signed and attested. There was no mistake; there was no misunderstanding. Here before him was clear evidence of the first mate's mutinous intentions and misconduct.

With all the documents now lying before him once again, the weight of the evidence was just as overwhelming now as it was all those years ago, and even now, to contemplate again the injustice of it all was a hard blow indeed for the old man. How professedly honest men, and some Kirk men too, could ignore such a weighty body of clearly written documentation and testimonial was beyond him.

It is a withering thing for a man to realise that his crewmen, who had sailed with him for so long and so successfully, were not the men he had supposed them to be.

It is indeed true that under siege or musket fire, or other pressing circumstances, men do sometimes show themselves in their true colours. In the smoke of battle, and as chain shot rends the rigging and sail, men's loyalties can change. They begin to think of their families, the comforts of settled life, or perhaps it is just that their courage fails them and they yield to cowardice. Battles are often lost, not because of superior numerical imbalance or the armaments carried, but because too often the will to fight is not there. So it was with losing the ship. Once begun, the mutiny had grown worse by the day, until even the most loyal of them saw it as the easier path to follow, for they could not find the courage to oppose it.

The mutiny was not brought about by storming the quarterdeck or taking over the helm. Not by cannon or cutlass, or such violence as befell so many unfortunate vessels that perished at the hand of brigands and thieves while peacefully engaged in their lawful trade and maritime employment.

Nay, murder and pillage was not the plan of the mutineers. They neither drew sword nor threatened life or limb, but knowing how vulnerable the captain was in his advancing years, and that his whole company business was, as it were, totally dependent on them, it was therefore only a matter of united agreement and the ship would be theirs!

CHAPTER 11

Do or Die?

They had given him a choice. He could remain as captain, but in name only. They would chart their course and make the business decisions. No one would know a change had taken place; outwardly, all would appear just as it had been, and the continued custom of the long-standing traders would keep them all comfortable. In pursuit of this plan, they had even offered to divide a portion of the profits for the captain's own use from every voyage made, so he would not be penniless in his new role. In the event, however, that Angus would not yield to this request, the second plan they forwarded left little room for doubt as to their evil intention to steal the ship at whatever the cost.

They would put the captain off at the first uninhabited island, of which there were many in those parts, leave him ball, powder, flint, and musket, some tools and provisions, and enough old sailcloth, spar, and rigging to provide shelter, and the ship would be theirs!

Before they reached Aberdeen again, a full two years or more would have passed, and it would not be difficult to make a report that the captain had perished in a storm, or died of some malady or other. The passage of time would help in no small measure to prevent any great interest in the matter. Moreover, small independent companies were not greatly represented as far as investigation was concerned, so no one anticipated any difficulty in explaining the captain's absence!

Another wind was in their favour in their evil scheme. Knowing very well that mutiny on the high seas was punishable by death would effectually seal every man's lips, and so it would be to every man's advantage to conceal the truth of what had actually taken place. Old Angus remembered the day well—indeed, how could he forget it?

He was enjoying the voyage that day. It was a beautiful May morning, but spring had been late in coming, and there was some ice on mast and rigging. They were leaving behind the cold and inhospitable northern climate of his native shores, and he was anticipating the soft warmth and balmy days of solitude and quiet contemplation as he waited for the vessel to unload at her destination and take on board her return cargo.

They were around 15 days out from Aberdeen on their way to the Gulf of Guinea, West Africa. They were crossing the Bay of Biscay, and three more days would see them clear of the heavy swells and westerlies that made this part of the journey the most dangerous of all. Heavy weather had hindered them initially as they came into Yarmouth Roads, but since then, the vessel had made good headway.

Although the best time of year for the voyage, now and then a swell would break over her bows, but the ship was in no danger. Spar and sail, windlass and capstan were all in good repair. Cable, hawser, and bars were well secured. All deck cargo was tied down and fastened with stout rope and cable. The rigging had been renewed where needed just before they left for the voyage, and so the 'Endeavour' was in good shape and in good hands. The experienced eye of the master mariner took it all in, and his sailor's heart was satisfied.

They were carrying full sail, and so long as the wind held, they had hopes of crossing the Bay within the next three or four days. This put heart and hope into all on board, for there is nothing quite so exhilarating as being under sail in favourable conditions, with only the soft murmur of the bow wave to break the silence, or the flap of a sail, or the shouts of the crew to one another as they kept a steady course and trim, using to the full advantage the stiff breezes that had augured so well in their favour.

It was in times such as these that Angus thought of the Psalm, and what it had to say of the seafaring life: *"They that go down to the sea in ships, that do business in great waters; these see the works of the Lord, and His wonders in the deep."*

In a reverent and honest heart, Angus thought that the Lord must have had a tall ship in mind when He gave those words to the sacred penman, for where else but on such a vessel could the wonderment of life at sea find a more apt expression than on a tall ship with a fair wind in her sails? On an ocean vast, such as no other scene on earth can be vast, a vastness empty of another living soul, a man sees himself as surely as God must see him—weak, helpless, a mere pitiful speck on the surface of creation, and the majesty of the Almighty is never more plainly seen than through the eyes of those who have first seen themselves for what they are.

CHAPTER 12

The Tropics

Angus had every right to enjoy that day and the anticipation it brought to him. He had his health and a prosperous and honest business, and the Gulf of Guinea was a very profitable destination. Indeed, wherever he chose to drop anchor, he could be assured of a good return for his cargo of trade goods. His reams of brightly-coloured cloth, clothes, blankets, axes, knives, metal cooking pots, and a thousand other things that would be highly sought after by the native dwellers of those climes.

In return, Angus would fill the 'Endeavour's' hold with ivory, furs, breeding pairs of exotic birds and small animals for private estates, peppers, spices, palm oil, beautiful seashells, and dexterously carved handcrafts. There might even be gold waiting for him, for it was in abundance in those parts, and the natives had little use for it except as an ornament. Perhaps most prized of all, if he could procure them, were the pearls, brought up from the depths by lithe and intrepid divers, their little baskets of crude matting filled with the oysters they had gathered. To see these glistening bodies bob to the surface, gasping for air, proudly holding their baskets high, never failed to stir a European visitor.

In the depths beneath the ship lay their harvest field, and could there be one more beautiful? White sand and coral reef, the water clear as crystal, sometimes jade, sometimes emerald, and sometimes a soft azure, and the myriad shoals of brightly-coloured fish that twisted and turned this way and that in perfect unison. Surely *the heavens do declare the glory of God, and the firmament shows His handiwork."* Angus never failed to admire and enjoy this particular business potential in operation, and if he could barter for the oyster's hidden gem, he would count his efforts well worthwhile.

All these and more would be the 'Endeavour's' return cargo, but only these and more of the same, for Angus never carried slaves.

There were those who scorned him for his sensitivities and for allowing such a lucrative opportunity to pass by. But Angus never regretted his decision to shun the traffic in human flesh. The very sight of those poor wretches, chained and shackled to each other foot and neck, marching to the gangplanks of filthy, unsanitary, disease-ridden slave-ships, to suffer and endure the most degrading and dehumanising voyage ever undertaken by mortals, shocked and sickened him.

Although it was mostly local native slavers and inland tribal leaders who rounded up these unfortunates and brought them to be sold at the coast, Angus often wondered how civilised nations could condone and engage in such brutality and wickedness against such innocents, and vowed that the decks of the 'Endeavour' would never be stained with their blood, and that her holds would never witness the untold misery and suffering of the greatest human injustice the world has ever known.

Yes, Angus was happy therefore as he paced the deck that day and thought on the good fortune Murdo's legacy had brought him. He was happy that his trade and business dealings brought no hardship to the native people with whom he traded, but had in so many instances improved their lot in life, and he himself had felt himself enriched as he came to know them.

But, as so often happens in life, nothing remains the same for long!

CHAPTER 13

The Visitor

He had not long entered his cabin when he was interrupted by a knock on the door. It would be the last time Angus would hear that sound. As he bade entrance, there stood before him McPhail, his first mate. This was the man whom Angus trusted above all others. He had given his cabin to him when he first came aboard and joined the crew. This was the man to whom he had spoken about actually inheriting the ship and all its trading business—the close companion he had treated like his own kin.

But this was not the man who now stood before him. Angus had been long enough treading life's path to recognise a change in the eye of a betrayer—a subtle, but nevertheless a very real difference in demeanour, stance, and spoken word.

McPhail had a letter in his hand, and he quickly crossed to the captain's table and presented it: "For you, Captain," then hurriedly left without another word. It was a cowardly act, his guilt and treachery plainly visible on his countenance, but then he never was one for courage, and in his own heart, Angus reproached himself for those times he ought to have taken the warning signs and the crew's earlier advice more seriously!

The letter, sealed with McPhail's own seal, was clear enough in its message. The first mate was not happy in his present position. He had notified the crew of his dissatisfaction and planned to depose the captain and take over the running of the entire business enterprise. It was signed by the captain's trusted and long-standing crewmen, and it was clear that there had been plans already prepared for this moment and time. Angus looked hard and long at the letter, and he took careful note of the signatures and conditions laid out.

Without the support of the crew, Angus knew he had no hope of saving the ship. He was on the high seas and far from a safe mooring. His company was an independent business with no established organisation to appeal to, so it was simply a matter of them against him! He was outnumbered—it was as simple as that—and the morality of the situation would not be a consideration. But the mutiny, coming as it did when he, and they, were in the prime year of a very successful twenty-odd years, was a heavy blow.

Angus slowly and carefully took in the situation as he sat in his cabin and pondered the first mate's letter. This was no time for rash or foolish action. A wrong move now would spell disaster.

It did not take him long to conclude that at all costs, he must get off the ship. Reasoning or pleading would be of no avail, and to beg was unthinkable. If he delayed, abandonment on some uninhabited island would very soon be his fate, and a fate worse than death itself. To die of thirst, hunger, or the madness of loneliness itself must surely rank among the very worst of human departures to the other world.

He had no time to lose. They had given him three days to decide, so he must contrive to escape. But how? Any thought of physical action would be doomed to failure and bring about his violent death in the process. No, he had to devise a plan—a plan that would be both quiet and unobserved, and above all, successful.

In their haste to establish their new status as owners and traders, the brigands had taken no precautions with Angus except to put all muskets and pistols under lock and key. He was allowed to continue in his cabin quarters as before, and still had freedom to go abroad at will for fresh air and exercise. They even continued to bring him his food, but they no longer knocked for entrance to his cabin!

As was his custom, Angus frequently spent much time on the poop deck, which was directly above his cabin, and from that vantage point in the stern he could observe the quarterdeck and helmsman below, and also beyond, and therefore appraise himself of the whole ship's company and efficiency at a glance.

Angus thought it good, therefore, to continue this habit. He had been given only three days to make up his mind, and any change in his frequent appearances on the poop might arouse suspicion. Suspicion was the last thing Angus wanted, for he now had a plan, and surprise would determine whether or not his plan would succeed as he hoped.

CHAPTER 14

Escape!

That night, after he had retired as usual and taken the food they brought him, he took a small empty powder cask that served him at times as a footstool as he read a book or studied a chart before retiring for the night. It had lain gathering dust in a corner of the cabin for years, with twine, reefing tools, blocks, light tackle and other small accoutrements of shipboard life, and had long since ceased to be noticed by either the captain or anyone else who entered.

Taking a sheet from his cot, Angus carefully wrapped the cask in it. Then, twisting the loose ends as tightly as he could on either side, he tied them off securely close to the cask with the ship's twine. When this was done, he then folded the remaining length of twisted sheet back on itself, tying it again, but this time bringing the uncut twine over to the other end and tying it in the same way. He now had a cask safely enclosed and tied in a sheet, and the twine forming a sling!

Since Angus had to leave the ship, he needed something to support him during the long hours in the water. With the heavy twine sling passed over his head and under both arms, the cask could not drift away, so there was no possibility of losing it. He was confident of his plan as far as the cask was concerned, but he knew they were approaching waters that were well known for sharks. There was nothing he could do about this except to trust in the Lord to deliver him, but as far as he was concerned, he had prepared as well as he could, and what more could he do in the circumstances?

With the little cask hidden under his cot, he lay down to sleep. The means of his escape were now ready; he must soon take the opportunity!

Dawn broke to another bright and sunlit day. The wind was still favourable, and the helmsman had held to the charted route passed to him the day before. Angus himself had charted this course, and in doing so had, without knowing it, given himself the means of deliverance!

Because of the heavy swells further out from the Bay itself, Angus had kept as far inshore as he could, and had charted a course right across the bay's mouth, straight between the two points of land that formed its outer boundaries—France to the north, and the most north-westerly point of Spain, which formed the southern boundary. He had reckoned the ship was making eight knots, and if the weather held fair, it would bring them to the southernmost point, Corunna, in three or four days.

Three days later, the night would be as dark as it could be in these waters, for it would be between moons, and Angus needed such conditions for his plan. He would make his move towards the end of the middle watch, around 4 a.m., when the night would be darkest and the crewmen tired. What he planned to do was a daunting prospect. To give oneself to the dark waters miles from land would strike fear into the stoutest heart, and Angus was only human after all. But to allow the ship to be commandeered by brigands and thieves, and further allow them to invent some story as to his demise, perhaps even add some scandal, was more than he could live with. He would expose them, or die in the attempt.

Angus spent the next two days as he had always done. An onlooker would not have perceived anything amiss. But he was ready! The next few hours would determine the truth of the scripture: *"Them that honour me, I will honour."*

It was just then that a great difficulty arose that would render his plan of escape useless unless he could remedy it. He was on the poop as usual when he saw something that caused him great consternation. Well forward of the bows and to the port side, he could make out the distant headland that marked the Spanish side of the bay. The water being very deep in these parts, they would pass within a mile of that promontory. This was crucial to his plan.

But they had made better time than he had anticipated, and the point where he had intended to depart the ship would now be on them by nightfall. If he missed it, all would be lost, and so he determined to attempt regardless of the risk of detection. He could not now afford to wait until the end of the middle watch; another four hours would take them past the headland, and he must make his move as soon as darkness would conceal him.

Of course, it would not be difficult to make a run for the gunwale and jump over if he were detected, but that was not his plan. He had a motive in mind in his secrecy of action. When the moment came, just as the first watch was changing with their comrades and their attention was on one another, Angus made his move.

CHAPTER 15

Survival!

With money belt carrying as much coin as he felt safe with, for he was careful lest the weight of the belt would render the cask ineffective, Angus made his way softly to the stern. Looking from within the small circle of their lantern's wan light, would only make the crew's vision worse against the darkness of the poop deck, and apart from the changing watch, all was quiet. Breathing a prayer for safekeeping and clutching the little cask tightly to his chest, Angus committed himself to the dark waters twenty feet below.

The shock of the cold water took his breath away, and for a moment or two he felt a great sense of desolation and failure in what he had just done, but he could not let these things deflect him from a last and final survey of the ship, and he struggled to gain composure and apply himself to his plan. As the dark hulk towered above him, receding now in the darkness, Angus watched and listened carefully all the while. Until she went out of sight, there was not a shout or lantern glow. Not a sign of alarm. Not a sound except the soft slap of water on his own face. He had made it! He had escaped undetected. Now he needed to survive.

Had the crew heard or seen him go overboard, it really mattered not to his aims.

They would never have turned the vessel about, and most certainly not in darkness, to search. But Angus wanted them to be left with the uncertainty of what he had actually done!

His cabin was as he left it, his cot unmade, and no last note for the crew—not a word to suggest why he had so suddenly just simply disappeared. He had deliberately left his pocket watch and compass on his cabin table, and only carried his captain's registration document inside a small Bible. Pressed tightly closed and wrapped in oilcloth, the water might spoil it somewhat, but tightly closed, it would remain serviceable, of that he was sure. Either way, he would take it just the same.

When his absence was discovered, a search would be made of the ship, and the crew would arm themselves. Every nook and corner would be carefully examined for the stowaway, and every eye would be on the watch for a sudden and violent appearance of the one they had so wronged. If he were on the ship, they would find him—only this time, there would be no mercy.

As he bobbed now on the wake of his own ship, a tiny speck on a dark and fearful ocean, his woe was now complete. He was alone and afraid, but once again, as so many times before, the psalmist came to his aid: *"Yea, though I walk through the valley of the shadow of death, I will fear no evil, for Thou art with me."*

Breathing a prayer of trust and petition, he committed himself to the providence of Almighty neither a compass bearing, nor even to see the Pole Star, for the prevailing westerly and tide would eventually carry him inshore. When he was clear of the ships wake, and began to feel the wind carry him forward, he simply clung tightly to the cask and let the ocean, and his calculations, do the rest. Movement and kicking would merely draw unwanted attention if indeed sharks were in the vicinity, and Angus knew that if that happened, all would be over for him in a few violent and gory seconds.

In a few hours it would be dawn, and one of the small fishing boats that were numerous in these parts would surely pick him up. The law of the sea, which his former friends had so cruelly broken, would perhaps find kinder hearts to administer it.

CHAPTER 16

The Providence of God

Old Pedro Menéndez and his wife María were poor people. His family had farmed in Galicia and its regions for centuries, but for all their industry, they never seemed to get any richer. Pedro had brought up his own family just a few miles inland from Corunna, where he had a small vineyard. His two sons, now grown, managed the few acres and, with a cow, some goats for milk and meat, and a few chickens, they eked out a living. Things were difficult now—much more difficult than formerly.

Their rulers, kings, and powers that be, in their never-ending quest for expansion, dominance, and subjugation, had impoverished the country in the ongoing need for finance and the materials of war. Heavy taxes and levies were laid upon people who had barely enough to eat. Their crops were taken to feed the armies. Their timber was cut to build their ships, and their olive yards and vineyards were plundered to provide for the ever-hungry mouths and thirsty throats of the king's court.

The calamitous loss of the great Armada had impoverished the nation, the consequences of which were still being felt, and it was the poor who suffered the most in all these things.

Yes, Pedro Menéndez was a poor man. Made poor and kept poor, he lived poor and would no doubt die poor.

Every summer, Pedro and María made the few-mile journey to an isolated part of the coast, where they had built a small dwelling. It was nothing grand—more descriptive as a hovel than a house—but as it was mainly for shelter and shade, it did not need to be grand. It served them well in the summer months, and being built from raw materials that Pedro himself had gathered, the outlay was such as he could afford. The purpose of Pedro's annual summer migration was twofold. Fish could be caught in the bay, and this annual good fortune was always a much-needed addition to the family purse.

Moreover, Pedro knew the ways of the sea, and he knew how every tide left behind the evidence of its visit! Old Pedro, therefore was a familiar figure on the shore. Out early and home late, either fishing or gathering the flotsam and jetsam that the tides left behind, Pedro and his little donkey cart could be seen daily. Fishing floats, lengths of rope, old crates, pieces of rigging, a broken spar or sail—sometimes in poor weather, larger items would make their way to the beach. A bale of hides, milled timber or planking, a ship's lighter (small boat), or casks of fruit, all swept off the decks by heavy seas.

Even the smaller items Pedro salvaged were of great value to the local inshore fishing community, and so he had a ready market as the reward for his labour. Now and again, a body would be among his pickings. Some poor seaman, tempest-tossed and in great danger, had been swept away in seconds to a watery grave and an uncertain eternity. When this happened, Pedro always buried the corpse in the sand above the tide-line, first removing anything of value. It was never much—a few coins, a knife stuck in a waistband, perhaps a ring or two on the gnarled fingers, and very often a small key on a tarred string round the neck. He never found identification on any of his gruesome finds, and if he had, he would have taken it to Corunna, where one of the many ship masters would have sought out the ship he came from.

Once, Pedro found a man whose arms had been tightly bound, and a blindfold still covered his eyes. A victim of man's inhumanity to man, he had been made to 'walk the plank' for some misdemeanour or crime, or perhaps mutiny, and had suffered a terrible death as a consequence. The least Pedro could do was to bury these unfortunates, and he always did so with respect and sadness, for he had lost a brother to the sea, and his body had never been found.

CHAPTER 17

Recalled to Life

When Angus opened his eyes, he did so to a semi-dark room and the smell of new bread being baked. He never moved. For long moments, he lay there in that semi-conscious state between sleep and wakefulness, trying to bring what he was seeing into the reality of his understanding.

In one corner, an old woman tended bread over a small fire, her long grey hair in a single plait that reached almost to her waist, while a stray wisp fell over her face, already smeared with flour from hands that had tried in vain to contain the wayward lock.

The dwelling was a single room, a lean-to against the honeycombed cliff face that formed its back wall. Rafters, rough-hewn from the forest, formed its roof support, the ends of which had been chiselled into the soft rock above Angus's head, while the other end was tied securely against uprights from the same source.

The walls, hand-made earthen bricks, kiln or sun-dried, were unplastered, and festooned with oddments of maritime salvage, and an earthen floor held more of the same. From a beam over against the fire hung an assortment of hams and sausage, both taking advantage of the smoke that curled in soft flowing rhythm around them, as it made its way through the rafters and tiles above, and the sight brought Angus to feel just how hungry he was.

On the floor, an upturned fishing creel served as a small table, and on it he recognised his Bible, his captain's registration document, and his money belt! It was then that last night and all the terrors it had held suddenly came into focus. He had escaped, he was alive, he was safe! A wave of thankfulness swept over him as he lay there, and tears of gratitude welled in his eyes when he thought of how the Lord had given him safekeeping through it all.

His clothes were nowhere to be seen, but he supposed them to be outside drying in the now bright sunshine, that showed itself through the doorway, and in many other places where it found access through the rustic tiles above.

Before Angus could beckon to the woman at the fire, Pedro appeared. A small man, stooped with the toils and cares of hard labour, his face browned and wrinkled, saw that Angus was awake. He greeted him in his local dialect, and his face broke into a wide smile when Angus returned the greeting in the same.

Corunna was a busy port, and exports like tobacco, whale oil, iron, timber for shipbuilding, hides, and Spanish cocoa made their way to England's shores. Since Angus often carried the same in times between his longer voyages, he had many acquaintances in the port itself and had picked up a competent grasp of the Galician dialect over the years.

In this way, Pedro was able to relate the story of finding Angus, more dead than alive, two days ago, and how he brought him to the lean-to and nourished him, keeping him warm and comfortable in the hope he would revive. Reticent as the old man was to relate the tale, Angus wanted to know the details.

Through miraculous circumstances, he had been delivered by the providence of God, and he did not want a morsel of this miracle to fall by the wayside and be forgotten.

<h1 style="text-align:center">CHAPTER 18</h1>

<h1 style="text-align:center">Pedro's Story</h1>

The place where Pedro had built his summer shelter was on a solitary stretch of coastline just a few miles north of Corunna. Just half a mile below his stretch of beach, the coastline became impassable on foot. A rocky headland jutted out to sea and effectively cut off all further access. Had Angus drifted another half mile, he would have perished. Pounded against the rocks by an unceasing surf, he would never have survived.

On the morning he had been found, the tide had already receded, and as Pedro made his way to his daily task, he saw the dark shape on the tide-line not far from his shelter. Heavy of heart, he made his way there first, only to discover Angus, white and still in death.

In prising apart the dead fingers to break them free of the sheet-wrapped cask, he was astonished when the fingers closed again in a tight grasp, and only then realised that life was still within the inert form before him. Since he was not able to lift Angus onto the little donkey cart, he simply passed a length of rope under his arms and dragged him over the sand to where María helped him get the sailor to bed and begin their aid to his recovery.

Pulling their little cot near the fire each evening, and using their own bed fleeces, the better to warm the dying visitor, Pedro and María took it in turns to sit with him through the next two days, now and then pouring a little French brandy through his lips, and vigorously rubbing his legs and arms in an effort to revive him.

When Angus had been found, his right arm had been over the cask, and his left hand had been clenched tightly to the bound sheet at the end, his head resting, as in a sleeping position, on the cask itself.

Immediately seeing the cask as a means of survival, Pedro became aware that it was no accident that this prostrate figure lay before him. This man, whoever he was, had planned this desperate and courageous venture, and Pedro would do his best to help this unknown fulfil a plan that had already almost taken his life. Later, in his little shelter, when Pedro saw the few personal items Angus carried, he was more and more convinced that, come what may, this sailor that lay at death's door before him must be saved.

Angus listened quietly as the old man related his story. When it was finished, the old man asked Angus if he was hungry. Before Angus could answer, the light in his eye at the mention of food was enough for Pedro to call to his wife to make ready.

As they sat at the makeshift table, the viands there were as no other ever tasted, for Angus had not eaten for almost three days now, and he was weak from lack of food alone. Ham, fresh bread, olives swimming in their own oil, fish, Spanish rice, and soft goat's cheese, washed down with the contents of a wineskin that Pedro had taken from a peg on the wall and poured generously for his visitor.

The generosity of his hosts touched the heart of the old sailor, and he marvelled that one of a pagan race could so far excel in honour and trust above those of the Christian nation to which Angus belonged, and some of them Kirk men too! *Truly the ways of God are mysterious, and quite past finding out.*

Before they rose from the table, Angus considered something that was barely comprehensible to him, and yet it came to him now as overwhelmingly true. From this moment onwards, all that he would ever have, or say, or accomplish in this life, would only be because of the old man and woman sitting across the table from him.

Moreover, all that he now had, all that he owned, was in debt to this couple, and as long as he lived, he must acknowledge and honour that fact. Only those who have been snatched from the jaws of certain death can experience this reality, and Angus found it a humbling lesson, one that would remain with him until the end of his life.

After they had eaten, Angus told his own story. Mutiny, pure and simple. An uprising by ingrates against one who gave them employment when they had been overlooked by others. Jealous, callous men who had trampled on every moral principle of decency and honour, and had coveted a vineyard they had never planted, and appropriated a business they had never earned.

When Angus had related all to Pedro as to how he made his escape, he made arrangements with him to go to Corunna the next day and seek out the next ship bound for Britain. Angus did not relish the task of being seen as a Briton without a ship in a foreign port, and perhaps drawing unwanted and adverse attention. When Pedro brought back word, Angus would go directly to the ship and seek passage from the captain. He was sure he would not be refused. Even if civility failed, the colour of gold would always overcome that difficulty.

CHAPTER 19

Reflections

As Angus looked back now to that remarkable deliverance, and his safe return to the Highlands, even after so many years he thought again with fondness of the old couple who had so faithfully brought him back from the very brink of the grave. Angus had taken to the sea on 18th May, midnight, at the end of the first watch. Pedro found him on the 19th morning at dawn on the tide-line, left there from the ebb tide.

Angus knew he had jumped on a full tide—that meant he had endured being in the water, without making much forward progress, until the next running tide bore him shoreward. He had therefore survived the cold waters of the Bay for around twelve hours. Without the little cask, all would have been lost. But, cask aside, it was a miracle of sovereign grace.

Angus was faithful in return—how could it be otherwise? Pedro's last years were spent in modest comfort; it was the very least Angus could do when such a great debt was owed!

After the old captain reached Aberdeen, he had sought out those who he thought, at the very least, would punish those who had done such a great and cruel wrong, but he was to be sorely disappointed.

With the help of a crooked lawyer, whose wigged species were as numerous as the ship's rats that scuttled about the quays and wharves, sniffing out some morsel of human misfortune on which to feed, the port officials, friends, and relatives of the mutineers, had come up with a disingenuous argument. Since no one had been charged with any criminality—apparently no foreign power had communicated any evidence of criminality—they would not enter into the issue!

Moreover, since there were no insurance claims against the cargo, and as Angus was an independent company, and not registered with one of the established local companies, they felt no obligation to help him!

Even today, so many years after it had all happened, the captain could not understand it. The old man had taken all the letters and forgeries pertaining to the mutiny, to an honest lawyer. He was told the forged letter was a clear case of criminality, and also that a moral duty lay heavily upon the authorities to act in the matter. The Procurator Fiscal from Inverness said he could pursue this very successfully at the Assizes, but health and age were against him, and even if Angus won compensation, he could never rebuild again his former success. The damage had been done, and it was irreparable. Angus finally satisfied himself by publishing an affidavit with all the correspondence, evidence, and names therein, thus absolving himself from any involvement in wrongdoing, or giving any cause for the mutiny or loss to the creditors.

The affidavit was merely a plea to all honest men for justice in the matter, and although it did not recover his ship, he had the great satisfaction of knowing it was never challenged by any of those named within!

Aye, those were days of rough seas and ill tides, the old man thought—tides that had brought his voyaging days to an end. He was now on a fast-running ebb, and the little crofter's cottage on the Nairn shore would be his last moorings.

CHAPTER 20

Shipwreck

There is an old saying in the Highlands, and Angus had often heard it from his father, "Ye cannae dae ill an' guid follow ye". He had first thought of this old Highland proverb as a child when the news came from Killiecrankie that Graham of Claverhouse had fallen, and he had thought of it many times since.

He was only three years old, but the sight of his father kneeling, with hands upraised in prayer and tears streaming down his cheeks, had never left him. Nor had the words of Scripture he had invoked in prayer, *"Oh Lord God, thou hast surely avenged our blood on them that dwell on the earth"*. There was no merriment, no sense of joy, no vulgar or unseemly behaviour, but rather a deep sense of the judgement of God falling for God's own righteous ends and purposes.

His father had known Richard Cameron, and many a time had given him shelter when he was being hunted like *"the partridge upon the mountain"*. He had travelled to Edinburgh to console Cameron's father in his hour of great and bitter sorrow, and had witnessed the unholy spectacle of the head of the young man on a pike as it was paraded through the streets of the city. Yes, at Killiecrankie the Lord surely honoured the Scripture, *"Be sure your sin will find you out"*.

Today Angus thought of the old saying once again as he considered the sad end of the ship he had so cherished.

Angus had come to know his crew in his years working with them. He did not pry into their personal lives, but as far as he was aware, they were all kirk men. In the times of communion they would be the first to hold out their hand for a token, enabling them to sit at the Lord's Table as responsible and repentant worthies, and to partake of the emblems that represented the Body and Blood of Christ, and signifying before all their desire to live in obedience to Christ's vicarious sufferings and to share in His love, compassion, and guileless conduct towards their fellow men. This was the most perplexing thing to Angus; being kirk men, he often wondered about their inner thoughts, both then and since.

When they saw their mutinous venture fail so shamefully, did they not have any misgivings? Did they never feel any sense of impropriety, or experience any recognition of misconduct in the performance of those things that were foolish, criminal, and immoral?

Although Angus had not had the privilege of a proper education, at least he could read, and he read extensively. That had proved a blessing to him in his many lonely months and years at sea. Even now, while the light in his cottage permitted, he still read. From his books, he would often remember a phrase or paragraph and, like a cudding stag in some secluded corrie, he would recall a line or two worthy of use and application.

Such a line came to him now—a quote from Cromwell, an enemy it was true, yet even enemies can speak words of counsel to those who are willing to listen. Cromwell's words were written to the General Assembly of the Church of Scotland, just before the battle of Dunbar, and the disastrous consequences that followed.

"I beseech you in the bowels of Christ, think it possible that you may be mistaken."

Aye, even the victor must make provision for the weaknesses and betrayals of the human heart, Angus thought, and even former friends who have proved unfaithful must in grace be allowed to consider this possibility.

As far as extending his forgiveness was concerned, the old captain was not at all troubled. In his reading of the Good Book, forgiveness was something that must be preceded first by repentance. Forgiveness was therefore the divine response to sorrow expressed for wrongdoing, the fitting and proper answer to a truly penitent heart. To offer forgiveness without the required recognition and acceptance of guilt is in itself rebellion against the clear and stated words of Christ Himself. Grace must match grace in the Divine order. When the grace of repentance is shown, the grace of forgiveness must follow.

When Angus heard of the shipwreck he was not surprised; neither was he glad. No man can welcome the loss of such a ship even though she be in pirate hands. Heavily laden with a cargo of wheat, she ran aground in heavy seas off Finisterre. Lifted on a great swell, she came down heavily, breaking her back, and thereafter she was lost. She could never survive now in such a sea.

In a few terrifying minutes, all the craftsmanship and glory of that worthy and graceful vessel was reduced to matchwood until she finally slid off the rocks and disappeared into the green and turbulent depths of the ocean. One of those who witnessed the end of the vessel swore to his dying day that before the stern finally disappeared, he saw the ghostly figure of the old captain standing in his place on the poop!

It was the beginning of the end for the mutineers and their ill-gotten gains. From the relative safety of a small boat, they had managed to launch, they watched in horror as the wheat poured from the hold in a tawny stream, only to be lost to the sea and scattered like spindrift on the waves. But worse was to follow. Merchants will not risk their goods and trade with a company that shows itself incompetent, and when the word got out that the vessel ran aground in daylight, and in good visibility, the next annual accounting proved disastrous.

When the mutineers called their traders and customers to report on the business, many had already sought new ventures. Of those who remained, there were barely enough persons to justify a legally registered accounting.

In a few short years therefore, their stolen hopes and future plans were but a shadow of what once had been.

CHAPTER 21

Another Day Over

The light was fast fading as Angus carefully folded the papers, rolled up the charts, and closed the manifests and logs before placing them again in the old trunk. As long as he kept these safe, he need never fear the private gossip and whispered threats of prosecution by the mutineers for daring to publish their names in the affidavit. There were libel laws in Scotland, and those who neglected to use this bulwark of character protection must have good reason for doing so!

As he folded away the last of the charts and papers, he did something he had never done before. He made a vow to himself, and he made it as before the God of Heaven. He would never open these documents again. He had done so too often already, and still no answer satisfied his perplexity of heart at the injustice. The time had come to yield to God's providence alone. He had done what he could; that much he had felt obliged to do as his duty. Nothing further could now be gained by traversing this path, and he must let it rest, allowing the words of Abraham to be his onward guide in the matter: "*Shall not the Judge of all the earth do right?*"

The old captain, rising slowly and painfully from locking the trunk, glanced at the clock. The widow Ross would be here in little more than an hour, and he had a chore to do before then. As was his custom, he always took an old peat creel to the end of his path and left it there so his purchases could be carried easily from the road to the cottage. When he returned from the road, Angus built up a good fire, for he had carried the peats in earlier in the day during a respite in the rain, and he was now comfortable in the knowledge that after supper his habit of settling near the inglenook would be undisturbed.

Apart from those times of recurring thoughts on the mutiny, old Angus was happy in his circumstances. It had taken a while to come to his present state of contentment, and in the meantime he had experienced a wide range of emotions.

But the Lord has many ways of working in a man's soul for His own glory, and Angus had come to realise that a faith that cannot trust God for personal hurts and disappointments—yea, even tragedy itself—is no higher in value than the heathen's blind worship, or his darkened image of some mysterious higher being who must be served through fetish and witchcraft.

As he read and applied the Word of God to himself, Angus saw that when an offended one sees the awfulness, the solemnity, and the eternal consequences of the Judgement Seat of Christ, it is not difficult for thoughts of revenge to turn away from the offender, and to leave them to the overriding and overruling providence of God. The Last Judgement is either true or it is not true. If it is not true, then none of the Book is true, but if it be true, then we must accept, *"It is a fearful thing to fall into the hands of the living God."*

Things happen to men in life, Angus thought, and some men do bad things, but for those things every man must give account. Angus had found his own peace after the mutiny, a mutiny that had robbed him of his life's work, and he would leave the others with their own reflections.

He would let them weigh their own contribution and work during those years under his own successful captaincy, against their motives and determination to seize a ship that was never theirs, and the great loss they had brought about as a consequence. It was a 'Naboth's vineyard' they coveted, and, like the wicked Ahab, they never got to enjoy the yields it had produced for its rightful owner!

Angus was happy within himself, however. In old age, the comfort and satisfaction of having sought to be just and honourable in life's dealings with our fellow man becomes very important. Satan is a masterly opponent, and adept at causing men to regret former decisions and dealings. This regret is designed to destroy the memory of our life's service to Christ, the only King and Head of the Kirk, and to besmirch His wisdom and providence in guiding us on our journey. Happy is the man, therefore, who can parry Satan's blows and wicked insinuations with the words of another worthy, and from the Good Book as well: *"I have fought a good fight, I have finished my course, I have kept the faith."*

CHAPTER 22

Contentment

Another day was almost over. Apart from these periods of reflection on the mutiny, little things, never before seen or recognised in the flush of youth and business of manhood, far outweighed them. These were now seen for the blessings that they were. Perhaps the eye of old age can see more clearly than the eye of youth. Whatever it was, Angus knew it to be true.

The evening fire in the hearth, a sound thatch overhead and the door tightly closed against the Highland storms, the smell of a tasty supper cooking, and the softness of the chaff in a well-filled mattress. When at length his weary bones lay down each night, these were the things he treasured.

Thankfulness filled his heart to overflowing when he placed these blessings under the shadow of the Big Stone at Drommossie Moor, and thought again of that moment when, as but a boy, he passed from death unto life.

A verse of the Old 100th came to mind:

"Know that the Lord is God indeed,
His mercy is forever sure.
His truth at all times firmly stood,
And shall from age to age endure."

He had first heard it sung as a child in many a moorland conventicle, watchful eyes on the surrounding glens and passes for the dragoons, and he sang it again now in his mind with a picture of those outdoor gatherings still vivid before him.

The new fire had taken hold, and its warmth and light filled the little cottage with their soft and flickering glow. He turned his old chair towards the hearth and made it ready for himself. He had salvaged the chair from his cabin when the ship returned to Aberdeen, along with a few other personal effects. It was his captain's chair: battered and well worn, but still sturdy and strong, and well it might be too, for it had been crafted from timber that had been growing five hundred years before Angus was born.

In the confines of the little cottage, it was always a prominent reminder of his years at sea, and although his former crew had stolen much, they could not steal his years at the helm, or the great and gratifying success he had enjoyed in them. They could never steal that. Now, in later years, he and they, had seen the evidence of their own incompetence. They had made shipwreck!

As he lowered himself wearily into the cushioned bosom of the old relic and stretched out his feet towards the fire, he was grateful once again for these moments of sensory delight. With his eyes closed in the pleasure of it, he experienced a twofold gratefulness. The warmth and comfort not only met the requirements of a frail and failing frame, but over and above those physical needs, as the old man felt again the support and embrace of those ebony arms, in those moments, he was 'The Captain' once again.

The End

OTHER TITLES BY THE SAME AUTHOR

From out a Poor Cradle

A memoir

Dark Strangers

Stories from an African Mission

Fornenst the Glow

Fireside Tales. Musings from a Parson's Pen

Fame Mission – The Untold Story

An Expose

Changed Times

Social, Ecclesiastical and Political Corruption in Ulster

What a Friend we have in Jesus

The History of Joseph Scriven

ABOUT THE AUTHOR

Alan Dunlop brings an authentic Highland voice and deep cultural knowledge to his historical fiction, drawing from a lifetime immersed in Scottish Presbyterian heritage and maritime tradition. His previous bestseller, which told the remarkable story behind the beloved hymn 'What a Friend We Have in Jesus,' demonstrated his exceptional ability to weave together faith, history, and compelling narrative.

Married to Irene for over fifty years, Alan and his wife have raised six children and delight in their thirty-one grandchildren and one great-granddaughter.

Contact the Author

Email: dsclevel1@hotmail.com

Are you inspired to write a book?

Contact

Maurice Wylie Media
Your Inspirational & Christian Book Publisher
Based in Northern Ireland and distributing around the world

www.MauriceWylieMedia.com